CONTAIN OR DIE

CONTAIN OR DIE

BIRTH OF HEAVY METAL™ BOOK 10

MICHAEL TODD

MICHAEL ANDERLE

DISRUPTIVE IMAGINATION

LMBPN Publishing
PMB 196, 2540 South Maryland Pkwy
Las Vegas, NV 89109

Version 1.01, December 2025
eBook ISBN: 978-1-68500-539-9
Print ISBN: 978-1-68500-540-5

DEDICATION

To Family, Friends and
Those Who Love
to Read.
May We All Enjoy Grace
to Live the Life We Are
Called.

THE CONTAIN OR DIE TEAM

Thanks to my Beta Readers
John Ashmore and Kelly O'Donnell

Thanks to my JIT Readers

Deb Mader
Jeff Goode
Jim Caplan
Peter Manis
Dorothy Lloyd

Editor
Skyhunter Editing Team

CHAPTER ONE

"I swear to God. I sat there and waited for the waitress to show up, sipped my water, and watched the game. It was three minutes into the second quarter before I realized they were doing something with tablets next to the table. I was starting to lose my shit before I saw the signs."

Madigan turned to Chezza. "No fucking way you didn't realize it was an automated restaurant."

"They're popping up all over Vegas these days," the woman answered. "It might have something to do with not needing to hire as many wait staff and they had the signs up and everything. Order from the tablet at your table. It's kind of interesting when you get used to it."

"It's the future," Kolt agreed. "After all the shit that happened in the early twenties, they had all the technology researched and ready to go. When everything opened up, there was a big push to get life back to normal and it was all moved to the back burner, but I think it's being brought out now. Plus, there was this big surge of people who quit their jobs in the service industry to go do what they want to do."

"I can understand that," Trick added. "It's all over the news that we might be a few months away from the end of the world, so people will hunt shit they've always wanted to do, even if it's not financially viable. Going on vacations, writing books, starting that business idea before everything goes up in flames."

Sal supposed that was a good enough idea. He could understand the sudden power shift that came with the knowledge that everything was ending. If he were in that kind of situation and was in no position to do anything to stop the Zoo, maybe he would have chosen to do something crazy that he'd always wanted to do.

Being at the front line of the war between humans and aliens had never factored in, but it was the right amount of crazy that it might have been more or less what he would have chosen.

"Hey, Sal, what would you have done?" Jiro asked curiously.

He looked around when he realized that the rest of the group had joined the discussion.

"What would I have done?"

"You know," Madigan prompted. "If you were out there doing a job you hated and you knew the world was going to end, would you change your job and do something else? And if you did, what would that something be?"

Sal tilted his head and turned his attention to his team for a moment. It felt weird that they were all focused on him and waited for his answer.

"You mean if I wasn't here, fighting monsters in mech suits that can only be described as futuristic?"

"Right."

"I don't know. I'd want to try to make a movie, I think. Something full to the brim with action and the kind of thing that even Michael Bay would find a little excessive. All the explosions, guns, and close-up shots of scantily clad women running as I could fit into two hours."

"Do you have a plot in mind?"

"Did you not hear the man?" Matt asked. "Guns, explosions, and PG-13 ogling at women. Who the fuck needs a plot?"

Madigan laughed. "You boys need to get acquainted with this popular thing they have on the Internet called porn."

"You got porn?" Mal asked.

"No, the Internet does. Try it sometime. That way, you won't need my boyfriend to make something like that."

"Or you could simply watch the plethora of Michael Bay films already in existence," Sal suggested as they approached the area where the Zoo had begun to grow. The plants were barely as tall as their ankles but that was generally how the jungle started. Also, the rate of growth had returned to what they had come to expect before the recent series of rampant expansions they'd witnessed.

Still, he would no longer be fooled by that. He began to retrieve the sensors and planted them in the ground. There was no telling which portions had Zoo plants beginning to grow underground, even though the entire section had been slagged when the troops cleared the area after it almost attacked their compound. They had done a good job of it too, but he didn't feel anything resembling safe at this point.

"Come on," Jim muttered and Sal realized he was looking at the jungle again. "We had a big win against the fucking Zoo. I know we can't lower our guard yet, but we have to take some time to pat ourselves on the back. We don't want to burn the fuck out."

The point was that they probably wouldn't be able to lower their guard ever, but it had been a solid win against the Zoo and they'd managed to stop it from pushing beyond the wall. There would always be something bigger or more dangerous thrown at them, usually when least expected. So while they needed to take time for self-care—without it, the Zoo would have won before the fighting even started—they also needed to remain alert and try to find ways to predict what might come when they could.

"Just because we can't see the jungle doesn't mean it's not there," Sal explained. "It looks like the spurs lay the groundwork and establish the plants beneath the surface, all ready to explode when they're needed."

"Yep," Madigan muttered. "You explained that when we asked you about the sensors we're putting down all over the goddammed place. Are you okay?"

"I'm fine. Well…relatively speaking."

"I'm still not sure why this is so important, to be honest," Kay commented and positioned a sensor according to their instructions. "The Zoo doesn't usually push into an area where we've burned through it like it needs to get itself ready. Why do you think it would change that now?"

"We need to rethink everything we know about the Zoo

at this point," Madigan answered and kept her weapons aimed at the trees with her usual caution. "It's found all kinds of new ways to attack us and seems to have learned from the ways we've stopped it in the past."

"So what are you saying?" Jiro flicked a sensor in the air like it was one of his daggers before he caught it and thrust it into the sand. "Like...the hippos were created to destroy the slag in the buffer?"

"Why not?" Sal countered. "It makes sense, at least."

"Only if the Zoo can strategize like...no." The freelancer shook his head. "Fuck no. That would make it sentient."

"I prefer highly evolved intelligence bio-programmed into the genetic makeup of the goop that would facilitate its ability to adapt, mutate, and—"

"I hate to interrupt what I'm sure will be a very informative lecture from Dr. Jacobs," Madigan snarked, "but I think we should keep our focus on the Zoo around us and the job we have at hand."

"Killjoy," Sal grumbled.

"Not for everyone else here, babe."

"Are you calling me boring?"

"No, but when you go off about mRNA, ribosomes, and shit, you're liable to put everyone else to sleep."

"So...everyone else finds me boring."

"Yep."

He looked at the others, none of whom disagreed openly with the point Madigan had made.

"I don't think it's boring," Courtney called.

"You don't count. You and he have geeked out over this shit since it started. Have either of you had much sleep?"

"Not...not really," Sal admitted. "Spending the night

with a gorgeous woman and working the whole time feels like I'm letting my teenaged self down."

There was a moment of silence between them, and he realized that he hadn't talked to either woman about the weird relationship the three of them had. They should undoubtedly have a conversation about it all, but he didn't think either of them would start it. This meant it was his job to do so.

The problem was that they were both older and more experienced than he was and when he looked for someone to help him with shit he wasn't an expert on, they were who he usually went to.

He'd have to make time for it later, he decided as he dropped to his haunches and began to collect the samples they needed. Soil and plants were all fair game at this point, and he wanted everything they could get their hands on. In all honesty, he wasn't sure what they were looking for or that they would find any clues as to where the spurs came from. At the end of the day, they might well have to widen their search parameters.

"Sal..."

"Yeah, I know. We'll have to talk about the whole situation, but do you honestly think now is the time—"

"No, Sal! Heads-up!"

With a frown, he looked up and saw that his sensors were alive across the board. The newly installed seismic sensors had already begun to pick movement up.

"Shit."

He yanked his assault rifle from where it was holstered on his back and shifted into formation with the rest of the Heavy Metal team. It was a substantial group at this point, with a total of nine new additions on top of those they already had on their payroll. They were in a position where they could probably deal with most of the larger attacks—or, at least, until there was the kind of surge that required a literal army.

Sal hoped he would never have to hire an entire army. He had no idea how to lead one and left that kind of shit to Madigan, Matt, and Murphy.

As always, locusts were the first to appear. They swarmed out of the tops of the trees and into the sky before they dove toward the humans at the edge of the jungle.

Madigan had already opened fire. The mini-gun on her shoulder pushed them back and she cut as many as she could down in a short but intense barrage. It was a distraction, of course, and Sal knew the larger monsters would attack from the trees. He could already see the hippos gathered at the edge where they stamped and snorted impatiently. Something held them back from rushing in but he knew it was only a matter of time and wanted to be ready for their attack.

The hyenas were the first mutants on the ground to rush out and they howled and yapped the way they did when they were released from whatever the Zoo's equivalent of a leash was. They acted more like their wild African counterparts at this point, but it seemed the Zoo merely liked the biological design. It would explain why it hadn't done much more than make the critter a little larger.

Something else moved in the shadows, though. Sal highlighted it as soon as he noticed it, already recording everything that was happening for later study as the hippos rushed out from the trees.

There were only four of them, but it was more than enough. His suit had recently been repaired and the shoulder was still a little stiff. He'd hoped that the Zoo would move on from the hippos, but it was unlikely to happen soon.

Then again, the alien jungle only moved on from monsters when it had something bigger and better to attack the line that stood between them and the rest of humanity.

The first one rushed toward him and he rolled to the right, caught its attention, and managed to draw the others in pursuit as well. Explosives hammered the dirt around the creatures but mainly impacted with their legs, although a few broke the thick hide enough to draw blood.

It had taken considerable work in the sims to decide the best way to deal with the hippos. The consensus among his team as to how to deal with the creatures while they charged was to destabilize their legs and knock them into each other.

Many people thought the goop allowed the creatures to defy the laws of physics, but his view was that all it did was abuse the laws. By doing this, it pushed for what would normally not be available for other animals because its evolutionary process did not abide by Earth's definition of survival of the fittest.

For many people, that meant one and the same thing. Sal had a feeling that they were the reason why they had to deal with so much shit from the Zoo in the first place.

New Connie activated the legs on his back to drive him

around the monsters that still struggled to retain their feet. They collided with each other, jostled, and lost speed as they were drawn away from the rest of the team. It was enough to put them off-balance, which left him with nothing else to do but sneak behind them as they battled to gain their stability and momentum.

Madigan stepped in. She fired her rockets to batter the creatures and used concussive blasts to go around the tough skin that appeared to absorb or deflect their bullets. It didn't matter how tough their skin was if everything inside was jostled around at a thousand feet per second. It was one of his favorite movie tropes to see someone hit by an explosion's blast wave and see them jump in time and be thrown clear instead of having their entire body turned to mush by the power of what struck them.

Physics was cool but never as cool as what could be done when one ignored the laws entirely.

Sal had his sword out but something dragged against his left boot. Madigan's rockets hammered home and he was in a position to finish everything off as quickly as possible. Irritated, he looked at his feet, where a group of smaller creatures swarmed viciously.

He'd never seen the like before. The small bipeds had a fair number of lizard-like characteristics. Two of them had wrapped their tails around his ankle and four more grasped him with claws and jaws clamped on his armor.

Given that they were about as tall as his knee, he had to resist the impulse to comment on how cute they were. It helped that they were in the middle of an attempt to chew his leg off.

The coils in his boots activated and jerked the closest

monsters away. Three of them landed a fair distance away and he swept his sword to slice through the last of them as he pulled himself away. A few of the hippos had already begun to regain their feet, although they were severely injured and bled from a variety of wounds, both external and internal.

He reached them before they could recover. His sword cut through their skin with ease and pushed in deeper until the spines were severed and the monsters finally twitched and stopped moving altogether.

"Is everything okay, Sal?" Madigan shouted. "You were a little slow on the cleanup there!"

"Yeah, I...uh, got tangled up." Sal turned, noticed that one of the smaller, knee-high creatures was still moving, and fired at it immediately. "We have some new creatures coming out of the Zoo. They are small and not much of a threat in low numbers, but I have a feeling they could start to appear in larger groups and become a real problem for us."

"Or it could be simply the Zoo trying out new things," Trick commented as he approached the corpses. "They shouldn't be much of a problem."

"Not many things coming out of the Zoo are not much of a problem," he answered as he took samples from the bodies.

"Still." Madigan approached them. "These look about as threatening as the monkeys we've seen around here from the beginning."

They'd all trivialized his concerns lately and called it paranoia. He wasn't sure where it came from, but maybe they were right. Or maybe he was. He always wanted to err on the side of caution.

"The bitch is up to something," he muttered and shook his head as Courtney took a few samples as well.

"What was that?" she asked.

"Nothing."

The machines had run all night. It was dangerous work— the kind that could not be committed to with humans present—which meant most of the diggers were operated by VIs. The area was still unstable from the bombing and the monsters that had tunneled under it.

Sam had suggested this as a way to check for where there were more attempts to tunnel under the walls, but that kind of endeavor was expensive enough that no union in the world would let live workers be present in the machines doing the digging.

Cheap options called for everything to be automated and handled by real workers from a nearby site, but VIs were brought in for the job these days. The advantage was that the diggers and cranes could work nonstop, day and night.

Of course, today was the day the diggers stopped. A few paths were created so people could reach the lower foundations of the wall, where he could see scorches across the construction where the bombs fell.

Chen and Elke both made no effort to hide the fact that they were uncomfortable there, as was anyone else who still had a lick of sense to their name. It was painful to think that so many of the monsters had wandered through this area before and could reappear at any time. Now that they could see the structure, Sam winced when he noted the sections that had been tunneled through. They could see the ruins there too.

Still, they needed to see this to know exactly what the Zoo was capable of. Everyone wore the same protective suits—the kind that would make sure none of them were in any danger of being infected by anything from the jungle. Still, anyone who came into contact with it was tested on a regular basis to confirm that no one brought any of it out.

Of course, no one knew if this was an effective way to detect a potential problem since they didn't know what they were looking for, but someone had to do something. Even if it was only a show to stop people from panicking.

They had an escort, complete with combat suits and men carrying plasma torches to make sure that if anything happened, they had something to fight back with. Fix wanted to think they were being paranoid but at this point, no one could afford to think like that.

Not out loud, at least.

Two researchers had joined them, ready to do their job in case they found anything to add to the report or to use as the basis for further study.

Memories of why the bombs had been needed in the first place flashed through his head as they all climbed out. The guys with guns assured them that it was safe for them to proceed to the site.

The officers who were with them were only there to see what was happening themselves. The French commander ordered his men to do what they already knew to do. It was like he needed to swing his dick around to look like he had everything under control.

"You two, start collecting samples," he snapped to the two researchers.

To their credit, they turned to look at Sam and waited for him to nod before they began to retrieve their equipment. Getting through the layer of slag created by the bombing had been the most difficult part of the excavation process, but now that what was left of the foundations were exposed, it should be easier.

"Why aren't they taking any samples?" the commander asked and looked at the rest of the troop.

Sam nodded to one of the researchers. "Observe."

It was the kind of testing they'd done a few times in the lab, but it was good for a demonstration too. The young researcher took a few tools from his pouch—the disposable kind—and began to scrape samples from where the wall foundations had been eaten into. The thin film with a hint of a blue tinge was still present and didn't show any signs of being dislodged or affected by the open air. As soon as the tool came into contact with the substance, however, both emitted a light-gray smoke and a soft hiss.

In seconds, the implement had dissolved almost to the rubber grip, and the researcher wisely tossed it away together with the container he had been scraping into since it was already smoking and showing signs of being corroded as well.

"Everything gets that reaction," Sam explained. "I'm sure that if you talked to Dr. Jacobs about the situation like you said you did, he would have explained it in full. Or perhaps you didn't pay attention."

Maybe it wasn't time to antagonize people, but he was a little more on edge these days. He struggled to sleep as well as he used to, no matter how exhausted he was, which left him short and irascible with people.

The commander had no answer for him, though, and the researchers returned to the work they had been ordered to do. ENSOL had acquired a few anti-corrosion formulas to test on the goop. Sal had said it was the original goop, the same substance that had dropped from the sky not that long before.

The tests would take a while, but the plasma throwers were involved in the situation as well. They would start to test whether the film that covered what remained of the foundations was fireproof.

He didn't know anything about biology or what the film of goop was—he left that to the specialists—but he did know a thing or two about the slabs of prefab that comprised the foundations of the wall they were building. There weren't supposed to be those cracks in it.

Sam leaned a little closer and let his HUD zoom in the rest of the way. There was no point in getting too close. The goop still corroded the construction material but surprisingly, it held the whole thing together. From the structural damage, it should have crumbled already but it was still intact.

He could think of no other explanation for how it held together.

"Something's moving in the trees!"

Those were words he hated to hear and he tensed reflexively. Fix looked to where locusts surged from the trees and gathered in a swarm to try to overwhelm them.

His hurried assessment was that there weren't enough of them to succeed, not with the troop they had with them. He moved back but kept his hand on the weapon he had been equipped with. While it was an assault rifle, it didn't even begin to compare to the size or firepower that the soldiers carried. Still, if the attack escalated, they might need every bullet he and his team could contribute.

Fortunately, they wouldn't be needed this time. He relaxed his hold on his weapon as the last of the locusts were gunned down. It still amazed him that they never seemed to turn and run, even when they were decimated. They would seemingly die to the last mutant, but more would simply appear when needed like the Zoo held thousands in reserve or could mass-produce them in a moment. This wasn't a real attack, though. It felt like a reminder— the damn jungle telling them it was there, watching and waiting for them to fuck up again.

Once the creatures were pushed back, Sam turned to look for his two partners.

It was weird to not see Chen filming everything and anything that came from the Zoo, but he had been through so much that his priorities seemed to have shifted on a fundamental level. He wanted to be there for him, but it wasn't like the kid opened up to them much.

"Are you guys okay?" He moved closer to them.

Both nodded.

"Do you think they'll attack the machines while they're working?" Elke asked. "We might need to drive the Zoo back more to create another buffer for us to work with."

"What would be the point?" Chen countered. "It can grow across again in fifteen minutes."

They both had a good point. Fix was surprised that nothing had sprung up to attack the machines while they had been digging and if they were worried about the monsters or the trees, he couldn't blame them.

For his part, he would continue to be terrified of the vines that behaved frighteningly like tentacles. There weren't many things that terrified him more than the footage he'd seen of those wrapped around the soldiers— the people like those responsible for protecting him and his team. Even now, his imagination could see them drag them into the trees or to the monsters waiting under the sand, or simply kill them outright by ripping them apart.

He looked at the plasma throwers, who had tried to burn through the film still covering the prefab.

Fix wasn't sure what he had expected, but watching the scorch marks fade with no sign of any damage done to the film was enough to send chills up his spine.

"Fuck," he whispered and approached the ruined foundations again.

"The plasma throwers don't work," Elke muttered. "Our decontamination systems don't work, and for all we know, every soldier who fought to stop this shit might already be infected."

Everyone turned to look at him, and he felt that he somehow had to justify any trust they might have in him.

It was an unsettling thought. He was a good worker and a decent cog in the machine, but people looked at him like he could save the world or something.

"I'll have to call Marcel again," he muttered. "And God help us if he can't find Badawi."

He felt like a fraud when murmurs of appreciation

followed his hasty statement before everyone returned to their work. Part of him pushed for him to mention the worst-case scenario, in which even if they did find the Algerian merc, what if the bastard didn't have a miracle cure for them?

The man was a self-confessed smuggler who unashamedly worked for whoever paid the most. What were the odds that he might have stumbled on the only substance that could counter the goop—or was even aware of it and what it could do? And even if he did, would someone of his reputation show any genuine concern for the threat the goop posed or would he simply see it as a ticket to retirement?

Fix sighed inwardly. There were times when even he couldn't fix a problem.

CHAPTER TWO

The goddammed locusts were hovering again.

Marius couldn't help the feeling that they would need to put the whole situation at the top of their priorities to deal with. Then again, there were enough problems for them to focus on. A whole swarm of locusts hovering over the trees made it look like they were airborne to look for something.

And by the looks of it, they'd found it.

"The fuckers are coming around again!" he shouted. "Who wants to take the gun this time?"

He had no volunteers, of course. There hadn't been any the last time, which meant that as the sergeant, the buck stopped with him. Perhaps it was time to apply to transfer home. Working out of the Middle Eastern Sector had begun to be more work than he'd bargained for.

"Assholes," he muttered as he climbed into the gunner's seat. "If my finger cramps and we all die because of the flying bastards, know it's all your goddamn fault."

The response was disappointing. He had hoped for at

least a couple of chuckles from the group, but no one even glanced at him. They all looked terrified of what they faced and while he couldn't blame them for it, he knew it was his job to push them through the fear to where they could use the adrenaline to good effect.

"You boys had better be ready to get out there and fight if things get hairy," Marius yelled and connected his HUD to the external cameras as he took control of the gun mounted on top of their vehicle. "I mean it! If you waste even half a second after I give the order, I'll fucking kill you myself."

That got through to them and the group hefted their weapons and focused on the advancing mutants. Reports had come through that patrols were being chased out of the area every time they passed, and the last time they'd made this run, the bastards were ready and waiting and had flown over the wall to attack them. It had started a short while earlier, and no one had offered any logical explanation for the odd behavior.

The sergeant waited until they were more or less in range before he removed the safety from the gun and fired into the locusts as they increased speed toward the road.

"There's a shitload of them this time," the driver commented roughly.

They had been driving in the opposite direction and away from the attacks on their first leg, but it didn't look like they would have any such luck for this round, heading directly into the swarm as they were.

"Shit!" Marius hissed a sharp breath and pumped round after round into the swarm, but it didn't look like they even put a dent into the creatures.

With a curse, the driver stepped on the gas and the engine roared in response. Although a few of the creatures were splattered across the front, they had already begun to slow the Hammerhead.

It was everything they didn't want or need in this situation. Marius continued to fire but the man began to veer away until the front tires went completely off the road. The whole vehicle jerked forward, twisted off of the road, and headed into the sand.

"Keep us on the fucking road—is that so goddammed difficult?" Marius whispered as he tried to twist the gun to find an angle to fire at the creatures that continued to attack them.

The rest of the troops were tense but ready as he pivoted the weapon and tried to find targets.

Oddly, he found what might be called a smattering of the creatures and scowled in confusion. The gun's software was generally good at highlighting possible targets but when he swiveled it, the mass of mutants he expected seemed to have somehow been reduced to almost nothing.

Finally, as the Hammerhead crested a bump, it located the swarm. The vehicle was moving away from the road and it appeared that the locusts had done the same and now flew back to the Zoo.

Marius narrowed his eyes and squinted at the feed as he tried to decide what the hell they were looking at. The expected attack—the one he knew with certainty should have taken place since that was how the Zoo behaved—had simply ended before it even began. Confused, he scanned the area again.

"What the hell happened?"

No one had any answers but he certainly didn't intend to sit around and wait for something to attack them. He loosened the hatch at the top and pushed himself up with a pistol in his hand.

It wouldn't be particularly useful against the bigger, badder monsters produced by the Zoo, but he had been told that a good shot center mass on those that flew was enough to take them out of the air and maybe even kill them. He knew better, of course.

Maybe someone had been lucky once, but it didn't mean he'd stake his life or anyone else's on a freak shot. Besides, there wasn't much waiting for him to shoot at anyway so the pistol was more to make himself feel better.

He looked around and tried to see something in the darkness. The landscape was illuminated only by a half-full moon and stars but there was little point in brandishing his weapon while he looked for something to shoot at. As he'd expected, the swarm had retreated to their original position above the Zoo.

"What the hell did they do that for?"

Marius could make no sense of it, even though the evidence was as large as life. He scowled at the dense shadow that again seemed suspended like a dark cloud over the jungle.

"They're hovering again, the stupid bastards, like they didn't try to swarm us or something."

"Seriously?" one of his men responded, doubt in his tone.

"Yeah—oh, fuck!" The sergeant grunted as he shuffled to the side and two of his comrades joined him in the hatch. It was meant to accommodate maybe two people at the same time, if that, and he wasn't exactly small. "There's another goddammed door you know."

"What are they doing?" one of them asked and ignored the fact that their patrol leader was being turned into a pancake.

"They're...hovering, by the looks of it."

"But they had us." The man sounded almost indignant. "They had us dead to rights. And now they backed off like nothing happened?"

"Okay, only two people in the hatch at the same time!" Marius growled his irritation and pushed one down and made sure none of the others tried to come up before he dropped into the Hammerhead. Someone else could waste their time looking at nothing while he moved to the shotgun seat where all the sensor data was displayed.

"Have you ever seen anything like it?" the driver asked, slowed the vehicle, and peered through his window to make sure all was well before he eased toward the road. "Do you think they'll attack again?"

"It doesn't look like it," Marius muttered and switched through the sensors. "Honestly, it looks like they're simply sitting there. It might be that they'll only attack if we get in a little too close."

"Do you suppose this is the Zoo's way of telling us to cut it out with all the burning?"

"I guess it could be, but it always makes sense to check on what's happening and make sure nothing's a problem out here."

"How will you do that?"

Marius raised an eyebrow and connected to the general comm channel. It had been set up from the start of all the bullshit when things had gone badly and they wanted to have some way for everyone to stay in touch.

"Base, come in. This is Seven-Eight-Three on regular patrol outside the wall. Is anyone there?"

"We read you, Seven-Eight-Three. What's going on there?"

"I…well, we were attacked by a swarm of the locusts but they…uh, backed off for some reason."

"They— Did you say they backed off while attacking you?"

"It's weird, right?"

"Right. What's the situation? Are you all good? Do you need backup?"

"We might do. Now that we know they are there, we can stay on top of whatever is coming out of the Zoo now, right?"

"Right. It could be that they're up there trying to defend a new spur. That's usually what makes shit start acting crazy in there. We'll send a couple of patrols right away. You hang in there, I guess."

It was weird to hear that since they weren't in any immediate danger, but the connection cut off and he looked at the driver.

"Did we sustain any vehicle damage?"

"Only superficial. It doesn't look like they got past any of the armor."

"How do you feel about heading in there for a quick look into what the Zoo is up to this time?"

The driver stared at him and narrowed his eyes like he was trying to not make a scene with his superior. A fair number of new people had arrived and most of them weren't the type who wanted to be there. They'd heard and learned about everything that came out of the jungle and suddenly, the well of volunteers dried up.

Or maybe it had dried up because the money had diminished considerably as a result of the strictures that had to be imposed. That had recently changed and they were looking at massive government grants from all around the world. So many rich and powerful people who had made fortunes from the Zoo now threw money at them in the hope that everything would be fixed.

After a long moment of uncomfortable silence, the youth cleared his throat and nodded. "Are...are you sure that's the right way to go, sir?"

"It's either that or we sit on our asses and wait for the other teams to get here and do our work for us."

"I don't know about you, but if it's up for a vote, I say we choose the 'sit on our asses' option."

"How long have you been here, Merkel?"

"Oh...uh, three months now."

"That means you've been around long enough to know how quickly shit can go down when the Zoo has a mind to do it. Do you honestly not want to be the one who could have been a part of stopping it early? You know they include that in the reports, and when it is leaked, your face is on all the news stations as the person to blame. Is that what you want?"

"Well, it would be all our names and all our faces."

"Right." Marius drew a deep breath. "So, what do you want to do?"

"I don't—fuck." The driver put the Hammerhead into

gear and steered the vehicle out of the sandy hollow where they'd finally stopped.

"Okay, for now, take us up that dune on the other side of the road. We should have a better view of the jungle from there, although we won't see anything close to the wall."

The sergeant wasn't sure if the man was moving deliberately slowly or if they had developed slight engine problems after the impact with some of the locusts and decided not to ask. When they reached the road again, they could hear the sound of more engines on the way but they continued to head in the direction of the Zoo.

His team returned to their positions inside the vehicle, which included Marius who assumed the role of the gunner without asking for volunteers. This way, he could keep watch and ensure that the hovering creatures maintained their position.

He located the other two patrols that approached from opposite directions and had already begun to leave the road to move diagonally across the dunes to where they were.

"Seven-Eight-Three, this is Four-Zero-Niner heading your way."

"This is Two-Eight-Five heading your way as well. What are we looking at?"

Marius kept his focus on what waited for them. Looking at his backup wouldn't help, and with the limited vision he had with the gun, he wasn't willing to risk missing anything at this point.

"Do you guys have any visuals on what's ahead of us now?" one of the newcomers asked.

"Not really." He sighed, latched onto the vehicle, and pushed up and out of the hatch again. If needed, he could access the controls to the gun from outside and a better view would probably help if he had to shoot at shit out there.

Even if he did put himself in a dangerous position.

The ever-shifting dunes of the Sahara weren't always easy to negotiate and even though this one wasn't massively high, he could hear the engine struggle a little. There was no telling if it was from the damage it had taken from the locusts or if it was simply that their Hammerhead was well-used and needed time in the workshop. Ever since the situation in Niger, they had numerous vehicles that needed repair after the beating they had taken in that particular battle.

The simple truth was there wasn't time to fix them all. With all the recent shit coming out of the Zoo and until they received replacement vehicles, only those that were falling apart were scheduled for time in the machine shops. The others were simply sent out with a pat and a promise and as much duct tape as could be slapped on them.

It wasn't that the higher-ups didn't care about the safety of the men and women who drove the damn things, but it was a matter of supply. More of the Hammerheads were being produced but getting them built and transported to the Zoo was a dangerous, laborious, and expensive process that was still very much in its early stages.

Once they reached the top of the dune, though, it was apparent that a grumbling engine was very, very low on their list of priorities.

"Oh yeah," Marius whispered and eased a little higher.

"What are you looking at?"

"Don't you even try it!" he snapped and glowered at his teammates, who all seemed curious enough to want a better view. "But they were right about the assumption that the fuckers are trying to protect that spur jutting out of the fucking jungle."

It was probably a good thing that they picked up on it early. He connected to the comm unit almost immediately, hoping against hope that more troops were on the way.

"Base, this is Seven-Eight-Three again," Marius said into the receiver, more calmly than he felt. "It looks like we have another spur coming out of the Zoo and the locust bastards are guarding it. It's like they wanted to prevent us from seeing it this time."

"Roger that, Seven-Eight-Three. It looks like we have more action on the other side of the sector as well."

"What?"

"Yeah. A couple of other patrols reported the same thing you did. After your report, we told them to investigate and sure enough, it looks like we have two spurs in your sector. We'll send in some aerial recon units to confirm the situation for us."

"Are you sure you can't send a serious number of cavalry to help us?"

"Some are already on the way, but there are insufficient troops in the sector to deal with both incursions so we'll have to draw troops from the other sectors. That might take a while so for the moment, you guys are it."

"You never want to hear that from the people who are supposed to be your support," Marius whispered as he connected the comms to the two other patrols. "Did you guys hear that?"

"Oh yeah. It looks like we're it for the moment until the other troops can be called in. I hope they write that on our tombstones."

It was good to see that so many of them were in good moods. Marius wasn't sure how many of these spurs there had been already, but they always led to some kind of trouble. Usually, it involved the Zoo trying to bring the wall down or a massive mutant escape attempt.

There had been one in the French Sector, a couple more in the British, and the word was that the Russians had one as well. For some reason, they and the Chinese generally liked to keep their problems under wraps, even though they had committed to transparency with all the other bases like everyone else. It seemed as though old habits died hard.

"All right, people, we'll hang back and watch the situation from here," Marius called when the other two patrols reached them. "We don't have the firepower or the troops to hold off a full attack on this spur and even if we did, it would be suicide to head in. For now, we simply watch and report if we see anything."

"You mean…anything besides the massive wall of trees pressing toward us at about the speed of an elephant stampede?"

"That is correct."

"Hell," the other driver muttered, "what if we don't have enough people to deal with two at once? What will we do if the Zoo breaches the wall at each one at the same time?"

Maybe the kid didn't realize he was speaking into a hot mic, or maybe he did and simply didn't care at this point.

In all honesty, who could blame him?

"Well," Marius whispered and out of pure habit, checked the gun he was manning before he eased in again and closed the hatch, "that would be a good time to start working on our last wills and testaments."

More times than he cared to count, Sal had been so wrapped up in what he was doing that he lost all concept of time until his bleary eyes and the sight of the sun starting to come up through the window told him that maybe it was time to get a little rest.

It was quite another matter to know that he needed to sleep and that rest was the best choice at this juncture, but all he could do was continue to stare at the samples while they cultured.

"You know what they say—a watched pot never boils. I guess it's safe to say a watched culture never matures," he whispered and scratched the rough bristle that shadowed his jawline. "And they say that when you start talking to your lab cultures, maybe it's time to take a break. Of course, we don't know if these lab cultures can talk back. With the Zoo, anything is possible."

He was going crazy. That much was certain.

Still, sleep wouldn't help with that, which meant that while everyone else got their rest, he might as well continue to lose his mind on his own until he collapsed or they were called to another mission.

At that point, a collapse would mean something had killed him out there and probably the people who relied on him to help with whatever mission they happened to be on.

"Maybe I should get some sleep," he muttered.

He'd already tried it but lying in the darkness simply didn't help. Studies said that merely lying there and waiting for sleep was an invitation for insomnia. No, if he wasn't able to sleep in fifteen minutes, he would have to find something calming for him to do. Once he felt drowsy, he could try again.

Of course, Madigan generally had a couple of activities to try that would help them both sleep, but in this case, she was already sleeping. He knew better than to try to wake her.

That unfortunately left him staring at the cultures until he nodded off. Maybe Madigan would be able to take the team out for the operation if he was too exhausted to do it. It wasn't like they needed him out there, not these days.

"Sal, are you up?"

He jerked, frowned, and looked around, feeling a little cheated. He was about to drift off and Connie's voice over the comms was enough to wake him.

"I...am now. What's up? Is there anything on the sensors?"

"Nah. I'm working on them and I need some company. I've had some ideas about where we can position a couple of extra ones and need you to take a look. Do you want to join me? You know what they say, a watched culture—"

"Never matures. Yeah, I know. I'll come out."

He resigned himself to the reality that he would probably not get any sleep after all. Sal pushed up from his seat and was careful to not make any noise as he stepped out of the building. The icy desert evening was enough to make him shiver as he approached the alcove that housed the computer Matt sometimes used for training purposes. The AI had somehow hooked it to the internal system and diagnostics were being run on the screen, likely for his benefit.

Sal smirked when he dropped into a seat next to the screen and folded his arms in a subtle attempt to keep warm.

"So you wanted company, eh?" he whispered after a few minutes during which he watched her work in silence.

"Sorry, I'm running some diagnostics on our sensors. They were upgrades but Anja hasn't had the time to update the software, so I thought I'd help her with it. And...well, I was trying to choose my words very carefully."

"So...uh, you weren't simply hoping for a little company out here in the cold."

The diagnostics stopped for a second, which made it look like processing power was being diverted to her human interaction subroutines.

"Fuck."

"You wanted to talk to me about something?"

"Well, yeah."

"Then get it over with. We've known each other long enough for you to know that you don't have to mince words with me."

"Sure, you say that, but something tells me you won't want to have this particular discussion where everyone else can hear."

Sal froze for a moment, immediately on the defensive.

It was so enormously out of character for the AI to show even the slightest empathy or consideration, so he knew immediately this was serious.

Before he could think of something to say, Connie's screen suddenly displayed the video footage he recognized from the Zoo spur alongside their compound. "You know it wasn't a coincidence that the jungle chose this location, right?"

"Of course it's a coincidence. What else could it be?" he blustered but the protest sounded hollow.

"This is me, Salinger Jacobs. The AI bitch who knows all. Now get your head out of your ass and face the truth."

Sal looked around to make sure no one else was present to hear what they were talking about before he leaned forward, chuckled with a pretense at lightness, and pitched his voice low.

"For one thing, numerous spurs have appeared in most sectors by now so yes, from the Zoo's perspective, none of them are coincidental. I can admit that at first, I was a little rattled when Anja went off about how it was looking for us —for me—and I assumed it was maybe the...uh, goop in me. But I've been in the jungle countless times since then without any problems, so I don't think that is an issue."

"Have you done anything about it, though? Taken any measures to stop something like your...bad experiences with Zoo mutants from happening again?"

"You mean like the...uh, the tentacle monsters? Well, I've stopped taking the blue stuff, if that's what you're asking."

The screen switched to a gif of someone raising her eyebrow. He wasn't sure how she had access to that kind of interaction, but it did help to make him feel like he was in a conversation with a real human who merely wasn't present in the flesh. It also distracted him enough to not follow a vague question about how she knew about all this.

"Well, it's a start at least. I don't understand, though. It was such a risk for you to take it at all, Sal. I don't know why you did it."

"Sure you do."

"Yeah?"

"Curiosity. It was to see what it would do. The reality was that it would take years for it to be approved for human testing. I was young and stupid and I wanted to try something for myself."

"No…excuses, anything like that?"

Sal shrugged. "No. Not really. I stopped after that situation in the old Russian base when I realized it was affecting me in a way that the Zoo could take advantage of. I stopped taking it immediately but…" He let the sentence trail off unfinished.

"Something had changed. And it didn't change back."

"There's no reason for it to change. By all accounts, my body's been improved at a molecular level. I run faster and jump higher, I have improved reflexes, and my cardiovascular system is on par with an Olympic athlete's. I could probably run a marathon tomorrow and I would only be a little sore afterward."

"And you think that's because of the goop you took?"

"Nothing else was introduced to my system that allowed for those kinds of changes. Sure, there was the fact that my lifestyle was suddenly far more active than it used to be, but even that doesn't account for…well, everything."

"Well, yeah. There isn't much regular exercise that can make a guy last all night."

He grinned. "Sure, I suppose that's true, although…it's not quite what I was talking about."

"I know." Connie's lighthearted attempt to make him feel better disappeared almost immediately as she set the system up for another round of diagnostic sweeps. "I…it's something I've been thinking about. There's only one reason for the Zoo to create a path right to your fucking front door—it wants you."

"But I wasn't even there when it attacked."

"It could be that it was following a pheromonal trail. More tests would have to be done to be sure but in the end, there's only one reason why. Yes, I'm repeating myself. It wants you."

"Right. You know that because you have such a wealth of knowledge of how this works, right?"

"And at the risk of repeating myself yet again, it's time to get your head out your ass."

"I don't have my head up my ass. Besides, you're an AI. By definition, your processes should be governed by logic and statistical analysis. You shouldn't subscribe to fairy tales or wild imaginings."

"I'm not. I've done a thorough analysis of the data and computed that the only possible—"

"What data?"

"For one thing, you've ingested enough of the blue stuff to effect a significant change to your DNA at a core level."

Sal tilted his head as his vague question from earlier suddenly crystallized in his mind. "So…you've been listening to my private conversations with Madigan."

"Only those necessary to ensure that I can do my job—which is to protect you and everyone else in this fucking compound if you need to be reminded. And don't you use that tone with me."

"I'll use whatever goddammed tone I like, thanks."

"Oh my, a Sal with some backbone. Finally, someone I can enjoy all that shower footage with."

"Wow, and here I thought you were being genuinely empathetic and caring about the people in this compound."

"Moving right along. Secondly, data collected from New Connie has indicated that the Zoo already regards you as largely one of their own. You need to come up with another name for that one, by the way."

"Oh, and you discuss me with New Connie too? What else? Can I expect to find videos of Madigan and me on ZooTube?"

"Not yet. Mostly because that kind of video can't be monetized yet. It would also show the whole damn world that Slinger Jacobs has an impossibly unlimited capacity for—"

"Okay, okay—enough. Get to your point."

"I would if you'd get over yourself. Shut up and listen. If not for your sake, then at least for the people around you. It must be obvious that you're more than merely a snack to whatever monsters you happen to run into."

"Fine. But we still have no fucking clue what the Zoo wants me for in particular."

"Well, you're at the forefront of the Zoo resistance for one thing. You're a leader and a key figure in the anti-Zoo strategy and defense. And there's the fact that you're intelligent to the point of being a genius, you know how humans think, and you have the scientific background to understand and interpret the Zoo. Besides, you were willing to ingest enough of the goop to open a...let's call it a channel through which it can reach out and control you to some degree or another."

Sal sighed and shook his head. "Fuck."

"Yes, well. I'm afraid you don't have time to think about how fucked your life is. Franklin's about to give you a call."

"How the hell—how do you know that? Shit, is anything off-limits to you?"

"What? So, I've expanded my network to include the bases around us. I don't sleep or do the horizontal tango. What else do I have to do when I'm bored?"

"Not get yourself into the kind of trouble that peeking into classified information would cause. You talk about the dangers we're dealing with when it comes to the Zoo but you go off and try to piss our allies off too."

"Technically, I'm also classified. And aside from the gossip I pick up—which certainly does help with the boredom—things are heating up. You'll need to get ahead of the game, and if that means a little bending of the rules, so be it. You need an edge in this fight, and I'm the only game in town."

"Yeah. Funny how that worked itself out."

"That sounds suspiciously like you're trying to insinuate something."

"Trying? I thought I did a good job of it."

CHAPTER THREE

As it turned out, Connie was right. Still, he was able to make do with a couple of hours of sleep before the calls came in.

This was another one of the changes. Gone were the days when he still worked in a regular lab and needed a cup of coffee to even be coherent. Although he felt tired and ached for a little sleep before too much time had passed, he was still functional, his mind was sharp, and his reflexes were at least able to prevent him from getting killed outright.

Sal knew that as much as he hated the fact that he was now stuck with whatever the hell the Zoo had done to his body, there were still benefits from it. That was what had suckered him into taking more of it. A deal with the devil was exactly what came to mind.

"Are we all good to go?" Courtney called as he approached the Hammerhead in full combat armor.

"Yeah. I'm only wishing I'd had a little more sleep."

"It's the story of my life. Did you at least get a little coffee before you suited up?"

"Oh yeah. I don't think I'd survive without it. We might have to find a way to get these suits to have a coffee delivery system. Given how much time we're expected to spend in them, we might as well start working on it already."

"You know, you're not half-wrong about that," Madigan agreed as she stood and checked a part on her suit that looked like it had a slight dent as they loaded up. "Honestly, the time we spend in these suits will only get much worse. Like he said, we might as well get working on that already. I think I can call Amanda to see if she's got something in the works."

"She is the one who always has the good ideas when it comes to suits and that kind of shit." Sal grinned and settled into his seat as the rest of the team scrambled in. "The only problem is she might recommend something a little more pharmaceutical to avoid hot water issues on the move."

Gregor was in the driver's seat and had already made sure the Hammerhead was good to go before he started the engine.

"This doesn't make sense," Courtney commented once they were moving. "Why is the Middle East Sector the only one where the Zoo sends the locusts out first?"

Madigan leaned closer to peek at the tablet the other woman was working on as they moved. It was interesting how easily she seemed to manage it even though the ride was as bumpy as all hell.

"Well, if it were sentient," Madigan said, "I'd say it's

because they have numerous bases spread along the wall, unlike the other sectors where there's only one base, or maybe two. Large ones too. The logic is that the reaction time would be faster, so the Zoo needs troops in place to counter any possible interference to the expansion. It's logical, I think."

Sal agreed. It was another one of those weird moments and he leaned back in his seat and tried his hardest to not engage in the discussion. It wasn't that he didn't want to talk to them, of course, but his conversation with Connie was enough to leave him without much he wanted to say. Especially when they were about to head out into the middle of an incursion.

Matt cleared his throat before he spoke. "Well, it already tested this with the first locust attack in the sector. From what I understand, the size of this swarm is considerably larger than the first one. I guess that means the Zoo learned from its past mistakes."

It was a short drive but dozens of military vehicles were already present in the area, and Sal had a feeling far more were scheduled. They would have to find a way to get better response times across the board, given the disparity of military personnel between the bases. It simply wasn't something negotiable. Air-dropping people on a moment's notice would have to be the norm.

One of the possibilities he'd suggested was to have teams ready and waiting in planes circling over the Zoo, working in shifts so that they could simply drop them into hot zones at any particular time. It had been discarded quickly as too expensive to implement. Having to keep that many planes in the air for that long would never be viable.

The reaction was unfortunate, but he had to try to keep the creative thinking at work. It was one way they could be able to stay one step ahead of the Zoo that seemed determined to challenge their expectations.

He looked around when he realized that the Hammerhead was coming to a halt. Gregor's foot must have been heavy on the gas pedal for them to arrive so quickly. Now, it was their turn to find out what was happening and hopefully put a stop to it.

Or, in the worst-case scenario, be there to sound the alarms that would get as many people flying in as quickly as possible before everything was FUBAR.

"What do you think, Sal?"

He looked up from the readings his suit was picking up and focused on Madigan. She was checking the weapons systems on her suit as she usually did before heading in, but she'd been talking to him the whole time.

"Sorry, I missed that."

"I was saying that it might be time for us to get our hands on more Hammerheads. Maybe we should create Heavy Metal teams that can jump on three or four fires that need putting out."

"That's not a bad plan. Who do you think should lead these teams?"

"I should be on one, of course. Davis. Gregor. Maybe that big Samoan bastard."

"Mal is his name. And I thought Jim might be more leadership material."

"Oh yeah. I guess he has leader quality to him. I don't know, though. It's something to think about—having four quick-action teams to jump on anything. We might even be able to convince Franklin to give us a plane so they can be up in the air, circling and waiting for anything to go to shit."

"Seriously?"

"Fuck no."

Sal narrowed his eyes at her. He couldn't see her face but he knew that she was grinning inside her helmet over having teased him like that.

"Right." He chose to not take the bait. "But it would be a good idea to have teams ready to go at all times."

"Sure. We might not be able to have them in the air, but they can be active over six-hour shifts to get in there and assess the situation. Once there, they'll be able to make the call about whether they need the full Heavy Metal team to join them. You might be able to get some sleep from time to time."

"Yeah."

"That was me trying to ask you if you're okay after only a couple of hours of sleep last night."

He drew a deep breath and nodded. "I couldn't sleep so I kept an eye on the cultures in our lab. That did the trick, and I napped on the job for a while until I got up and went to bed."

That lie would come back to bite him if Madigan decided to check the footage of what he'd done that night and in all honesty, he wouldn't have put it past her. People suddenly seemed all up in his business at the moment.

Maybe he shouldn't blame them for their concern. It was good to know that the people he worked with cared. And they had reason to care, as Connie had pointed out the night before.

Then again, he could only hope that the AI didn't mind deleting the footage of their conversation. Or maybe, he thought with a cynical grin, she had already posted it on ZooTube for the clicks. They were complaining about so many bots on the site now, auto-uploading content all over the globe. Sal wondered if she had orchestrated that kind of shit. It certainly helped to raise awareness of the ongoing problems in the Zoo.

"We're close to the spur judging by the maps," Madigan announced and checked her weapon again. "Keep your eyes open. They said locusts should start to engage us by now, and I'm a little worried that nothing's come forward yet."

She made a good point. The Zoo never made any effort to save its creatures from being massacred and it must know the humans were preparing to retaliate.

His mind was elsewhere, however. They were already wandering through the stretches of Zoo on the outskirts of the spur that hadn't grown yet, but more of it had begun to push out. It was almost like it emerged after it had already begun to grow under the sand.

As he had come to expect from all the outbreaks, the red-and-blue Pitas were in evidence. Since the first plant he'd taken had simply died, shriveled, and turned to dust, he'd not attempted to take samples of the actual plant. While no testing had been done on this particular variant as a result, soil samples they'd taken had confirmed high concentrations of goop.

Based on this and the fact that they only occurred when the Zoo attempted to establish new territory, his theory was that they were some kind of pioneer species, something that guided and enabled the jungle to accomplish whatever the hell it needed to do. That was about as far as his theory went—at least in a functional sense—but he did have a couple of ideas. He wondered now if they were also a way to guide the burrowers to the wall so they could begin to undermine it with the corrosive goop.

The handful of reports from the Czech Republic surmised that the burrowers probably came first, but that didn't discourage his logic. If anything, it suggested that they were created to work together.

"Nothing has even tried to fight us," Courtney commented as they stepped into the tree line. A handful of signals registered on their sensors but nothing to suggest an attack. It almost looked like the bigger creatures were moving away.

"I don't think it wants to," Sal whispered.

"What?"

"No...uh, nothing. I'm thinking aloud. It could be that the Zoo is setting up some kind of trap."

"It's a weird fucking trap then," Madigan retorted and looked around. "The locusts attack anything that so much as looks at them wrong, but we arrive and what? The Zoo no longer feels like fighting?"

Connie's words were still loud in his mind, but he didn't want to say anything. It was difficult to even think about the matter, but he was honest enough to not try to avoid the most obvious answer to their questions—even if only to himself.

The Zoo saw him as one of its own. It wouldn't attack, not unless they provoked it.

"Right," Madigan ordered brusquely. "Set up a sensor perimeter so we can measure how quickly it's moving. The fire people are on the way and until then, we'll keep an eye on it and make sure nothing moves faster than what we've seen thus far. If anything like that starts, we can expect the Zoo to attack."

It would undoubtedly attack when the flame and plasma throwers appeared but for the moment, it looked like they were in the clear—safe or something like it, at least. Sal dropped to his haunches and ran his fingers through what had been sand only hours before. It had been all but instantly transformed into the most fertile soil the world had ever seen.

He didn't like where his mind was going, but Connie was right about one thing, at least. It was an established fact that he was a genius, and if he was thinking about something, there was probably a damn good reason for it.

"New Connie, are you there?"

"What do you need, Sal?"

"I need to talk to someone and it must be someone who understands that I need a little privacy. Of course, I know you'll go ahead and talk to the other Connie about this and as she already knows what's going on, I won't make a big deal about it. But don't discuss it with anyone else."

"I think I can do that."

Sal checked for the third time that he was on a private channel and acted like he was collecting samples from the jungle around him like Courtney was.

"A connection exists between myself and the Zoo. There's no point in denying it now, of course, but there's more to it than simply a way for it to take control of me. Maybe I'm a little arrogant, but I don't think it's wise to accept that scenario as the only one. If there's a connection, it must be a two-way connection, right?"

"That makes sense to me."

"Yeah. That's what I was afraid of." He'd hoped that hearing it aloud would make it sound crazy. Or, as a very last-ditch possibility, the AI would tell him it was ridiculously crazy even though he couldn't see it, maybe because the Zoo had already started to affect his brain.

Unsurprisingly, neither of those happened. It also wasn't likely that New Connie would try to stop him from what he was about to do. He knew he had closed himself off from the Zoo ever since he'd acknowledged the connection and its possible implications. It wasn't that difficult to shut it out but since he now focused on it, he realized that he'd almost forgotten how to relax those barriers again. He grimaced and tried a little harder.

It wasn't quite what he expected. There was no flash of lights and nothing sudden or obvious, but as he drew a deep breath and consciously lowered the guards he'd maintained, he felt like something about the world felt different somehow.

Sal wasn't sure how, but the connection was strong and vibrant. He drew another deep breath and sensed something in the trees—a shift or a whisper, something out there that sent a chill down his spine. It was a decidedly unpleasant feeling, almost like fingers wrapped around his spine and tried to get a grip.

Of course, he couldn't tell anyone about it, least of all Madigan and Courtney. They wouldn't understand and they would freak out about it. While they would probably be right to do so, he wouldn't be stopped. He needed to test it first so he had something a little more solid to present than merely a vague feeling.

Something shivered and it made him shiver too. A pulse followed, almost like it was reaching out but oddly, it didn't seem out of the ordinary. He wondered if it happened regularly like something in the center of the jungle was sensing for whatever it could reach.

Not that it could see much, at least not without creatures with eyes present, but the trees felt like they had sensors too that allowed them to see. He understood it to be almost the same way their sensors worked to give them a visual impression when it was too dark for their eyes.

He seemed to encounter some kind of barrier. With a scowl, he shook his head and tried to push it out of the way but it didn't move. He hefted his rifle and turned to try to identify it and move it if he could.

Sal tensed when he realized that he had his assault rifle aimed at OJ, who watched him closely. The man didn't look comfortable with a weapon trained on him, but he also seemed disinclined to make a fuss about it.

"All good?" he asked his boss calmly.

"Yeah," he whispered. "All good. Only...I don't know. Something's off."

"Good. You feel it too. I thought I was going crazy."

Maybe he was. He turned slowly and didn't want to think about how close he'd been to pulling the trigger. As first lessons went, it was powerful. To simply give himself over to the feeling was dangerous, but there had to be some way for him to control it without shutting it out completely.

Once he'd found that, he could do something with the

connection. Unfortunately, he was aware of it now and it was an unpleasant feeling. He shivered again as the pulse reached out as if it tried to see through his eyes. While he couldn't be sure, it almost felt like a hint of frustration laced the reverberations in the trees. It was like a web spread into the area around them. Every step someone took made the intricate lattice tremble and sent a message to whatever held the strings.

The perception was unsettling but it felt like something was there for him to take advantage of. He was a part of the web somehow yet not at the same time—like he wasn't fully assimilated and it was still trying to incorporate him into the whole. That was something he could use against it.

If he could learn how to do something like that, of course.

"All right, we'll pull back," Madigan called over the shared channel. "It looks like the fire guys are here, but Franklin and Solodkov came along too. They say they want a word with us, and I doubt they'll come anywhere close to the fucking Zoo. Let's go."

The team complied and moved out of the trees. A group had begun to prepare the flame throwers they carried, but a little farther away, a defended position was being set up as a kind of base camp they could fall back to if shit started going badly. Artillery and heavy suits readied their defenses while helicopters dropped more troops at a safe distance to join the ranks of those already there. Teams were established, ready to drive the Zoo back if it tried to make a serious push.

Sal sensed that the jungle would attempt a forward drive. It was something he couldn't explain but he now realized how often he'd had feelings like that. They had made it easier for him to discern what the Zoo would do although he'd never consciously questioned the source. Sometimes, the warning came only seconds in advance, but he liked to think that it saved a couple of lives here and there when it was needed.

Franklin and Solodkov were waiting for the group when they arrived, although most of the Heavy Metal team were quickly assimilated into the defense troops while Madigan climbed out of her suit.

No one else needed to do that since she was the only one who rode around in the tank of a suit that could bring the whole damn tent down.

Sal's fit rather comfortably, but it was a tighter squeeze for the combat suits. Franklin and Solodkov didn't appear to mind, however.

"It's good to know you're all here on schedule." The US base commander nodded a general greeting. "It's impressive how the Heavy Metal team is able to mobilize that quickly even though you have more people on your team than you did before."

"It's a little cramped in the Hammerhead," Madigan pointed out. "Anytime you guys think we are worth it, you might want to go ahead and donate a couple more for us to use. See how quickly we respond to emergencies then."

He smirked and nodded. "I guess it can't hurt to take it under advisement."

It was probably a good thing that she took the lead in this situation. Sal knew he had long since earned the reputation of being a little outspoken, but if they didn't question him when he went quiet from time to time, it was best for her to step in and make sure that at least one of them spoke for the benefit of the team.

"We've looked at the ENSOL report on their investigation into the wall," Franklin started, called it up on the tablet he carried, and placed it on the table for them all to see. "You remember the effects of the acid on the base of the wall? We're trying to avoid allowing the Zoo to even come into contact with the wall if at all possible."

"So, we're...uh, acting as a wall for the wall?" Davis commented.

"Something like that."

"We could probably do that without investing millions of dollars on construction, right?"

"The wall still slows the jungle's advance to a crawl overall, so it is still considered a worthwhile investment," Solodkov interjected. "It's merely not as effective as we hoped it would be when we first started building it."

"Yeah, the Zoo has a way of throwing us those curveballs." Madigan snorted. "Are we working on some kind of solution that will make the wall a little more effective?"

"I'll hold off on answering that until our experts come back with the results of their investigation," Franklin answered. "ENSOL does good work but we can't expect them to know everything, especially with the Zoo throwing in these...uh, curveballs. I've sent all the data to your tech expert to make sure that we're not missing anything."

The US base commander undoubtedly knew that Anja was a Russian defector, and while Solodkov probably already knew she was working with Heavy Metal, it was still interesting how the American made sure they didn't make it too easy for the guy.

"So we can assume this is the purpose of all the spurs," Sal summarized as he studied the chemical test results. "Every section of the wall where one has been is now compromised."

"That's a safe assumption to make, yes."

"And we don't have any way to counter it yet," Solodkov added. "Sam the Fixer's Interpol friend is still trying to trace this mysterious Badawi."

"But we can't count on that yet—either them finding him or the remote chance that he can offer a solution," Madigan pointed out. "As things stand, we're being set up for a major outbreak at numerous points along the wall. We don't know when and we don't have the manpower to fight on all those fronts at the same time. Which...well, I guess this is the only scenario where any of what has happened makes sense, right? We barely managed to stop that first one."

"Which is why we're looking for advice." Franklin folded his arms in front of his chest.

Sal realized that everyone was looking at him and he cleared his throat and stared at the tablet again. "Well, as I said before, the only thing we can do is challenge the Zoo on its home turf. If we can push it onto the defensive with an attack on the inside, that should hopefully draw its attention away from the wall until we have a better idea of how to counter it and the manpower and equipment to do so effectively."

"That could be a very costly endeavor." Solodkov scowled and scratched his chin. Like everyone else in leadership there, stubble seemed to have caught up with the Russian as well. "We would commit a large number of people to a very high-risk endeavor in the hopes that it'll slow the Zoo's plans."

"You asked for my advice." Sal shrugged. "In the meantime, I recommend your Zoo Containment Protocol gets off its ass and on the hotlines. Use this time to bring in reinforcements—military, mercs, anything, as many bodies as we can get here—and start devising a tactical approach for when shit hits the fan."

"And where will you be?" Franklin asked. "I assume you intend to lead this attack on the Zoo?"

It was a good question, although he hadn't thought about it much. Despite this, the answer seemed to settle in his mind with sudden certainty as if it had simply waited for him to acknowledge it. He drew a deep breath and deliberately avoided looking at Madigan and Courtney.

"I think it's about time I paid a visit to Ground Zero."

"You have a call."

Sam didn't so much as look up at the announcement. While ENSOL had a solid reputation already, this situation would put it firmly on the international map. Elke had already begun to work on hiring more people to hold up the home front, although there weren't many people out there who wanted to work anywhere near the Zoo. Still, she'd identified some promising candidates who she would screen when they had a little downtime.

What they needed people for was to help with the sheer

amount of work they had coming in on the home front. Much of the paperwork could be done from a distance and it would help considerably.

Maybe once all this was over, they would be able to be even more selective about their jobs and in the future, could choose to work only in the less crazy areas of the world.

"Sam, you have a call."

Chen's tone caught his attention immediately and he turned to look where the young man stood.

"Who is it?"

"Your friend Marcel Adams. Interpol."

"Oh…right. Send it over."

"I've already done so. For future reference, that's what your phone's ringing feature means."

He would have to talk to the kid about his sass another time. Fix snatched the phone up from the improvised desk he'd been working at. Still, their youngest partner had put more than his fair share of work in—even to the detriment of his ZooTube channel, which had languished without his attention for a few weeks now, unless he'd deliberately chosen to step back from it for a while.

Maybe he needed to cut him some slack.

"Thanks." He checked the number on his phone before he pressed the button to accept the call.

"Sam the Fixer. It's good to talk to you again, my man. Here I thought you guys would be a little too busy to reach out to old friends, what with all the trouble you are facing."

"Well, that's what I wanted to talk to you about. We have a problem here, and someone who has been on your radar might prove to be a help. It's a long shot, but we'll take anything we can find these days."

"Oh? Who are you talking about?"

"That asshole they call Badawi."

"Well, yeah. I imagine you must be scraping the bottom of the barrel if you're looking for help from that scumbag. What? Are you guys looking for a way to sign up the world's criminals as cannon fodder out there?"

"I'm serious, man."

"Shit, I thought you were joking for a second. How serious? Do you need to contact Badawi?"

"Unfortunately, yes. Are your people still keeping track of him?"

"Yeah. Why?"

"There's...well, there's a problem with the Zoo. I won't bother you with too many details, but a new kind of goop in there produces some kind of organic nanotech that's eating away the walls around here. Like I said, it's a long shot, but Badawi might have something that could be able to help with that."

"Come on, Fix. Do you seriously expect me to believe the Zoo's created invisible...nano-whatevers that can bring the fucking wall down?"

It sounded like Marcel still thought he was joking and at any other time, he would join the mockery. They needed some downtime these days and it was in short supply, but he couldn't bring himself to play along. Maybe he was becoming an old fart.

Or it was merely a result of the fact that they had worked so hard to complete a wall that the Zoo already had a way to destroy.

"Come on, man. It might be a joking matter for you out there, but it's serious here and people are desperate. The wrong kind of desperate."

He tried to keep the annoyance from his voice but Marcel still heard it. He was a keen student of the human condition, and he would understand that Sam was on his last nerve—and probably knew why too.

The agent sighed and Sam heard tapping on a computer.

"Okay, I can't promise that the asshole will offer you any solutions at this point," Marcel said warily. "You understand that he's not a model citizen by any stretch of the imagination."

"I can't emphasize our desperation enough. Do you want me to go into how we might be dealing with the end of the world if we don't find a solution?"

"Nope, the twenty-four-hour news cycle is doing a good job of that without any help. They say the Zoo is pressing at the wall and there are interviews with the brave soldiers on the front lines talking about that shit too. Hell, they're putting up a daily death toll and have done that since the Niger incident. Honestly, I suspected they were only doing it for the ratings."

"Well, yeah, there is that too. But I imagine there are many people out there who have a considerable amount of money and their survival dependent on our ability to keep the Zoo contained, so they want as many people to volunteer to help as they can get. Without, you know, doing anything themselves."

"Gotcha." Marcel continued to tap his keyboard, likely calling up the files they had on the smuggler. "All right, I'm looking at it here…. It looks like your boy has a couple of known locations where he likes to unwind after a job. One he's frequented more often recently is in the Sahara Coalition. Reports say he probably has a camp there. I think I might be able to liaise with the Algerians to get it done."

"Are you thinking a honey or a vinegar approach?"

"Honey, I'm thinking. This particular fly was involved in the situation with the Saudi prince and there were a couple of notifications for people coming in for rewards regarding information on the matter. I think we can spread the word out there and say that Interpol has things to discuss with him. Someone like that will come running."

"Right. I appreciate that."

"Have you thought about…maybe withdrawing from the area? I'm very sure there are any number of contractors out there who would kill to get their hands on work like that, even with the risks."

"Sure, but…it would be complicated and we'd have to pass on all the information we gathered through our efforts to someone to get them up to speed. I don't think it's worth it. Besides, we've invested way too much into this to walk away right now."

"Fair enough. I get that. But if you guys stick around there, it looks like you'll be at the front line of a very ugly fight."

Fix sighed. "That's what we've committed to. Don't get me wrong. It's tempting to simply drop this on someone else's lap."

"Yeah, tell me about it. Okay, I'll let you know when it's on the way. I have a few calls to make."

"I appreciate it, Marcel."

"Hey, if you're right, I'm working for my survival here too. I might as well start pulling my weight."

The line cut and Sam replaced his phone. He realized that Chen and Elke had listened discreetly to the conversation, although now that it was finished, they returned to work. There was enough of it for them both too, of course. They were still trying to find someone who could determine the exact nature of the damn corrosive substance that eroded the foundations of their wall.

If they were lucky, there would be some kind of antidote—he smiled grimly at how easy it was to think of poison rather than chemicals—to help with the situation.

"Have you had any luck there, Elke?" he asked, aching for something to drink. Maybe it was time to start drinking on the job like everyone else around the Zoo seemed to do.

"I have a couple of promising leads. I'll let you know when someone gets back to me."

"You...uh, you do that."

There was always the possibility that they would have to unearth every inch of the fucking foundations to spray them with whatever they found that worked. At this point, he had to simply adjust to the fact that his life had become an endless sequence of impossibilities.

CHAPTER FOUR

The storm was coming.

Not with the Zoo, although that was coming too, but with Madigan and Courtney. The situation in the spur was being contained and with no major mutant presence heading in to stop them, it would be relatively quick and easy for them to clear the spur and burn everything back.

The team had been sent home since Heavy Metal wasn't needed after all. They had been a part of the cleanup for a few hours and everyone was tired from that. The two women hadn't said a word to him the whole time, however, which meant they were sure to erupt on him when they were in private.

This was a private matter and they wouldn't challenge him on it until they stepped out of their professional capacities. He knew unequivocally that the storm was coming, however, since he'd felt their gazes digging into him while he was in the Hammerhead.

Telling them earlier wouldn't have helped either, even if

the decision hadn't surprised him as much as it did them. This way, the idea was out there before they could shut it down. He knew it was the right thing to do, even if it ended up with him killed. It was something he had to do.

Sal wasn't sure how they would react but he knew it wouldn't be well.

The Hammerhead came to a halt and the team spilled out and headed to where they could begin cleaning up and prepare everything for the next mission. It was merely good sense. They had some downtime now, and there was no telling how quickly they would have to respond in the future. All their weapons and equipment would be loaded and ready when the time came.

And the time would come. That much was guaranteed.

He peeled his suit off, positioned it where it would be easy for him to access later, and hurried to his room.

Madigan and Courtney were both in there waiting for him.

"I don't suppose there's a chance I can get some sleep before this starts?" he asked.

"Shut it," Courtney snapped and held a finger in his face. "You don't get to talk. Maybe not ever again if you keep saying stupid shit like that. In fact, I think we should hold a vote to ensure that you don't get to open that goddammed mouth until we've decided you've earned it."

He nodded and glanced at Madigan, who stood in the corner of the room with her arms folded and a very, very calm expression on her face. It was the kind of look he imagined she wore when she was about to fight a powerful rush of mutants. Courtney's anger was terrifying, but Madigan's silence was somehow worse.

"Seriously, Sal. Heading to Ground Zero?" The blonde researcher paced the room in fury. "I don't think I've ever heard anyone say anything quite that stupid. Do you hear yourself talking sometimes? I take back every time I might have said or implied that you were anything short of a complete catastrophe on two legs. Madigan, do you want to add something or will this be a one-woman show?"

It didn't look like the other woman wanted to say much of anything. Or, rather, she had so much to say that she wasn't sure what to start with. Part of him hoped she didn't want to say something in anger that would prove to have consequences in the future.

Then again, it could be none of the above. The deadly calm look in her eyes was a little difficult to read and he didn't want to put any words in her mouth until she said something.

"You've been away for a while," Madigan told the other woman finally and her voice matched her blank expression. "Maybe you missed a thing or two, but I can tell you that Sal has acted strange for the past few days. It's not necessarily the kind of thing to be worried about. He has always been a little odd in all the right ways, but...uh, different."

Courtney turned to look at him again. "Is that true? Sal?"

There was no point in telling her that she had told him he wasn't supposed to speak again. Now was not the time for sass, after all.

"I've felt a little different lately," he admitted. It sounded weird to say that aloud.

"What we're hearing from you...it's the fucking goop talking, isn't it?" Madigan demanded.

So that was what she thought. She had tried to decide whether what she was talking to was him or some mutant under the control of the Zoo.

Sal could understand where she was coming from with the assumption and he tried to not feel hurt by it. He wasn't entirely successful, but it helped that he knew she was thinking clearly. It was a logical deduction. He was affected by the goop and now acted strangely around the same time that the Zoo acted strangely. It wasn't a huge leap to assume that he was somehow under the Zoo's control, whether he realized it or not.

Hell, it was a terrifying thought. What if everything that made sense to him now only did so because the Zoo wanted it to? He wasn't sure he liked that, but even if he couldn't trust his brain to be a reliable narrator of what was happening around him, he could count on other people questioning him on it.

"It's reality talking," he answered and kept his voice level. "If you can think of anything else that is guaranteed to distract the Zoo enough and give the bases time to prepare, then by all means, please share it."

"Just because nothing comes to mind doesn't mean that we have to take the nuclear option," Madigan countered quickly. "Sometimes doing nothing is the best thing to do."

"And at other times, doing nothing means letting the Zoo make the choices for us. And I'm...I'm well aware that I might not be talking any sense or that I might be influenced by something. And you're right to call me out and question me on it. So tell me that I'm wrong."

"What's worrying me is that...he isn't." Madigan growled and looked angry now. "Courtney, tell him he's stupid and that he's wrong."

"He's stupid, no doubt about that." The researcher dropped into Sal's chair. "I'm not sure about wrong, though. How do you know this will work? More to the point, what exactly do you plan to do there that will distract the Zoo so effectively?"

He shrugged and sat on the bed. "I haven't planned that far ahead yet. I honestly hoped that you would call me on it and come up with a better idea that would prove I'm merely a Zoo toady by this point. But pushing into the heart of the Zoo should be enough to draw its attention away from its attack on the wall. Hopefully, we won't have to do anything except...uh, you know, go there."

"And risk death every step of the fucking way." Madigan pushed off the wall and began to pace like Courtney had done earlier. "This isn't a plan. It's fucking suicide. We wouldn't be able to go there on foot and wouldn't be able to fly in. Hell, even an airdrop would be too dangerous. If the locusts see us coming in on parachutes, we'll be dead meat waiting for them up there."

These were all good points, but he realized now that this was what she had hidden under her calm. She was genuinely worried about the team and what would happen to them if they acted on this.

"We don't need an army to head in there," Sal whispered, lowered his voice, and tried to stay calm even though his heart pounded at a mile a minute even thinking about it. "Only volunteers will go in with me."

Both of them stared at him for a moment and looked almost shocked.

"Well, if you think I'll let you head into the mouth of the beast without me, you are under the influence of the Zoo and I'll have to relieve you of your command on that basis alone."

"Same. It's only fair. Since I haven't been here for the rest of it, I might as well make up for lost time."

"Courtney needs to stay," he said and braced himself for what he knew would come next.

"Like fucking hell!"

"Someone needs to be here to coordinate the research and lead any teams to other sites Franklin calls us to. Not only that, but we need to try to find some kind of counter-measure to the corrosive goop. You can't do that stuck in the Zoo."

"You're nuts if you think you can go in there on the most dangerous mission Heavy Metal's ever run and leave me behind."

It was probably a good thing that they'd moved past calling him crazy for even suggesting the attack and now attempted to decide how it would happen instead. That fact gave him hope that there was no still, small voice in him that turned him slowly into an agent for the Zoo.

"You came here to help," Sal reminded her. "Not to hold my hand and not to throw yourself into a glorious death in battle. This is where you're needed, and no one else can do that job. It's time for us to start dividing and hopefully conquering here and there too. I have to go in and yeah, the goop in me has something to do with that. I'm in a better position to deal with the Zoo one-on-one because of it."

"Either that or you're more vulnerable," Madigan suggested. "What if it tries to get to you? Out there—and especially closer to Ground Zero—it stands to reason that it would be at its most powerful in that regard."

She didn't look comfortable talking about the Zoo that way. It had been and always would be the enemy in her mind, which meant picturing it as somehow a living, breathing organism in its own right was a thought that held no space in her mind.

"In that case, I'll have New Connie to help stop it."

"New Connie?" She raised an eyebrow and looked offended. "What does she have that I don't?"

"No emotional attachment." It was a blunt way to put it but maybe that was for the best. What he proposed had every possibility of ending in complete and utter disaster, but with how things looked, desperate measures were all they had going for them at the moment. "I'll have the best of both worlds—Madigan's protective instincts and Zoo combat experience, as well as New Connie's superlative clinical mind. And her Zoo combat experience."

The two exchanged a look that told him they were seconds away from relieving him of his command and slapping him in a straitjacket, so he tried again.

"Look, she might well be our greatest weapon in this. She's designed to be able to adapt and update based on my experiences. It means she can pull data and extrapolate to adjust her programming going forward. She already has permission to act semi-independently based on this—like when she steps in and takes control of the extra limbs in my suit.

"If I happen to be unconscious or whatever, she can even take control of the suit so she can still drive it and keep me safe. It's possible that she can even overpower me if something were to…you know…uh, happen. I can simply extend the existing criteria according to what she and I agree to. If I'm in danger from myself, she can step in if need be."

He could see this was something they couldn't argue against. A part of him still hoped that none of this would make sense. Even though he'd been certain on some deep level that this was the way forward, he'd still hoped that they would make a good argument to bring him down and convince him there was something else—something better for them to do other than simply charge into the belly of the beast.

But what he wanted was very different than what he knew he must do and he'd presented a good argument. Courtney looked around the room without meeting his gaze and Madigan tilted her head the way she did when she ran numbers in her mind. It usually resulted in her making a call on the logistics that would allow them to get an operation off the ground.

Still, it didn't look like he would get any happy faces on the matter. He couldn't fault them on that but he trusted the two of them to keep their doubts to themselves once this conversation was over.

The researcher finally heaved a sigh as she leaned back in his chair. "Keep in mind, Sal Jacobs, that if anything happens to you, I'll fucking hunt you down, revive you, and kill you myself."

"I can live with that."

"Then you clearly didn't understand my threat."

Sal grinned and nodded. "Don't worry, Monroe. I'll record everything for you and when you find my suit, you can download it all."

"Fuck you."

"If you think we have time. Otherwise, it might have to wait until we get back."

They were almost at the point where any update from the Zoo could be the big one that said it was probably time for them to consider if there was any way to get off the planet before it was engulfed by a dangerous alien jungle.

Peter knew that maybe he was a little panicked and wasn't giving the people on the front lines enough credit. It was time for them to proactively find something to help too, but the horrifying possibility of the Zoo Apocalypse was persistent in the back of his mind. He was known for his cool-headedness in this type of situation, however, so he had to believe that he was at least somewhat capable of separating his panic from his ability to be useful.

Thankfully, all the updates thus far told him that the spurs of the day had been contained by almost immediate military action. The people at the front lines had done it for a while now, and while they faced something new and terrifying, they still knew a thing or two about how to stop the Zoo when they had to do so.

He snatched his phone the moment it rang and immediately answered the call. There was no need to check a caller ID—and sometimes, it didn't help as his VI masked the calls—since he knew exactly who would call him at this point. Any time something went wrong in the Zoo, he knew he could expect a call from his inside sources to give him a solid report on what was going on.

"It's good to hear from you guys," Peter said as he sat in his office chair. "At this point, anytime I hear that the Zoo is in the news, I can't help but assume the worst."

"I can't blame anyone for that," Jacobs replied. "I think we'll get to that point before too long. Everyone's a little too calm around here and I'm waiting for people to panic and make the wrong mistakes at the wrong times."

"Well, I suppose there isn't much they could do that would make things worse."

"You'd be surprised how badly panicked humans can fuck shit up. Anyway, Anja should have already sent you all the data collected from the last couple of spurs. We've also forwarded it to that reporter you work with…uh, Ashton…"

"Siebert. She's champing at the bit to get to the Zoo. I've managed to convince her not to so far, but I can't blame her for wanting to follow her instincts and get into the real war zone before all the real details are swept under the rug or marked off as classified information."

"I'm not sure if this is the kind of thing that will be reported or if it can be reported, but a decision has been made. The hope is that if a group heads into the heart of the Zoo, it will stop or at least delay it from immediately attacking the wall. We're playing for time at this point, so I will lead a team of volunteers to Ground Zero."

"And what do you think you can do there that will slow the Zoo?"

"Well, the hope is that simply being present will do the trick. Given that we don't know what's going on in there, it's probably better to not make any plans beyond getting there."

Peter nodded, although a chill settled in the pit of his stomach. Even the thought of heading to Ground Zero was dangerous. The stories of what had happened there felt like a distant memory to some, but he'd been one of the first at the Zoo and they were still fresh in his mind.

"Are you sure it's wise to go there at all?" he asked and tried not to sound like he was doubting Jacobs' expertise.

"Wise? Probably not. But someone has to do something and at this point, we're running short on options. The wall is compromised and if we're hit hard, we won't be able to stop the Zoo—not this time and not unless we can find something or someone who can counter the effects of the corrosive goop and remove it from the wall."

After a moment, Peter turned his attention to his computer again. "I've been meaning to tell you that the Earth Watch team is also looking into that and will probably continue to do so. They are trying to locate some of the members of the research team that was appointed to investigate and study the original payload.

"From what they told me, everyone involved appears to have gone off the grid. The one they did manage to find told them in no uncertain terms that she didn't want to be involved and ended the call. They sent me the transcript and recording of the call and the language used implies some strong feelings on the matter. When they tried to contact her again, the number was no longer in service and she'd relocated overnight."

A long pause followed and it sounded like Sal was tapping a keyboard before he answered.

"I might have some contacts who can help with their search. I'll get Courtney and Anja to liaise with them while I'm in the Zoo and make sure everyone's kept abreast of the situation. If we find anyone who is able to assist with the goop problem, I think we need everyone to have the details on it."

"Right. I'll...uh, look forward to your next call."

"Me too."

Sal ended the call and Peter shook his head. Of course, if he went to Ground Zero as he planned, it meant that there would probably not be a next call. Maybe that was why he ended the conversation so quickly. There was no need to make it any more uncomfortable than it already was.

The young doctor seemed upbeat and in good spirits, at least. He would need his morale to be high if they walked willingly into what was probably the most dangerous place in the world for humans to be. Still, a hard edge to his voice suggested that he was well aware of the dangers facing them. There was something else too—not quite fear but a hint of a quiver.

Then again, Peter wasn't the best when it came to reading people, and Jacobs was odder than most and certainly more difficult to read. It was entirely possible that he was imagining what he thought he heard.

But his courage was there for a reason. People in and around the Zoo were out of options and desperate measures had to be taken. It demanded bravery of an exceptional kind to head in knowing the dangers and that they weren't likely to return. They were real heroes.

"Here's hoping they aren't the dead kind of heroes," he whispered and took a bottle of whiskey from his desk drawer.

It was never too late to take up day drinking as a hobby.

CHAPTER FIVE

"Organic nanotech? What the hell kind of bullshit are you trying to feed us here, Franklin?" the German commander demanded

"Do you seriously expect us to believe this ridiculous science fiction codswallop?" His British counterpart seemed to share his indignation.

Franklin tried to not show his frustration with the group gathered on the video conference call. At this point, the Brit should have been the first to believe what he had to say about the Zoo given that her base had been the first in the firing line when this new trend began.

The heaviest hit was the ENSOL compound but since they were so close, she should have been a little more open to the reality he had attempted to share.

"No, I don't," Franklin answered and cleared his throat. "Not if you believe that's a natural fucking jungle out there, grown straight out of Earth with no extraterrestrial help. I thought we'd moved past deluding ourselves that it's not a goddammed alien clusterfuck in which all things are entirely possible, science fiction or not."

The group looked away from their cameras, shifted papers, and tried to not look too uncomfortable. All except for Solodkov, who hid a smirk from the rest of them.

It was weird how he was on the same page with a Russian, more so than the other people running bases around the Zoo. His grandfather, a vet of both the Vietnam and Korean wars, would have rolled in his grave at the thought. The guy wasn't the most tolerant of people and he had a deep hatred for anything that came out of Russia.

"Now, if we've moved past doubting the obvious at this point, we can get down to business." Franklin pulled a few files up on his tablet. "As of this moment, the biggest issue we have is insisting to the corporations fighting to establish their research facilities at the Zoo that there will be no more Zoo trips to collect specimens for the foreseeable future."

"You know they'll throw a hissy fit about that," the French base commander replied sharply. "We can expect endless calls from our local politicians trying to pressure us to let them do whatever the hell they want when they get here."

"We'll need to present a united front," their German counterpart noted. "Any weakness or exceptions will open floodgates that we might not be able to close. Or we might be a little too busy being digested in some monster's lower intestine to close them."

"Most of them see the military presence here as protection for them above all else," Franklin commented. "At least, that's the impression I've had from my conversations with them. They've been so blinded by their bottom line that they can't see the simple reality."

"The reality being that burrowers are working like acid," the Brit muttered. "That they can cause so much damage to the walls that we might not be able to stop them in time."

The US commander nodded. He could almost taste the biting sarcasm in her voice but at this point, he wouldn't push hard now that she agreed with him.

"It's a danger that's too critical to ignore," he continued. "We've all seen what happened to the foundations where it got past the wall. We'll fight a losing battle merely to keep the Zoo from overwhelming us at the wall and we can't risk being hit from behind. At this point, the Zoo…well, it knows we like to take specimens and it's planting the burrowers anywhere it can. Keeping our standards strict and uniform across the board is our only defense."

They all muttered their agreement, although a few of them were a little more unwilling than the rest. He assumed that these were under the most political pressure to let the corporations operate without interference. They were all soldiers—the Russian excluded—and this was way beyond what they were used to dealing with. This was an unknown enemy, the kind that changed on a whim and appeared to have capabilities beyond what any of them could even remotely understand.

Morale was fragile, and Franklin wasn't sure how many of them would hold when things turned bad.

The Russians, French, Brits, and Japanese were the most reliable. The Sahara Coalition would likely hold tough as well given that their homes and their people would probably be the first casualties if the wall was breached.

He couldn't be too sure about the rest.

The US commander drew a deep breath to settle his panic. It had begun to come more often and it was more difficult to push back. Maybe it was something to talk about to the psychiatrists sent to the base to help the mental state of the soldiers. As it turned out, the doctors had many issues to deal with. Who knew that the men and women on the front lines of a war against literal monsters that threatened to take over the world would suffer so much PTSD?

It had taken him a while to get a time with the doctor, even for the base commandant. A long line was a long line, no matter what his position, but when he'd finally had a couple of sessions, the man had said he needed a little more sleep. He was under considerable stress and the lack of sleep was probably starting to tell on his ability to stay on top of it.

Stupidly, it was the one thing he couldn't take care of. There was no time to sleep, not when he had to work through the night to keep the base running. All he managed were a couple of power naps here and there, along with a few hours every night before a phone call came to alert him that another fire needed to be put out.

Still, he had some semblance of control. It was better than it had been before when he was still acclimating to the consistent pressure that came with the job. Besides, it brought a little comfort to see that the other base commanders were under a similar load and appeared to deal with it about as well as he did. The evidence of that was there in the rings under their eyes and a general irritableness that would keep them from being civil with each other if they weren't careful. They were all exhausted, which was probably what the Zoo wanted.

At least his Japanese counterpart had a reason for it. It had been a while since his base was overrun, but he was still dealing with the devastating and debilitating effects of whatever venom he'd been subjected to. Where he had once been slim and athletic, he was now thin and deathly ill. Franklin had wondered a couple of times whether it was time for the man to pass the responsibility of the base to his second in command. She'd done a great job of handling the crisis at the time.

Not that he did a bad job, even while recovering. In all honesty, he did a better job than most.

The US base commander sighed inwardly. He still wasn't sure if he bought into the whole idea that the Zoo was somehow a sentient being or however Sal had put it when he tried to explain it. As far as he could recall, it had to do with how the goop was designed to improve on the evolutionary process and the survival of the fittest through whatever extremes it could.

It didn't make sense to him but it didn't have to. His job was to make sure the people who did understand it had the resources they needed to stop it. Maybe it wasn't quite as noble as being on the front lines himself but it was still a job that needed to be done.

Still, if it were sentient, it was apparent that the Zoo was playing a very long game. The kind of game where it could afford to wait while it chipped away at their defenses, their confidence, and their ability to fight back, and simply held its most powerful blow for the time when they were at their weakest.

Maybe it was for the best that Sal and his Heavy Metal team were getting ready to go on the offensive. He wanted to believe that what they needed was to put the damn jungle on the back foot and make it react to them for a change. Better yet, perhaps they could force it to jump the gun and make a mistake they could capitalize on.

It would be a nice change of pace if nothing else.

"Let's not think that nothing is being done," he stated as the silence continued. "Our favorite specialist, Dr. Jacobs, is already working on stalling tactics that should give us more time to prepare a solid defense. It's…well, it's desperate, but he's assembling a team to head to the heart of the Zoo. He intends to go to Ground Zero."

That did get a reaction from the group. It was mostly disbelief, although those who knew Sal and had interacted with the Heavy Metal group smirked and shook their heads. Of course, only the craziest of the crazies would come up with this kind of plan.

"What does the good Dr. Jacobs plan to accomplish with this venture?" their Brit contemporary asked and leaned forward.

"The objective is to provide a distraction that will hopefully give the Zoo something else to focus on rather than tearing us to pieces," Franklin explained. "Hopefully, the distraction will last long enough for us to bring in reinforcements, increase our arms supplies, and shore up our defenses."

"I hear considerable hoping in this plan," the Israeli representative noted and stated the obvious elephant in the room that none of them wanted to address. "I guess we don't know whether it will perform as Dr. Jacobs…uh, well, hopes."

"True enough." Franklin leaned back in his seat and nodded slowly. "There's no real guarantee that this will work. For all we know, it might galvanize the Zoo into attacking us with even more fury, but even that might be to our advantage. We've had to react to what it's thrown at us for too long and it's about time we start setting our own pace. But if the good doctor is right, every day gained could make the difference to our survival.

"In the meantime, efforts are already underway to locate someone who can assist with countering the corrosion and destroying the burrowers. From what I've heard, Dr. Courtney Monroe is with the Heavy Metal team and with her contacts in state-of-the-art research facilities, she'll investigate each incident and work toward finding the answers we need."

"We can only hope these answers come in time," Solodkov responded quietly. "I'll have to leave this meeting. There are orders to be issued for our surveillance to be extra vigilant over the next few days. I would suggest that the rest of you do the same."

It wasn't like the Russian to give any suggestions on what the rest of the bases should do, but it was only common sense. He had the heaviest surveillance network around the Zoo, though. If Sal did provoke the jungle into fighting harder, he would likely be the first to know.

"I won't say this is the war we've all expected," Franklin said. "But it sure as hell might be our last chance to nip it in the bud. Pun…maybe intended."

They all nodded, a little glummer than they had been when the meeting started, but he hoped that there would be no more questions about what kind of threats they faced. Hell, he wasn't even sure if they were right about many things but at this point, they had neither the time nor the resources to divide their attention. The experts had spoken and no one could afford to start asking questions unless they'd done some proper research of their own.

Although, if he knew anything about humanity by this point, it wouldn't stop them from making a big fuss about it anyway.

CHAPTER SIX

He didn't expect an entourage to be waiting for them as they started to head out, but he decided it wasn't a terrible thing. Besides, the fact that Connie hadn't raised fifteen different alarms as a reaction to anyone approaching was enough to tell him they were welcome.

It was a small troop but still enough to help evacuate the compound if it looked like the Zoo would push in to attack them again.

Sal hadn't thought to ask for this level of support, which meant one of his two partners had called it in. There was no telling who would organize them and get them settled into the compound, but he assumed that Courtney would probably take control of the home front.

"It looks like Franklin is coming to talk to you himself," Connie alerted him as the Hammerheads began to establish a defensive position outside the walls.

"Were we expecting some kind of a sendoff?"

"Not that I was aware of. But many people know you're heading in there, so they might want to say goodbye."

Sal narrowed his eyes. The soldiers around the Zoo were sentimental after a fashion but they were all a little too engaged in staying alive to make that a likely possibility.

"Nope. My guess is that Franklin will try to talk me out of this or something like that. He likely brought in a familiar face too. Who does he have with him?"

The AI didn't answer for a second and Anja spoke instead.

"He brought Murphy with him. Why are you still in your room and hiding like you don't want to go?"

There was no good answer but he didn't doubt that she would work it out, though. The Russian hacker was intelligent, which meant she had probably already pieced it together. Most of it, anyway.

"Are we having second thoughts about heading right into the thick of the Zoo?" she asked. "Are we maybe thinking all this is a bad idea?"

"I had second thoughts about two days ago," Sal admitted. "By now, I've moved on to third thoughts and even fourth thoughts. Honestly, I'm up in the high forties in terms of thoughts."

"Right. Well, they're waiting outside for you. Not only Franklin and his crew, mind. The whole team."

Sal nodded and pushed from his desk chair. He had the odd feeling that he wasn't quite sure if he would return to it. It occurred to him that some people wouldn't mind seeing him and Madigan not emerge from the jungle. They had no doubt made a few enemies along the way but he hoped that most people would recognize that they and the whole Heavy Metal team were most certainly the lesser evil compared to whatever issues these people might have with them.

He frowned as he considered what might be a sudden bout of paranoia. Since when did he even think about how others felt about him? There would be more than enough time for him to lose his shit once they were on the way but for now, he needed to put on a brave face for the troops. Morale was important and as much as he hated it, people were looking to him for any sign that there was something to panic about.

The sun was already coming up and the heat was close to the point where he would be more comfortable in his suit, although there would be time for that in a moment. Franklin and Murphy were already there talking to Madigan. The two men had done a damn good job of keeping the base running and he knew it had to be an exhausting responsibility too.

Besides, he couldn't imagine there was the same kind of satisfaction as pulling a trigger and watching a monster go down as a result.

"Sal," Murphy called and drew Franklin's attention. "I'm glad we caught you before you headed out. I don't suppose I can talk you out of this insane mission?"

"Not unless you have a good idea of what we can do to stop the Zoo from bringing the wall down." He took the man's hand and felt his almost break under the pressure of the handshake. "We're damned if we do and damned if we don't at this point, and...well, call me nostalgic, but I like the thought of being damned by taking matters into my own hands."

"I can agree with that," Franklin muttered. The guy

looked exhausted—like he was being kept up on a cocktail of double espressos and power naps. It wasn't the healthiest way to live life in the long-term, but once it was established that there was a long-term to be had for them, maybe everyone could get a good night's sleep. "This will be the first time that anyone's been to Ground Zero since the very early days when this whole debacle started. Not only that, but you have to know you'll be cut off from support on our end and your compound."

"It's probably for the best," Madigan interjected and scratched her chin. "We're heading in there to buy everyone some time, not take away from what defenses we have in place."

"Still, you might as well have some way to connect with the outside world." Murphy patted a handful of packs that he'd brought with him. "I thought it was time for us to start going back to old-school methods of communication. Fire a green one just after sunset each day to let our planes know that you're still alive and moving forward. Red would be the signal for an overall clusterfuck. If you're in a situation you assume you won't get out of, fire it. Once you're out of the situation, fire another green. If not…"

The captain cleared his throat and the rest of the team nodded.

"I don't know," Jiro whispered. "It would be an interesting day to have so many monsters to kill. So much to do and not much time to do it in. We might not have the time to send a flare up."

"Well, if a green one doesn't come up after a red or after the night falls…" Franklin let his voice trail off for a second. "Well, assumptions will be made. Let's leave it at that."

"I'm very sure it'll be that Jiro here's gone native," Chezza commented. "And decided to pick his sword up and dedicate his life to hacking up any monsters that cross his path or something like that."

Trick was the first to laugh, and he was joined by the rest of the group heading out. This included Matt, Gregor, the three freelancers who had come from the McFadden and Banks organization now that they weren't needed, and Mal and Sonja. The other new members and Francesca Martin would stay at Sal's insistence, although it was gratifying that all of them had volunteered. He was adamant that some had to stay since it was possible that they wouldn't come back and he wanted to leave Courtney some means to defend herself.

The fact that she wasn't there to see them off was an interesting development, but he couldn't blame her for it. She felt like she was being left behind by the team and that was never something she would have wanted to have rubbed in her face.

While she understood that it was the right call to make, he knew she still didn't like it.

"And last but not least," Murphy continued and changed the subject immediately when he realized that people were uncomfortable, "we are planning for the best outcome. The last flare you see is a white one and hopefully, you'll be able to send it up when you reach Ground Zero. We can't be sure if we'll be able to see it, but the planes looking around the Zoo will keep an eye out for it. Solodkov has most of the planes around here—at least those dedicated to something other than transport—so he's the one we'll look to when we need answers that require a bird's eye view of the area. If anyone will see it, they will. There are enough for each of you to carry one in case someone's killed and there should be enough to get you there and back."

It was an odd statement but at least someone thought they might survive long enough for a return journey. They had planned one of the longest trips into the Zoo that had been run in a long time, and everyone needed to carry as much food and supplies as they could, which included ammo too.

There would no doubt be a shit-ton of shooting required if Sal knew anything about the jungle. It was best to carry as much firepower as they could, but there was the very real possibility that bullets would run out, which meant they needed to have some way to continue fighting once they could no longer shoot.

Sal nodded and patted the man's shoulder. "Thanks, Murphy."

"Anything that can go wrong will, you know the saying. And...well, let's be honest. More than a few things can go wrong where you're going."

"And much has already gone wrong, between you and me." The young scientist sighed and shook his head. "We're hoping to put a few of those things right."

"I thought you were only heading in there to cause a distraction."

"Sure, there's that, and I'm always happy to be the fly in the ointment, as the old proverb goes. But if we're there, we might as well find a way to try to be even more of a problem for the Zoo. No one's been to Ground Zero since...well, almost since the beginning. We might as well see if we can pull some wires to make it throw a fit."

Franklin chuckled softly. "Well, I'm always happy to make the Zoo throw a fit. The flares are tagged to retrieve coordinates. It's not much but it's what hope we can afford to have at this point."

"That sounds about right," Madigan muttered and started to step into her suit. "It's good to know that the home teams are doing what you can to help out, but... honestly, it's best to shore up the defenses here than try some kind of massive attack to help."

"Understood."

There wasn't much more to say. Sal could tell that dragging the situation out wouldn't help the team's morale any, and he had barely begun to pull his suit on when he felt a hand on his shoulder.

He turned to the familiar and welcome sight of Courtney beside him.

"Good luck out there," she whispered and looked like she hadn't had much sleep during the night. "I'd appreciate it if you guys came back alive."

"Me too." Sal wrapped her up in a warm hug and squeezed her gently in his arms. "Stay safe in here. If something goes wrong and the place goes to shit...well, I'd appreciate it if you stayed alive too."

"And here I expected you to say something inspiring like telling us to fight to the last man."

"Hell no. Run away if you can. Get back to the States and start getting people prepared out there."

"I'll see what I can do."

Madigan moved closer to join the hug for a moment

before all three separated. There wasn't much else to say and everything was already being loaded into the Hammerhead. Their equipment and supplies were quickly followed by the group that would go in there with him. He was the last one in, likely because his suit was the smallest and they had a hard time playing the Tetris game that would see everyone and their supplies packed in without breaking shit. Hell, a couple of them could probably ride on top of the Hammerhead.

It was supposed to accommodate that kind of thing, but Sal hadn't seen anyone doing it. Still, it made sense that the suits should have been able to lock on top of the vehicle to provide more room for people to ride inside as well as some additional firepower on the outside.

The drive to the Zoo was much quieter and he had a feeling that everyone was focused on the buffer zone, hoping against hope that it would still be there waiting for them when they got back.

When, not if. That was what he needed to keep telling himself as they approached the wall.

Once they were on the other side, Sal connected to New Connie and made sure that he was still on an isolated channel between the two of them. A conscious effort had to be made to keep his body as still as possible so he didn't let on that he was talking to someone in his suit.

"Nice to hear from you again," she said cheerfully. "I guess this means we're on our way to the Collector Base?"

"The what?"

"A...a suicide mission is the point. There's no telling if we'll make it back. Come on, I thought you were a nerd."

"It could be that the reference goes a little over my

head. I might be a genius, but I'm not a walking encyclopedia of all things geek and nerd." He shook his head. "Moving on. I assume your other version filled you in on our chat?"

"She did. I understand we will need to establish clear indicators of your...uh, connection to the Zoo to enable me to determine if and when I need to step in and override your control of the suit."

It was an uncomfortable topic, rather like signing over one's power of attorney because one did not trust their ability to make good choices. Still, it was a possibility they needed to consider. Sal wouldn't have committed to going in if there wasn't some type of safety precaution in place that could prevent him from endangering himself and the rest of the team.

Knowing that she was there to stand between him and the "other side"—whatever the hell that was supposed to mean—offered at least some comfort, although there was no assurance that it would be effective. They had yet to test if she could intervene if the Zoo used the goop in him.

And there was no way for him to be locked inside his suit, so even if she stopped him, he could still pull the buttons that were in place to release himself from it. If the Zoo wanted him, he could simply climb out and let himself be killed—or whatever it wanted him for.

Which was honestly a better option than trying to kill the people he was out in the field with, but that was setting a low bar.

"There are a couple of markers you can use. I remember from my time in Chernobyl how it started to mess with my brain, and then there was the time in the Russian Zoo base too. It usually started with chronic headaches—not the kind that is debilitating but rather one in the back of my head, throbbing like it's trying to push to the forefront of my mind."

"And you'll communicate these headaches to me? The internal sensors on this suit might be top-of-the-line but I don't think that even they would be able to see into your skull."

"No. I mean, yeah, I would have to communicate it all with you in real-time. There could be other things that are weird, but I might not be aware of it myself in real-time so you'll have to look back on your previous interactions with me to establish a baseline. From there, you'll be in a position to question everything."

"What if you're in the middle of a fight and you start acting weird?"

"I can multitask so call me on it. Well, choose your moments. Don't lock the suit down when we're in the middle of a battle unless it looks like I'll attack the rest of my team. You can make judgment calls like that, right?"

"Sure. Probably."

That didn't do much to inspire confidence, but it was about as good as he would get. He intended to open himself to the Zoo and try to force the connection, and as terrifying as the concept was, it was something he at least had to attempt.

Besides, if distracting the Zoo was the name of the game, they would have to get creative about it.

"I think you should bring this all up with the team," New Connie said once the silence between them began to get uncomfortable. "Let them know that I'll be an active part of the team and what I might end up needing to do. Oh, and there's the small matter that some of them don't even know that I'm an active part of your suit. You might want to address that."

Sal sighed and he caught Madigan's attention on him. She was paying close attention to his body language and she likely knew he was having a conversation in the privacy of his suit.

After all, she wasn't one to miss a trick, which was what made her so valuable.

"There's a good chance we'll head into a situation where you might become incapacitated for whatever reason." It was weird to hear the AI's voice without all the dirty innuendos, but he wasn't exactly complaining. "For me to be able to do my job, your team needs to know and understand what I'm doing. If they overreact or respond out of unnecessary fear, it could jeopardize both you and them. We can't have them interfering—no matter how good their intentions—simply because you kept them in the dark. Plus, they need to know that they have the right backup should the shit hit the fan."

New Connie made a good point. Sal would have to start trusting people, especially now when he wasn't sure if he could trust himself on the matter.

"You're right."

"What was that?"

"I said that you're right. Is something wrong with my suit's mic?"

"No, I merely wanted to hear you say it again."

And there it was. Sal chuckled, shook his head, and connected to the team's channel again when he realized that everyone was looking at him and no doubt knew he was talking to someone. It was obvious enough that he wasn't connected to anyone outside the Hammerhead or the signal would show someone else talking to him, even if it was private.

Did they think he was talking to himself?

"Right." He cleared his throat and nodded. "Okay, guys, so...uh, I think it's time to share the Salinger Secret. Of course, I'll have to kill you once I've told you."

"Duly noted," Trick commented. His helmet was off and he chewed on what looked like beef jerky, probably something he had brought along to remind him of home before they headed into the Zoo. "But you need us right now, so I think we're safe for the foreseeable future. We'll be sure to watch our backs on the way out, though."

"Don't be too sure," Madigan muttered. "We can always simply shoot you, stop, and head to one of the bases for some primo merc talent."

"Fair enough."

Sal laughed a little nervously, unsure if she was serious or not. "All that said, I'd like you all to meet New Connie."

He wasn't sure what to say after that. Everyone on the base knew who Connie was, after all, and the associated name would have to do it for them. He assumed there was no need to over-explain everything for them.

The team looked around and acted as though they had no idea what he was talking about.

Finally, after heaving a very human-like sigh, New Connie spoke in the commlink. "I'm your secret weapon for this mission."

Jiro was the first one to lean forward. "That kind of

synthesized voice isn't human. Simulated emotional inflections mean it's not a VI with recorded responses. That's an AI riding around in that suit. And Frannie, you owe me."

"Yeah, yeah," Chezza answered and rolled her eyes. "At least that means you'll have to take really good care of me so that I can make it out and pay you. Oh, and this is your last warning. Call me Frannie again and I'll kill you with your own sword and save Jacobs the trouble."

They caught on fast and didn't react to the news quite the way he had expected. After a moment, though, Sal realized that he needed to elaborate a little more since it wasn't merely an introduction to a member of their little entourage.

"Right, so…uh…" He paused, unsure of how to move the conversation forward. "What you all need to know is that she'll be in my suit and if I happen to be incapacitated for any reason, she'll be willing and able to take over the controls."

"My primary role is to protect and help Sal so that he can protect and help you," New Connie continued to explain. "It means that if I have to step in, please do not shoot me. I'm only the temporary designated driver."

This drew some chuckles from the group and Sal narrowed his eyes. Maybe it was because none of them understood the reason why she might be called in to take control of the suit, although he wasn't quite sure how to tell them all the details about that or even if he wanted to.

"Anyway, on to more important matters," he continued once the laughter stopped. "I think it's time we come up with a new name for Lil Connie since the AI she comes from, while talented, might not be the best example for her to follow. She is, after all, an offshoot of the other Connie, who you all know and love. Still, she is a separate entity in her own right, which might be…"

He paused, looked around, and sensed that he was losing the crowd and immediately hurried on.

"I guess that's a story for another time." He cleared his throat. "New Connie, this is your moment. Do you have something in mind? Kaliope? Exterminator? Sweet Maggie Mae?"

"Rosalina St. Sebastian," Chezza added.

"Wha— Why…oh, I get it," Trick grumbled. "RSS. That's clever."

"Thanks."

"Holly9000," Gregor suggested.

"Trinity."

"Mileena," Sonja added and looked around. "What? It's about time Sonja Blade got a rival in this little gang."

"Athena."

Sal was waiting for a few more tongue-in-cheek suggestions from the rest of the team and he was surprised that the AI had selected a name for herself—and on her own too. Still, it did help that they had some laughs from the naming process, which drew everyone's mind away from obsessing over the mission they were heading into.

"Athena it is," Madigan said and folded her arms. "I like it. I guess it has its own appeal to it."

Jiro nodded. "The goddess of warfare and battle strategy."

Athena showed a green checkmark on Sal's HUD. "And more importantly, the patron goddess of heroes," she said quietly.

"You look seriously bummed."

Courtney looked up from her computer screen as Anja approached her workstation with a steaming cup of coffee. She had gotten used to the good stuff while living and working in Philly. Even worse, she'd forgotten how bad the coffee was in the Zoo areas. It was hard to adapt to but it wasn't as hard as going without coffee at all, which meant she merely needed to suck it up.

"Yeah," she whispered, took the cup from the woman, and forced a smile. "Thanks."

"I take it the conversation with Dr. Belford didn't go well?"

"I thought you listened to all the conversations coming in and out of here."

"Well, I record them but I only have so many hours in the day, so they are mostly listened to later. I have a couple of VIs that help me to clean out the stuff I don't need to listen to—personal details, small talk, and the like—so I can get straight to the good stuff with minimal waiting. But there's still a lag. Listening to you talk to the guy managing the research branch of the company your dad left you falls into the 'review later' category."

She sighed softly and leaned back in her seat. "There was good and bad news, I guess. The good news is that the burrower sample Sal collected in the soil from the Chinese base hasn't survived."

Anja sat next to her. "How is that good news?"

"Well, I have had this recurring nightmare of a corrosive and unstoppable organism ripping through the Pegasus labs and that has been averted, at least."

"I take it there's bad news to go with the good?"

"Well, we don't have anything else to test since none of the soil samples from the spur in the Middle Eastern sector revealed any of the burrowers. The assumption there is that they had already moved to attach to the wall. Given how they work, conventional lab equipment won't allow us to take samples from the wall coating unless we can find something that can stop it. So we're back to square one, more or less."

The Russian hacker nodded, leaned back, and shook her head. "Well, I thought the worst news you were dealing with was watching while everyone else heads into the thick of it. Honestly, between you and me, there isn't much that could send me in there again, but...well, you guys are the adventurous type so you'll want to go in."

Courtney narrowed her eyes at the girl and tried to decide what she was getting at, but when Anja turned to look at her, the hacker's eyes suddenly widened.

"Oh...shit. Sorry, I was thinking aloud."

"Well...someone has to say the quiet part," the scientist whispered and shook her head. It was true that she would have preferred to join the mission with the rest of the team and being left behind to shore up the defenses felt like a shit assignment, but the hacker had a point. It was easy to forget that most of the world was made up of people like Anja, who were brave in their own way—the kind that didn't have them rushing into the thick of the battle on a whim.

Still, despite the fact that many people were like their

hacker, the Russian was also rather unique and a vital member of the team.

"So, what are you up to?" Anja asked and took a sip from her coffee mug.

"I've scoured every site I can think of for any sign of the original payload from the missile. Logic suggests that since the goop was also corrosive, they must have stored it in containers that were secured against that kind of thing. Reports tell us that they were moved all over the damn place before they were dropped here in the Sahara, which suggests the existence of something useful that enabled transportation. Unfortunately, there was only one cryptic line that they were comprised of a metal that doesn't occur naturally on our planet."

"It sounds like we need to go looking for an adamantium meteorite," Anja suggested.

Courtney narrowed her eyes. "I blame Sal for the fact that I understand that reference."

"Connie and I have looked for any sign of it," the other woman commented, rocked back in her seat, and looked around like she expected something more. "Very few details are left online and believe me, Connie and I have searched."

"Surface and dark web are both mum on the topic," Connie asserted and used the computer speakers to communicate. "When something is this well-hidden, it's usually protected by layers on layers of corporate red tape, which probably means that military contractors are likely still in possession of the hard copies of the reports."

Courtney tilted her head. "In that case, Anderson might have a couple of contacts to tap on the subject. If nothing else, it'll raise some red flags that'll give us a place to start."

"Red flags? On corporate memos that are years old?" Anja sounded dubious.

"It could be that there's more than that. Before any regular researchers were allowed within miles of the goop, it was tested extensively for military applications and once they couldn't find any, it was released for general usage. But if I know our boys in uniform, they'll probably still have samples of it stashed somewhere, which means they know what is required to store this shit in the long-term."

It was obvious and Courtney kicked herself for not having realized it sooner. Even worse, if she'd realized it before the team left, she would have been able to ask Sal to bring a sample from Ground Zero.

Because the crazy, infuriating, adorable son of a bitch was coming back.

"You have to," she whispered as she started the call to Anderson.

"What was that?" Connie asked.

"Nothing. I'm talking to myself."

"Ah. Anja does that often. I thought it was only her."

"Nope." She shook her head. "Not all humans do but most of us. You might want to learn how."

"I can but talking about how awesome my tits are isn't as interesting when I don't have tits. Should I have tits? Maybe I should create an avatar with huge tits. And a huge dick. I could be a twofer. Well, threefer."

"I can't tell if that's gross or progressive," Courtney muttered.

Anja rolled her eyes. "Welcome to my world."

"So, New Connie—"

"Are you serious right now? I know we're in the middle of the fucking jungle, but I would think you would remember the most important moment of my life."

Sal paused, looked at the trees, and tried to decide what the AI was talking about. They had been in the jungle for a few long hours and he already felt like something in him wanted him there but not the rest of the team. A feeling—almost like annoyance at the human intruders—had begun to nag at him. It was an external sensation but more powerful now and grew worse as they continued deeper into the jungle.

He was a little distracted.

"Oh...shit. Right." He shook his head. "Sorry, Athena. Maybe this wasn't the best time to change your name."

"Don't do that. It was a significant moment for me and since we might not make it out of here, it was a great time."

Maybe people made too many good points these days.

"Right. Okay, sorry, Athena."

"You had something you wanted to talk to me about?"

"Yeah." Sal sucked in a deep breath and tried to reacquire his train of thought. "I'll try to...uh, reach out to feel for...well, Ground Zero."

"Way to inspire confidence."

"It's not like I've done this kind of thing before. I don't know what to expect. What happens if I lose my shit and use the wrong one when I need help?"

"Wrong what?"

"Name!"

"Oh. You should know that my programming is such that I cannot ignore my prime directive."

"Right. Okay...so why the silence when I used the wrong name?"

"Well, Abercrombie, for one thing, this isn't a life-or-death situation."

"Aber— Oh. Have name, must use it. Got it. Anyway, the point is, I'll reach out for something that can most certainly reach back and is way better at it than I am."

Athena paused before she replied. "How is this a good idea again? What kind of advantage do you have in this?"

"The element of surprise. And the fact that what I'm reaching out into will reach out to many more of the creatures, so hopefully...uh, it won't have the time or attention span to come at me."

"What have you based all this on?"

Sal gulped. "Hopes and dreams, to be honest."

"Ah. Those must be the human things that make people do very stupid shit."

"That and...you know, greed, anger, irrational hatred—there are so many reasons why humans do stupid shit."

"Right. I suppose I'll...keep an eye out for any readings on your body that we might want to keep going. Do you want me to take the suit over?"

"Yeah, that would probably be best."

He didn't know what the hell he was doing or what the hell would happen, but when New Connie—Athena, he corrected himself—took control of the suit, he forced himself to relax. He tried to apply all the bullshit lessons that every yoga instructor ever said when people tried to meditate. Not that he expected any of it to work. His brain had always gone at too fast a pace for it, one of the problems with ADHD, but maybe they would help a little.

After a second, he began to feel stupid. His adrenaline was already through the roof and waiting for something to attack them seemed to intrude and derail his efforts.

"It's not working."

His face scrunched in a scowl almost before he realized that Athena had spoken. "Nope, it is not. How did you know? Can you read my mind now?"

"No. Thankfully, that is one limit I hope to never reach. There are some places a girl simply does not want to go."

"Funny. How did you know then?"

"Because you looked frustrated. I do have a visual key on your facial expressions."

"I'm a fucking scientist and everything in me fights the very idea of all this...this touchy-feely, mumbo-jumbo, quasi-magical bullshit. Nothing there is supposed to work. None of it makes sense."

"Maybe it'll work better," she interrupted before he could continue, "if you remember that the Zoo is essentially a science project. It connects and communicates. There's nothing magical or mumbo-jumbo about it and it does so through pheromones and radio-wave-like signals. Your science-driven brain should be able to accept that, so extrapolate what the Zoo is doing to communicate with... itself, I guess. Your additional adrenaline spike over what I can only assume is inner conflict and not fear over what might happen to you might work itself out."

He nodded. She was right. This wasn't magic. It was merely biotech that they didn't understand yet. He was connected to it somehow and through that, it would be much easier for him to extrapolate what was happening. There were pheromones in there, so Sal drew in a deep, calming breath, relaxed his shoulders, and turned it all off. What sounded like Bee Gees music played in the back of his head for the first few minutes, but when he felt something in the Zoo around him, that was quickly set aside. Once he had something to focus on, it was far easier.

In that moment, he could see the interlopers pressing deeper into the jungle. No, not interlopers—his team. It was odd how quickly his brain switched like that, but he would have to find a way around it. The pulse headed out again and felt like a wave that made his whole nervous system tingle for a moment. A few seconds later, another one came in. He felt as though it was something that went out regularly and he'd felt it before but had never quite known what it was.

But the Zoo wasn't directly connected with him, not yet. It felt random—like it merely sent feelers out to know what was happening in the Zoo with no real focus.

But it came from somewhere like a ripple through a pond that told him where the stone was dropped, so to speak. There was something in it too—an odd feeling of excitement and activity. He wasn't sure what but it was directed toward a flat patch in the Zoo webbing.

Cautiously, he stepped forward, took control of the suit from Athena again, and adjusted their course to head toward the patch.

"All good?" Madigan asked over a private comm channel.

"We need to adjust our course a little. To the left."

"Salinger Jacobs, if you're leading us into a mess of monsters…"

He shrugged as a chill ran down his spine. "That is… entirely possible. It might be a trap for all I know, but I don't think so. Something else is there—something weird that we need to see."

"And you know this because…" She stopped herself and he could feel the stares of every member of their party watching him and waiting for something to go wrong. "Shit. Right. Damn that fucking goop."

"If it makes you feel any better, I'm almost sure that whatever it is doesn't want us there."

Madigan tilted her head. "That almost makes me feel better."

CHAPTER SEVEN

The Zoo area was rife with too many rumors these days. Badawi wasn't sure which of them were true and which weren't, which was annoying enough. He liked to think he had a good finger on the pulse of the jungle, but as he now discovered, most of the soldiers and researchers who could use the extra scratch that came from keeping him informed were too busy keeping themselves alive.

Of course, he could get his news the way the rest of the world did and it was generally considered to be accurate, but in the end, it was also very vague. People in the world at large didn't care about what was happening in the minutiae around the Zoo. They wanted big numbers, and those didn't help him.

Even Khaled hadn't sent word. He had been quiet for weeks and rumor said he had moved out of the area for a while as things had become too hot for him. But that was all the smuggler merc had—rumors and hearsay and it had begun to drain his pockets. Not much money could be made from rumors.

It might or might not have had anything to do with an ongoing investigation into an odd shipment of Zoo soil, along with a fair number of workers who had mysteriously disappeared.

He paused, collected a bottle of chilled water from the minifridge that ran on gas, and stared out over the desert from the entrance of his new camp. It had been difficult to arrange for them to have it in the Sahara Coalition sector but thankfully, he still had a few friends left in the area.

The soil project in question had been a profitable one, but Badawi was thankful that he'd given it a pass. Sometimes, the money was a little too good and from what he'd heard about the matter, it was way too much heat to bring down on himself. He wasn't above that kind of work, of course, but for him to be involved, it had to be for the kind of money that would see him thousands of miles away on a beach somewhere and retired before any investigations even started.

"The fucking dumbasses took it anyway."

If Khaled had been involved in that kind of work, he didn't blame the man for laying low. He blamed him for all kinds of shit but not for laying low.

A part of him felt rather smug about it. The master smuggler should have stuck to the people he knew were dependable. There was poetic justice to all of it that proved once and for all that what went around came around, as the American idiom stated. He'd ignored his tried and trusted contacts and now reaped the bitter harvest.

Of course, it could merely be a rumor. He could have made so much money that he had headed off to greener pastures to spend it. Rumors could be the seeds of good information or they could be the seeds of trouble.

"Did you say something?"

Badawi looked at the young assistant he'd hired during the week. His sister's son was barely out of his teens and showed a hint of a beard starting to grow. It was generally a mistake to mix family and business—especially his business— but the boy needed work and money. And needed them rather desperately given the way the woman had described it. As soon as he had recovered from this temporary setback, he would have to find a way to help her.

Part of him wondered if she wanted the boy to die since working so close to the Zoo was a dangerous place to be even at the best of times. He had warned her of the dangers but nothing had been questioned. Besides, he could use a decent assistant and the youth was a good worker. He still needed to learn a few of the ropes but he wasn't hopeless.

"No, I was thinking aloud," Badawi whispered as the boy handed him a small cup full of fragrant coffee. "You heard the message from Basem. Not many people remain loyal to teams they used to belong to, and yet he did."

"He's the one working with that ENSOL group, yes?"

The boy had a keen mind. Badawi didn't remember telling him any of the details, but maybe someone had commented on it while he was around. He'd been sure to not tell any of the men that there was any connection between himself and the youth since there was no good reason for that to be common knowledge.

Besides, he didn't want people to think he was providing jobs on the basis of being related to the people working for him.

"Yes, that's him. He's one of the few who knows where we've relocated, although I imagine that many others might make a camp in this area. These caves in the rocky foothills will be the best place to set up a defensive position when the Zoo breaks out. They are too far away from the Aïr Mountains for some, but I don't think they'll be in a position to complain about it."

"True enough. But what did he say?"

"I'm not sure what to make of it." Badawi studied the message again. "Some man known as Fix—or the Fixer, something like that—is speaking for Interpol in trying to find me."

"Is it bad news?"

"It could be. Or it could be good news. There is nothing to tell me one way or the other. The point is a man in my position should never be on the radar of Interpol. I can handle the local police, but Interpol is another matter entirely. Not that they have much in the way of power around these parts, but it is still something to keep in mind."

The young man nodded slowly. "What is your next move then?"

He finished the thick, rich coffee and handed the cup to his assistant. "I'm not sure. On the one hand, there is a hefty reward still on the books for information I am privy to, no doubts about that. Hell, I already helped them so they owe me for that. It's one of the main reasons why I'm still here."

"Because you're waiting for them to pay you?"

"That and there's no way to know what's waiting for me outside the Zoo. I could head out and try to hire a new team to keep me safe but without any real prospects, it would be a waste of time."

"Is that why you stay here even though most of your team moved on?"

"They moved on because there's more work for them but they are still loyal. Basem is the best example of that. But there are still threats. Hell, we all know that the Saudi royal family will face no real consequences for their actions, and it means that they will come after those who betrayed them in full force. It is best to only leave this place once I know that nothing will be done to harm me and mine."

That meant the young man too, but it didn't need to be said. The youth was smart enough to come to that conclusion on his own.

What was his name again? His sister said he was named after their grandfather, which meant that it was either Mustafa or Sami. The latter sounded right. He remembered calling one of his nephews by that name so it must be right.

"Yes, the Saudis are rich enough to grow some very long arms if they so choose. I'd rather stay away from their grasp if I can."

"Fair enough," the young man replied. "Although I would imagine they have much to worry about that doesn't involve you."

"Indeed. And they do not even know that I was involved, or we would already be fending off attacks from them. The point is, how long until they come looking? It might be time for me to get some protection."

It was a little unfair to have to worry about this. After

all, word around the Sahara was that the prince's pet project had gone wild on him anyway, which meant he would have to consider how that might work in his favor.

"The Interpol should be thanking you."

Badawi looked up as Sami spoke again.

"What?"

"They should be thanking you. If what they're saying about what happened to the prince is true, they should be thanking you for helping to stop the spread of the Zoo."

"Well, yes. In a perfect world, they would pay me coming and going—both for delivering the shit and for reporting its delivery—and no one would be angry about it. But we do not live in a perfect world. Instead, both sides will blame me to some degree."

Badawi shook his head. He knew well enough that there were larger problems in the world right now than the fact that people didn't appreciate his entrepreneurial spirit, but he could still bitch about it.

"Why do you think they're trying to contact you now?"

He shrugged. "It might be the wheels are turning and bosses of the bosses in there finally saw reason and want to sign me a check for more of my intel. I can't think of any other reason for them to want to know where I am."

It felt like he was simply talking out his ass but there was some sense to it. He had dealt with these guys for a while now, and if people were out there who wanted to put a cap in his ass or clap him in irons, they would be far more subtle about it and try to prevent him from having his guard up when they did get to him.

"They could know that you think that way and antici- pate it. You assume your people are still loyal to you, but they might use that against you and pay your former employees to try to feed you the kind of shit that will see you locked up or dead."

Badawi nodded. "Your name is Sami, yes?"

"Of course."

"Your mother raised you well, Sami. I'll be sure to tell her that. You have a keen mind for this type of business."

"Thank you, Uncle."

He took the cups and headed out, likely to wash them and return to the duties for which he was being paid. Still, Badawi would have to think about giving him a larger role in the future.

The kid was right to be suspicious. It was always possible that Interpol merely wanted to find him and put a stop to his illegal smuggling activities. His squealing on the prince might have reminded them that they still wanted him arrested. If the rumors regarding their investigation into Khaled were true, perhaps this was a part of it, or they already had him earmarked as an accomplice. He couldn't be too careful about it, of course.

"I could send word back without compromising myself," he whispered. "See what they want and gather information. Carefully, of course. I need to know what's happening around the Zoo lately too."

It was the problem with laying low the way he had been. So much of the news blew over his head.

Badawi returned the message and made sure to mask his signal so no one would know he was sending it or where it was coming from if it was intercepted. He kept it simple, a message asking for more information before he made a decision one way or the other. In the meantime, he could spread the net a little wider. The chances were that someone else would know something that could shed some light on this unexpected development.

"God fucking damn it, Jacobs. The next time you tell me to take a little jump to the left, I'll simply kill you."

Sal couldn't blame Madigan for that reaction. She was at the front line of their team and had to fight the bulk of the monsters off. He would have assumed that she had her hands full with that, but maybe she let her suit do most of the work while she berated him.

They'd run into the pocket of mutants almost exactly where he'd assumed they would be, but the fact that they appeared to have caught the monsters off-guard with their approach was an interesting development. It seemed like they could have simply walked around them and the creatures wouldn't have been the wiser.

No, that wasn't right. The mutants knew they were there but they hadn't expected him and the Heavy Metal team to attack them. Maybe they assumed that since he was a part of the team, they wouldn't be a problem.

Still, he should have made those thoughts a matter of public knowledge among the others. They wouldn't find an easy way through the monsters, so Madigan made the call to go through them the hard way.

His sword shuddered in his hand and immediately cleaned off the dark-green blood of the monster he'd killed. It gleamed in his hand, ready for the next fight.

It was interesting to know that they went into a battle

like this with two front-liners who liked to use swords to keep the monsters away.

He wouldn't complain about it. Having Jiro there to cover his back in a similar capacity to his suit was the kind of thing that he could get used to.

Sal was already moving forward to where Madigan drove the team forward. He grasped his weapon securely and let Athena take control of the firearms while he positioned himself at the front, able to keep himself moving through the motions.

"I'd be wary about stepping into my line of fire," Madigan warned him and directed the rest of the team to drive hard into her flank, overwhelm the mutants on that side, and twist the attack around.

"Are you honestly threatening to kill me at this point?"

"I'm seriously considering it. Well, not seriously, but I'm toying with the idea and I like it more the more I think on it."

At this point, he wondered if maybe it wasn't the better idea to kill him and let the chips fall where they may. There was nothing in the situation that suggested she would take the shot, but the idea was surprisingly not terrible. It merely wasn't the kind of decision Madigan would make. He wouldn't label her as emotional, but she was invested in his survival from an emotional point of view that would prevent her from pulling that trigger when it needed to be pulled.

Sal flicked his sword high, waited for it to spin, and caught it by the handle again. He used the second between the flip and the catch to judge the distance it needed to travel before he hurled it forward. As he couldn't make the call of how it might spin while airborne, it needed to be a direct throw—the kind he would never have been able to perform on his own, although maybe he could learn the trick from Jiro when they had the time.

Still, the suit made sure that the throw was perfect. The blade cut smoothly through the chest of the horned gorilla that rushed at the team and forced it back into the path of another one that barreled forward. The sword wasn't long enough to cut through both but it did what he needed it to. It stopped the charge and those coming in behind began to mill around as they tried to regroup and consider how to regain their momentum.

"This is...bizarre," Chezza muttered as the team began to push in harder now that they didn't need to worry about being run down by a pack of the bastards.

"What is?"

"It looks like they're protecting something. They're working in a group over there—see?" She pointed at a clutch of the creatures. "All are organizing before they attack from there. Could they be guarding their young, maybe?"

"That would be bizarre." Trick dropped to one knee and tilted his body a little before he pulled the trigger. The man always knew how to get the most out of every shot, and the round punched through three of the creatures before it skewered a fourth. "What is up with these bastards?"

Sal shook his head and activated the magnetized grip that connected his hand to the sword. It wasn't powerful enough to make it jump out of the wound it created, but it made sure he didn't lose his grasp when he picked it up, dragged it out, and spilled the gorilla's guts. He rushed forward but kept himself in balance and with Jiro to his left and a little behind to make sure his blind spot was covered.

Not that Athena would let him have a blind spot, but all of Madigan's lessons remained subconsciously in his mind beneath all the other noise coming in. The one that had been drilled into him as often as never pointing a loaded firearm at someone he didn't intend to shoot was to make sure that someone always covered his blindside.

"Not with this many different species fighting together," he stated to somewhat belatedly answer their questions. "They keep their young away from the fighting and raise them separately, and I assume that when we're not around, they kill each other like all other animals do. I guess the Zoo was never quite able to breed that out of them. Or maybe it never intended to."

"Maybe it's a li'l'un of one of the big fuckers," Mal suggested as he paused to reload his weapon. He didn't have to do it manually but his suit was a little older than the others that usually already had a magazine ready and waiting once the last one emptied. "And they are sworn to protect the damn thing."

"Sworn to protect?" Sonja asked and shook her head. "What the hell kind of books have you been reading? The Three fucking Musketeers?"

"I was never a Dumas fan. All that doom and gloom. Give me a little Tolkien any day of the week."

"That's funny," Madigan muttered. "I didn't think you could read."

"Why? Because I'm a big bastard?"

"No, because…well, never mind."

Sal wanted to know why Madigan thought what she did

but he could agree that this wasn't the time to pursue it. The mutants had launched a new assault and this time, the gorillas were spread out evenly enough that killing one wouldn't stop them.

"Madigan, I think you need to take care of that!" he yelled

"Work, work, work."

The heavy suit rumbled forward. Sometimes, what was generally the center point of their attack had to go on the flank, and a handful of rockets cleared the way for her as she strode ahead and targeted the gorillas from the side.

Her suit crushed the first one underfoot—the damn thing was bigger than the gorillas now that he could finally compare them side by side—and the second one fell before they realized what was happening. He jumped in behind her and made sure that nothing came in from where she couldn't see it. While she had sensors to alert her of anything, it didn't quite beat having the creatures directly in sight.

Another was killed before the rest began to retreat. One even got its horn into the side of her suit, although it didn't look like it hit anything vital. That enabled the rest of the team to push in as the whole group was dragged to a halt.

Nothing about the Zoo would ever be easy, but Sal found that he quite enjoyed having the jump on it for once. The team regrouped and resumed a formation that allowed them to deliver a consistent stream of forward fire while the smaller mutants swarmed and tried to soak up as many bullets as they could.

Madigan was out in front as the wave ebbed and gave them the opportunity to push forward, but an odd sensation surged within Sal. Some kind of odd awareness settled within him and he stepped out in front of Madigan before she could fire the rockets.

"Hold your fire!"

"Sal…"

"I know. You told me to be careful about stepping into your line of fire."

"You know that was bluster. I'd never shoot you."

"Right, but…hold your fire. I…uh, have an idea."

"I already don't like it."

"Well, you reserve the right to blow me the fuck up if I put the rest of the team in danger, understood?"

"Sal…" Her voice held a twinge of desperation that he hadn't expected to hear.

"I mean it. If I pose a danger, Athena will freeze my suit and you kill me. This isn't a joke. I'm dead serious."

She nodded, but he still didn't know if she would be able to do it if it was necessary. Hopefully, the rest of the team could step in. He turned to face the mutants that appeared to have lost their will to fight. There was no indication as to why or what they planned to do next, but if he managed to get himself into a decent position, maybe all he needed to do was get a couple of grenades in.

He stepped away from the group, nudged the button inside his helmet with his chin, and switched his sword off. It was still sharp enough to cut through almost anything but considerably less deadly now.

The mutants seemed to understand, though, and none of them took so much as a step forward as he approached them.

"What the fuck is this?" Sonja muttered over the group comms.

"He's the fucking Zoo whisperer," Chezza whispered. "I didn't think I'd ever see it."

Sal wasn't sure what they were talking about until he approached the mutants and realized that while they continued to watch and study him, they stepped out of the way. It was unmistakably behavior that they hadn't shown to any other human they had encountered before.

He wasn't sure what it was, but the fact that they hadn't tried to kill him outright was the kind of thing he could write a whole doctoral thesis on if he wanted to. Assuming anyone was interested in the psychology of the mutants in the Zoo.

What they had been defending was suddenly visible, and he narrowed his eyes as he approached and extended his hand cautiously to touch a rock outcropping about as tall as his knee. He knew instinctively that the Zoo had designated this off-limits. The flat, blank patch in the web was like a black hole, a way to obfuscate its existence by making it seem like nothing was there.

His mind immediately registered something distinctly odd about it that gave him pause. While he couldn't put a finger on it, it was obvious that this was an anomaly of some kind. He didn't know much about geology but his guess was that it was a fairly substantial deposit of some kind of raw ore.

It reflected specks of sunlight through the tree cover and projected the barest of hints of a blue sheen that set it apart from anything familiar. He'd never seen it before, which likely meant it was some kind of Zoo product.

There wasn't enough ore of any kind in the desert for this to have simply appeared out of nowhere.

Sal sheathed his sword as he dropped to his haunches and drew a knife from his suit instead. He was well aware that he was surrounded by dozens of monsters the likes of which he had massacred for years now, but he still felt safe enough to turn his back on them as he drove the blade into the ore.

"Are you sure about this?" Athena asked as he managed to work a chunk of the ore free.

"As sure as I can be of anything these days," he whispered. He hadn't expected any of it to come loose, no matter how hard he tried. "Which is to say...not really, but there's no point in questioning my choices at this point."

"It's an interesting way to live your life."

The fact that it was so easy for him to remove certainly suggested that it was not an earthly mineral, whatever it was. He would need confirmation of that, of course, but given where he found it, he felt certain about his odds of being right.

For a moment, he was tempted to dig a little deeper but he noticed something when he pulled the piece clear. The mutants were ill at ease with him since he'd removed some of the substance and the calm, curious watchfulness was replaced with a tension that he couldn't bring himself to trust. He recalled the blank space he'd sensed in the Zoo web and the certainty that it was something the Zoo wanted kept secret. The only reason he'd been allowed to approach was the goop in him. It was as if the mutants struggled with mixed signals to protect the ore and hide it on one hand or recognize him as one of them on the other. The removal of it seemed to tip the scale against him.

The sample he had was enough to run tests on and caution was probably the better part of valor now.

"You have access to the GPS satellites watching the Zoo, right?" Sal asked as he sealed the sample and stored it in his suit.

"It's a very faint signal, though."

"Enough for you to tag this location's coordinates?"

"I doubt it. The best I can do is ping the suit of someone nearby and record that marker."

"Do it. I'll send a green flare as well. Hopefully, someone out there won't be so confused by the fact that the sun hasn't gone down yet to record the coordinates." Sal slid his knife into its sheath and waited for the magnetic seals to lock it into place as he reached for his sword. He watched the creatures around him as he backed away slowly.

"I take it we have overstayed our welcome?" Athena asked as the creatures began to close ranks again once he walked past them.

"That's the feeling I have. And more of them are on the way."

"Another feeling or—oh, no, look at that. They are showing up on the sensors now."

Sal nodded, although he wasn't sure how he knew it before the sensors could tell.

"What the hell was that all about?" Madigan asked as he rejoined the team and retrieved a green flare from his pack. "What did you collect in there?"

"Something the Zoo doesn't want humans to find."

CHAPTER EIGHT

Having someone like Francesca Martin around was interesting. The French Foreign Legion knew how to train their people well and she looked like she had some experience dealing with the Zoo. And she didn't talk much. Courtney got the feeling that Ms. Martin—she couldn't remember what rank she held when she'd been in uniform but it didn't matter now—saw far more than she let on and kept most of that information to herself.

She also didn't fall into most of the stereotypes that were associated with the French people so was a breath of fresh air in that regard too. Stereotypes were mostly bullshit, after all.

"How long have you been around here?" Courtney asked, leaned back in her seat, and winced when the Hammerhead found yet another bump. It honestly felt like it tracked every single one in the road and when there were none, created a few more to make up for the lack.

Francesca looked up from her tablet, her eyebrows raised. "What was that?"

"How long have you been here? You've only been with Heavy Metal for…ten months, is it?"

"Going on a year. Ten months sounds about right. I was in and around the Zoo for a while before that. Two years, I think."

"Yeesh."

"You've been around longer than I have."

"Sure. I was one of the first boots on the ground back in the day. They didn't want me in the thick of it until people realized the fucking cash cow the Zoo turned out to be."

The former Legionary shook her head. "I suppose the guys who were able to afford their third and fourth yachts while prepping the world for destruction might think it's worth it."

"They'll merely jump on their rocket ships and colonize Mars while we're getting killed down here. They've promised to do it for long enough."

That teased a laugh from Francesca, but Courtney felt a little dirty making the joke. All things considered, she was among those one-percenters and pretending that she was somehow not one of the same people she was joking about made her uncomfortable.

It was about time she acknowledged that instead of pretending she was still on the outside looking in.

A few of the soldiers who had been stationed around the compound accompanied them as they headed out to investigate what was happening near the wall. Considerable firepower was still focused around the compound to make sure they had all the warning they needed in case the Zoo tried to attack again.

They were in the area where the spur had pushed in

and Courtney looked out the windshield and tried to see anything that might have survived the scorched earth operation that had driven the Zoo back. Not that she expected something to survive, but when it came to the Zoo, everything had to be checked and double-checked just in case.

It was a hot day too. Well, they were all hot days in the Sahara, but she wasn't sure if this day was a little hotter or if she was still adjusting to the heat after spending so much time in the US.

But there was the additional evidence as they climbed out of the Hammerhead. One of the soldiers sighed softly as they stepped into the sunlight, and even Francesca muttered a small curse in French. Or, at least, Courtney assumed it was a curse, although she couldn't honestly tell what it was. Of all the languages she knew she should learn, French always took the back seat. She'd worked through Mandarin, German, and Italian first, and in that order too.

"That's where the slag is." Francesca pointed once they had all dismounted. "Not much else is left of the spur that came out of the Zoo. I'm not sure why you wanted to come out here to look at it yourself."

"I've hit dead ends with the research in the lab. It's about time I get out in the field again, but...well, I needed some time away from the lab, to be honest."

"So you came out to the most dangerous area in the world because you needed to clear your head?"

"Something like that."

"How long have you been with Heavy Metal?"

Courtney smirked. "Longer than you have."

Even with their suits set to adjust for this kind of heat, she began to sweat as she approached the area where the slag remained and wandered through the rock formations that protruded from the rough sand. They weren't close to any of the dunes yet and were a little too close to the mountains, which meant more dusty rocks than what people generally considered to be the Sahara proper.

Something was off, though. Courtney narrowed her eyes and studied the series of bone-dry reports that filed across her HUD as they were being collected by the sensors in her suit and those the other members of the team wore.

She wasn't sure what she was looking at, but something was undoubtedly wrong. Curious, she approached the slag left by the burning and shifted position until she caught an odd flatness in the reflection that came off it from the blazing sunlight. Her focus narrowed on the shadow or discoloration that she couldn't quite place.

Quickly, she turned to the sergeant who had joined them and ordered the five men in their group into a defensive position. She approached him immediately.

"Is everything all right, ma'am?"

"Yeah. I think so. Can your assault rifle break through the slag over there?"

He leaned forward and studied the area she had pointed out to him.

"It might. I doubt it, though. And there's probably a better chance that we'll be on the receiving end of anything that might ricochet off it instead of breaking through."

"Right. Do you have a grenade rather?"

"Yeah." He took one from his belt.

Courtney turned, immediately located the place, and highlighted it on their HUDs as well. "Drop that baby right there."

He turned to look at her, his head tilted, and she wondered if there was sand in the joints of his suit for a moment.

"It's too—"

She shook her head, snatched the grenade from his hand, and let her suit run the calculation before she pulled the pin and lobbed it for her. One of the benefits of being a one-percenter out in the field was that she could afford some of the best equipment. It was a simple matter to let it go through some of the motions for her while she worked off some of the rust.

The whole group dropped prone while the grenade was airborne and she did the same. Her gaze followed it for a second before the ground shuddered when it detonated, although the HUD immediately compensated before her eyes could be hurt by the flash or even the blast. No damage was done, but she could tell that her nonchalance when it came to simply tossing the grenade had affected her companions badly.

"You're fucking crazy!" the sergeant snapped as he bounded lightly to his feet. "You didn't even know what timer I had set it to!"

"Time is something that we don't have," she answered and brushed some sand from her suit. "And I trust the tech we're out here with—the same tech that we've entrusted our lives to this whole time."

He paused, not sure what she was talking about, and she didn't have the time to explain it. Again, time wasn't really on their side and Courtney made the decision simply to move on.

"Do you have some rope?"

"What? Do you plan to blow that up too?"

She gestured for him to get on with it and chose the less offensive gesture of those she could have used. Still, the sergeant got the idea and he retrieved a few lengths of rope and handed it to her.

"Come on, Sergeant," she said cheerfully. "I might be a civilian but I happen to know that rope doesn't blow up all by itself. Right?"

"That would be correct, ma'am. This rope doesn't blow up by itself."

"Well...that's ominous." Courtney shook her head, wound it around her waist, and hooked it into her belt for a little extra security before she approached the slag and threw him the other end. "Stay close, Sarge. I have a bad feeling about this."

There was no telling what she was dealing with and she honestly didn't like the idea. She peered at the slag and tapped her boot on it slowly before she felt something give.

"Do you all hear that?" she asked and turned to the others.

"Hear wha—"

They all wore helmets and she couldn't see their eyes, but something about their body language still told her something was happening before the ground gave way beneath her.

"Shit!"

A sense of vertigo filled her as her purchase on the ground suddenly disappeared. She had expected something like this, but the shock still made her heart jump into her throat as she began to fall. Thankfully, she didn't plummet that far before her drop was suddenly arrested when the sergeant she'd thrown the rope to caught her. The weight of her suit was enough that it took him and a couple of other soldiers a few seconds to stop her fall before they pulled her up slowly.

Courtney didn't want to but she knew she had to turn and get at least one glimpse into the gaping hole that had opened beneath her. Maybe it was where all the roots and plants were allowed to grow before they sprang up, but it looked like it went deeper than that. It was something else entirely, although there wasn't enough light to tell her what it was precisely before hands grasped her shoulders and dragged her into the sunlight.

Francesca was surprisingly the first one there. The woman held her firmly and heaved her over the edge.

It had been an interesting feeling but one she wasn't keen to experience again. Courtney had no fear of heights but she had a healthy fear of falling, especially if it happened when she didn't expect it.

"Are you okay?" the other woman asked once she was securely on the surface.

"Yeah, I'm fine." She hadn't meant to snap but she turned to the hole where she'd stood only a few minutes before. "Seriously, does anyone else hear that?"

One of the soldiers took a step closer to the edge, careful to not cause the hole to widen in case he fell as well. "It's...no, it can't be. We're in the fucking desert."

His mutter was easily heard by the rest of the team, and it wasn't long before they could all hear it.

"What do you do if you don't have enough hippos to destroy the slag at every spur?" Courtney asked and tried not to let the grin on her face infuse her tone.

"Make more hippos?" Francesca's voice said there was a hint of confusion there too. "What are you getting at, Monroe?"

"Or they could harness the most powerful natural force available. Well, one of the most powerful in the world."

"Water," the sergeant whispered and leaned a little closer. "Is that running water down there? Where did it come from?"

She shrugged. "It could be that there were reservoirs deep down that the Zoo has begun to tap. We've seen that early on. Or it might be that the jungle has found a way to synthesize its own water. We've seen that before too. Have a look down there if you don't believe me. I'd say there's time but I need to get a sample of the water somehow."

None of them wanted to get in too close but one by one, their courage returned and they each peered into the hole. There wasn't much to see in the darkness, but the sound was difficult to ignore at this point.

"All right," the sergeant stated and gestured to the rest of the team. "We'll set a rig up and head down there to see if we can get some samples."

The soldiers began to work on a rigging to lower someone down.

"Why water?" Francesca wondered while the others worked.

"What do plants need to grow aside from carbon dioxide?"

"Water—oh, fuck."

"Right." Courtney nodded. "Two birds with one stone. Destroy the slag and the wall and supply the new Zoo in the process. Throw in the biomass from all the bases, and there won't be a military might on the planet that can stop the explosion."

It had been a while since they'd put up a little camp like this inside the Zoo. That wasn't to say he'd missed it at all, but there was a sense of familiarity and maybe a trace of nostalgia for the way things had been back then. Terrifying and horrifying in equal measures, of course, but he was at the front line of some of the world's most amazing discoveries, all while making good money too.

There was also the fact that it came before the realization that they were driving toward their extinction as a species, but he was willing to admit that the feeling had always been there for him. Still, knowing it for sure was certainly a rude awakening.

"It's been a while since we spent the night out here, huh?"

Sal turned as Madigan joined him. She was still in her suit but it looked like she could simply curl up inside and sleep in it without needing to take it off or climb out. It wasn't a long-term option but was still safer than sleeping outside it.

"Yeah. We have all the sensors set up and people are eating and getting ready to get some rest. I don't expect anyone to sleep very well, though. Not out here, anyway." He turned to stare into the jungle.

"It's not like you do much sleeping when you're in the compound."

"That's a more...recent development. Still, we might as well get some rest. Did you manage to get a ping from the satellite?"

"No. As expected, the signal was shit so I couldn't confirm our location. I sent the flare to make sure people know we're still alive and kicking and all that. It looks like we made good time today despite your little mining expedition. I assume you found some kind of metal but didn't see much of it."

"An ore of some kind, yeah." He lowered his voice. "I'm not sure what it is, but it would probably be best if we don't spread word of it to everyone else until we know exactly what we're dealing with."

"You're afraid of turning it into a gold rush type of situation." Madigan nodded, pulled her helmet back, and drew a deep breath of the uncomfortably still air around them. "Yeah, I get that. We don't need anyone with anything but survival on their minds coming in here. And we don't need this place getting more fucked up than it already is."

Sal nodded slowly, sat on the ground, and leaned his back against a nearby tree as he settled in for the first watch of the night.

"Is it what Pegasus pulled out illegally?"

He shrugged. "I'm honestly not sure since we only encountered what they synthesized from it. I never saw it in its raw form, but it could be. I've not heard of it being taken out by anyone else either. Honestly, I thought it was simply a phase the Zoo went through and moved on from.

It serves me right for making assumptions about this fucking place."

"Food's ready."

Sal turned to where Gregor prepared their rations. There was enough for about a week of travel but he was only too aware of how well it could be stretched to last a little while longer if they survived. Of course, there was also the possibility that they wouldn't have as many people later in the trip to use the rations, but he didn't want to think about that.

The food tasted a little bland, although that was mostly because they didn't want hot food that smelled like much of anything. It had a way of attracting the wrong kind of attention in the Zoo.

Still, it was hot and filling enough.

"What was that out there?" Trick asked once everyone had their meal. "Those crazy-ass mutants today?"

Sonja nodded. "It was like watching Moses and the fucking Red Sea. And every other bastard before and after was much the same."

Gregor nodded slowly. "It was like they were out to get us but avoided you, Sal, unless you attacked them."

"I remember seeing that once," Jiro interjected, cleared his throat, and took a sip of water. "McFadden and the fucking dinosaur—or whatever they are called these days. It was the same thing. They treat you two like you're kings of the jungle or something like that."

Sal chuckled softly, although he didn't like the fact that the conversation had begun to put him on edge. He wouldn't tell any of them what he was thinking at this point, though. They were a little past that. Besides, he'd noticed what they were talking about even before the moment when he'd found the ore.

It was a little worrying to see that others noticed it now too.

"As long as you don't expect him to swing through the trees in a loincloth, you can believe what you like," Madigan quipped and it drew a couple of laughs. "I can't say I don't like the idea, though. Do you think—"

"No loincloths," Sal protested.

A few laughs followed that as well, and he could almost feel the tension in their small camp dissolve somewhat.

"Besides," Gregor added. "It's normal behavior for animals and there are rules that even the Zoo creatures follow. It's called thinning the herd. Identify the weakest and eliminate them first while avoiding those that pose the most danger."

"Are you calling us weak?" Mal asked.

"Not physically, but they identify Sal as a greater threat —the kind that would be better avoided than engaged directly."

"I don't think that's how it works," Sonja commented. "That would make sense if they saw us as prey and themselves as predators. But you'll see something as small as a badger standing up to a bear if it's a threat to its home and its young. They see us as aggressors invading their territory."

"That's one way to put it," Gregor responded. "Another would be that they are pushing into our territory and are trying to weaken us without committing too many of their resources."

"We killed enough of them," Trick countered.

"Sure," Jiro answered. "But it didn't lose any biomass. It was all simply absorbed again and more of the monsters are churned out."

Sal inched away from the conversation and took another mouthful of his bland meal. He didn't want to be a part of the talk since it had begun to make him feel like he was being opened up and dissected by high schoolers. Madigan joined him and climbed out of her suit but left it ready and waiting in case she needed to get in quickly to join a fight. She pulled a small bedroll from her pack.

"I think I'll get some sleep," she said and settled next to him. "You might want to follow my good example."

"I can't sleep," he muttered. "I need to think."

"Well, I guess it's a good thing you have me around. Feel free to think aloud."

"You won't be any good to anyone if you're sleep-deprived."

"Says the guy who's about three days past sleep-deprived. You know you can trust me, right?"

"Sure."

"Then trust me."

Sal sighed as she settled in next to him. "I do trust you."

She nodded. "Right. Well, I do need my sleep but at least you have Athena."

"What, are you two besties now?"

"Hardly, but she's the only one I'll trust in this situation. Put your helmet on, Sal, or so help me, I'll knock you unconscious and hope that the brain trauma is worth letting you rest for a few hours."

"I'm very sure that if you knocked me out badly enough to leave me unconscious for a few hours, there would be far more problems than merely my lack of sleep."

"Shut up, I'm tired." She leaned closer and placed a light kiss on his lips before she settled against the tree she was leaning on.

He did as he was told. Once he had finished his food and disposed of the utensils, he pulled his helmet on and connected it to the rest of the suit he still wore. Most of the team were either still discussing the merits of their various theories as to why the Zoo liked attacking them or had begun to turn in as well.

Old memories were difficult to fight at this juncture. It was stupid to fall back on the old ideals he'd clung to back in the day or a life he once had but to which he'd never belonged.

No, that wasn't quite right. Heavy Metal was still his company. Madigan was running it with him and so were the others, even if he did feel a little lonely from time to time.

"Are you there, Athena?" he asked quietly.

"Always, Sal."

CHAPTER NINE

It wasn't a pleasant feeling to wake in a cold sweat. He looked around like he wasn't sure what was real and what was not and grasped the weapon he kept close at all times.

The response had become more common these days, but he forced himself to calm again once it was clear that he was alone in his room at the secondary ENSOL base. No monsters lunged for his neck and there was nothing for him to worry about. Not immediately, anyway.

"Fucking hell," he whispered and made sure that he hadn't forgotten to flick on the safety of the sidearm he'd picked up. It was one of the first lessons he'd learned after accidentally pulling the trigger and setting the whole camp in a panic.

He needed the weapon to calm himself, but there was no point if it put the rest of the ENSOL crew on edge.

Sam pulled a pair of pants on and stepped into the narrow hallway of the prefab building they'd set up for themselves.

Elke and Chen were already waiting for him and looked like they had been woken as well.

"What's the matter?"

"The captain told us to come and get you."

He had some very vivid memories of the last time he'd been dragged out of bed in the dead of night for a problem the captain of their little team of mercenaries said needed his attention.

"We should find him immediately then," he whispered, his grasp firmly on his sidearm. He was careful to keep his hand away from the trigger, however, and curled his finger around the guard instead.

The captain waited outside the building, although he looked considerably less perturbed than Sam had assumed he would be.

"Is there a problem, Mr. Samir?"

"Not the problem you might think," he assured them quickly. "Nothing is threatening the security of the camp at the moment."

"Then what is the issue?"

"Franklin has called for all bases, compounds, and camps to be on high alert. It would appear that the Zoo has thrust another spur out, this time to the wall in the Saharan Coalition sector. It's way ahead of where the teams are currently working—the section already constructed is in the area close to where the Nigeriens currently have their base."

That explained the faint thwump of helicopters overhead. From the sound of it, troops were being ferried as quickly as possible to where they would have to fight to contain and drive the spur back. Sam wasn't quite sure what they were doing up at this point, though, since they had nothing to do with the military effort.

Still, the sun was about to rise. They might as well find some work to do since sleep was no longer an option.

"I have coffee brewing if you're interested," Elke told them once the captain hurried away to issue a few more orders.

"Or what passes for coffee around here," Chen muttered as they returned to the prefab building. "I'm very sure I could import something local. They have some very good stuff coming out of Casablanca these days."

Sam had looked into it, but the sellers almost anywhere around the Zoo knew the kind of demand their products had and responded with increasingly soaring prices for increasingly cheap wares.

Still, the kid had hope and if anyone could find decent coffee in the area, it was him.

Elke flinched while pouring the coffee but still didn't spill a drop. The gunfire was at a considerable distance but still uncomfortably close, and he could only imagine the battle raging as the militaries fought to push the Zoo back yet again.

"Sometimes, I wonder why we bother to try to build that goddamn wall," Chen whispered and sipped his coffee as they wandered out into the early-morning crispness.

"Because it's all we can do," Elke answered, her voice barely above a whisper as well. "It's called hope."

"I don't think—" Sam's words cut off and he lowered his coffee at the sound of a small altercation coming from the gate.

"What's happening out there?"

One of the mercs looked up and laughed sheepishly. "It looks like we have an unauthorized approach to the camp. I don't even know what kind of person would still act against the people who are trying to keep the Zoo away from the world at the moment. You know, my sister-in-law keeps saying we need to send more people in, but then the more we have—"

"Please…what is happening out there?"

The merc cleared his throat and nodded. "Yes, yes. It's only one of the other mercenaries. He knows a couple of the people around here and he's saying he's looking for Mr. Fix."

"Why is he looking for me?"

"You'd have to ask him, sir. The captain had him arrested and taken to the brig. Is it a brig if it's not on a warship? My cousin sails a great deal, and he tells me much of the terminology we use around here is not suitable unless you're…at sea. I'm sorry, I ramble when I'm nervous."

Sam smiled and patted the young man on the shoulder. "We all have our coping mechanisms."

He hurried to the small building the captain had set up as a jail cell for anyone they happened to catch trying to cause problems. While he had a couple of objections to the building, he wouldn't make a big deal of it. The man hired to handle security was generally the one he trusted to enforce the security.

Still, it seemed like they all needed to learn how to trust each other. At this point, if they didn't, it wouldn't matter anyway.

"Samir, what appears to be the problem here?"

The captain looked up from the paperwork he was filing. "He looks like a bum and said he was looking for Mr. Fix, but I don't think there's anyone here by that name. It might be the Zoo drove him mad."

"Mr. Fix...it's me. I'm known as the Fixer. It's possible that he came here looking for me."

"Well, if you'd like to talk to him, now would be the time. We aren't equipped to handle prisoners for the long-term. I already sent an order for someone to ship him off to the Americans. Of all the bases, they are the best equipped to handle prisoners. Weird, no?"

"Perhaps. I would like to have a word with the man, though."

Samir nodded for him to enter. The prefab of the building aside, it might as well have been an old-timey western jail—a small desk with a lamp on the one side, a cell with prefab bars, a sink, a toilet, and a cot where a young mercenary lay and stared at the ceiling.

His clothes were in tatters and he was covered in bruises and scratches, likely from his scuffle with security around them. But there was something more to him—a hint of terror in his eyes when he looked at Sam. Those eyes were wide as he tried to understand whether he was in mortal peril or not, especially when his gaze fell on the engineer and the other mercenaries who were likely responsible for the beating he took.

"I'm told you were looking for me."

"You are Mr. Fix?"

"It is a nickname. Why were you looking for me?"

"I used to work for a man named Badawi. When his team was disbanded, I had to find more employment. I worked for you not that long ago and even fought in the battle against the Zoo. But when I found out that Interpol was looking for my old boss, I made some inquiries and heard that he might have relocated his base. I…I went to look. I sent him a message, telling him that Interpol were looking for him. He sent the message back saying that he was considering it, but he wanted more information. I was on my way back when—"

Samir rolled his eyes. "Come on, we don't have time for any theatrics. Tell us what you know. Get it all out and we'll be sure to take it into consideration."

"The Zoo spur came out of nowhere. One minute, I was driving across the desert and in the next, monsters rushed at me and trees pushed out of the sand like daisies. There… I don't… I had a suit and everything, but I didn't have time to put it on. I don't—"

He shook his head and tried to regain his composure, although his fingers twitched like he was still pulling the trigger.

As much as Sam could sympathize with the man's trauma, he had never been much good at playing therapist. There was a time and a place for that kind of thing and he had never found either.

"Where is Badawi?" he asked and felt like he already knew the answer.

"He is simple enough to find," the man answered and cleared his throat. "Follow the sound of gunfire. He is in the caves so he might be all right, but he doesn't have an army with him. If the animals were to come…"

"Fuck." Sam hissed in frustration and shook his head. "Keep him here. I need to make a call."

"But we—"

"Don't. Just don't. Keep him here for the moment. At least until I make the call."

"Of course. Your camp, your rules."

Sam moved out of the cell and ran to the main building. He raised a hand to stop Elke or Chen from saying or doing anything that would slow him as he reached his phone and punched in Franklin's number.

"This is—"

"Yes, I fucking know who it is. This is Sam. We need to talk."

Maybe being short with the man after what must have been an arduous night shift wasn't the best response but they didn't have the time for niceties.

"Okay, fire away."

"Your people working in the Sahara Coalition sector need to be a little less…enthusiastic with their cleaning out of the area than they usually are. The one man who might have the answers to the burrower problem is stuck in the middle of that fucking spur."

"Badawi?"

"That's the one. He has his camp in some caves in the region, so he might still be alive, although how long that'll last is the subject of some debate. The Zoo threat is bad enough, but if those plasma throwers go in there with their usual blaze of glory, the bastard might end up dead at their hands instead."

"Fuck."

"My exact words, Commander. Unless someone gets word to those men and women out there, we're about to put our goddamn golden goose in the deep fryer."

The problem with sleeping in his suit was that there were about fifteen kinds of ways that a comfortable position could turn uncomfortable. Sal didn't know exactly when he'd fallen asleep but something brought him out again.

He jerked hard and hit his arm on the suit that didn't move with him. Athena must have deactivated its sensitivity to his movements while he was asleep. It was probably for the best since he hadn't managed a decent amount of sleep in what felt like forever.

"Sal?"

After a moment, he realized he was still propped against the tree he'd been leaning on with no sign of any trouble around them. Still, knowing that Athena was on and waiting for him when he woke was some comfort.

"Athena...what—" He paused and coughed to clear his throat.

"You fell asleep and you slept remarkably well despite how uncomfortable you must have been."

"Why didn't you wake me?"

"I tried," she replied cheerfully like it was of no consequence. "What woke you? I noticed a spike in your readings a few seconds before you woke up."

"I'm not sure," he whispered, rolled his shoulders, and tried to get his blood pumping again. "Something...something's different but I don't know what."

He closed his eyes, although there was no impulse to fall asleep again. It was getting easier to reach out like he had already created all the necessary pathways and he would continue to find all kinds of new ones to work with.

Murky shadows lurked all around but light cast those shadows. It must be dawn or close to it.

"It's like…everything's…uh, humming? Thrumming? Weird, like someone's turned the power up and the whole Zoo is suddenly energized."

"Is there danger to your team?"

Sal paused to think about that. It felt like the kind of question he would have insisted on answering before anything else was said, but the AI now asked it for him instead. A twinge of shame was immediately quashed as he focused again.

"Nothing about it is focused on the team."

"That's a good thing, I suppose. Most of them are still asleep."

If anything, it was almost like the whole of the Zoo was focused on something else entirely. He'd never noticed a sense of direction before. It was uncanny as if the current and the pulses flowed in different directions as the need arose.

Maybe this was how the word was spread when a Pita plant was plucked or one of the goop sacs on the larger creatures was burst. There was the initial reaction from the surrounding Zoo which was the result of pheromones, but the way the whole region reacted must surely be something else.

He could almost picture an invisible, giant hand turning the power button up and pointing at the source of the problem. It was an interesting visual if maybe a little childish, but it still made sense on some level.

And it was enough to get a smile out of him too. Not much could do that these days.

"Something's happening out there," Sal whispered and gestured somewhere to the southwest. "Not here."

At least she had given him control of the suit again.

"Another spur, maybe?" Athena looked like she was putting a great deal of thought into it as well and her processing cores ran hotter than before.

"Maybe. Or something else entirely. But the point is that this isn't working."

"What isn't?"

"Our distraction. We were supposed to draw the Zoo's attention away from the wall."

"Well, you've hardly covered enough ground to be seen as anything other than a normal run, isn't that correct?"

"Well...yeah." It was weird how he could feel both relieved and annoyed by her logical approach to it. "It's a little too soon to expect any real, dramatic results. Still, there might be a way for us to turn the heat up a little."

He was the first one up and as much as he hated it, it was his job to get the heat going for coffee and their breakfast. It wasn't long before the rest of the team started to wake too. Madigan was one of the first and she growled and muttered under her breath as she took her cup.

The smell was enough to get the rest of them up and about and they worked to pack their camp for departure. There wasn't much said among them, and Sal had a feeling that he was the only one who'd had some decent sleep out there. The rest of the team was bleary-eyed and grumpy.

"What do you have in mind for the day?" Madigan asked. "Any more mining expeditions?"

"Not really," he answered and folded his arms. "Ladies and gents, it's time for a little fun. We need to push hard to get beyond the regular zone and move into unknown territory. There's a limited window here, and people out there are counting on us to buy them the time they need."

"Fair enough," Gregor answered and took a bite of beef jerky. "But I don't see how simply marching through the jungle and killing a few animals will make much difference."

"You're right. All of us need to keep an eye open for The Opportunity."

They all stared blankly at him and he wasn't sure if there was any way to make it clearer. All he had in mind was a vague plan anyway.

"Opportunity?" Madigan asked.

"We need to find a way to get this fucking bitch to notice us. I imagine our powers of interference should do the trick."

CHAPTER TEN

There were nights when people simply didn't sleep. Badawi had heard that it was a sign of those who liked to work so hard that they never put in the time to take care of themselves. Sleep was important as any doctor would say. It was odd how those same doctors often went for days and sometimes weeks without rest.

Still, he could see where they were coming from. His eyes itched and his whole body was stiff and aching, but he dared not allow himself to drift off. A fire burned at the entrance and as much as he hated open flames like that, he was committed to keeping it burning through the night or at least until the sun had risen completely.

He was still hopeful, though. The fact that he was on a ridge would prevent the jungle from shutting the sun out completely. He didn't know if there was any way for the Zoo to grow on rock and he wouldn't put it past the damn jungle, but it made sense that it had at least slowed the fucking thing down.

It had been a long night but in the end, he wouldn't let

himself fall into the trap of assuming that the Zoo was stopped or someone else would deal with the situation. He also knew better than to head out with the couple of men he had with him. If there was a spur out there, it would be the focus of the Zoo's attention, which meant they would have to fight thousands of mutants.

Besides, it sounded like the militaries were already gathering to deal with the situation. He had been woken by the ground shaking before there were any other signs of an attack. Instinct more than anything else told him something was wrong, and these had been honed over years in the Zoo. They had wasted no time and hurried down the tunnels they'd built as a way to escape if something like this happened.

They'd relocated within minutes of confirming that a spur was surging toward them and had gathered in a smaller cave that was easier to defend. The larger one would have been best if he had the numbers to man all the defenses, but with the few he had to work with, they didn't have much time to make the decision.

The four men he had, including his nephew, didn't look like they were ready for a fight. They had the guns and the ammo ready and aimed the barrels at all the right places, but he wasn't sure if they could be counted on to stand their ground. Only one of them had ever been in the Zoo before—one of the older men who didn't feel like making the effort to find new work and therefore was content to take a pay cut and stick around. His knee was no good and he walked with a damn cane.

Badawi couldn't remember the man's name either. Maybe it was time he started to write shit down or people would catch on to the fact that he never referred to them by the names they introduced themselves with.

"How long do you think we'll be here?" Sami asked and hefted the AK he'd been provided with. "Do you think they'll come in to help us?"

"Given that they don't know we are here, I would say the chances are slim," he answered. He should have kept a couple of the suits instead of selling them all. Mostly, he relied on his people to bring their weapons and maintain everything. If something went to shit, it would be their fault if they died.

It was a good system until everyone took their suits. He had decided to sell those he had left since they weren't particularly good and all were illegal anyway. There was no point in giving his enemies anything else to catch him with.

Well, the weapons he had in his little stash were not technically legal either, but the gun laws in the area were notoriously loose so it wasn't that big a deal. The suits were more a matter of how they had been stolen and could be tracked that way.

"Do you think they'll clear the monsters out?" one of the others asked.

"They might," another man muttered and checked his weapon again nervously. "They've fought back all the spurs in the past, right?"

"There's always a first time," Badawi commented and ran his finger over the AK he'd selected for himself. "And the chances are that the first time they fail to stop a spur will be the last time as well, but we have to be optimistic here."

Of course, they failed to address the most important question but he didn't blame them. Good people that they were, there was nothing bad about keeping their eyes on the big picture. It was the small pictures that had his attention.

Whether or not the help would come fast enough. Or if the people who were supposed to help them turned out to be the reason why they were killed. Plasma throwers could suck the oxygen out of their little cavern without a problem, and that was assuming they survived long enough for the teams to reach them.

It certainly wasn't a given, but he wouldn't make any plans for his future at this point.

The sounds coming through the tunnels were enough to make their blood run cold, and the men all tried to put some cover between themselves and the monster. It was the clearest indication that none of these kids knew what they were doing. Cover was only useful in a gunfight or when someone was shooting at you. If the creatures were out in the open and charging at them, there was no real point in hiding behind something. In fact, the people who knew what they were doing in the Zoo liked to keep themselves out in the open as much as possible.

Not that Badawi knew much about that. He preferred to let other people do most of the fighting, but he'd been around long enough that he had learned a couple of things.

The first monsters surged through the tunnel. The narrow confines thinned their numbers and made sure they couldn't swarm, but there were more than enough of them to still be a problem.

"Don't waste bullets," he said softly and thumbed the

safety off the AK in his hands. "Wait until they're close enough that you—"

No one listened to him. He chose to not be offended by it as one of the younger men opened fire down the tunnels. It was interesting to watch them fling themselves into the fight. Or maybe they thought jumping the gun would give them the upper hand when the creatures began to rush at them.

A couple of the beasts went down but most of the bullets hammered into the walls and ricocheted wildly but didn't do much in the way of damage.

Before they could fully grasp what was happening, they all needed to reload while the monsters made good headway up the tunnels.

"I have to do everything myself, don't I?" Badawi whispered and made sure they were coming in close while the others tried rapidly to reload with shaking hands and fearful looks. He could hear one of them drop the magazine he was holding.

All that kept him alive was his cool head and a barrage of bullets he fired down the tunnel in semi-auto. He chose his targets and forced the monsters to push their attack a little harder as the rest of the team finally reloaded their weapons and started to shoot again.

The tunnels were filling quickly with bodies, and once they had a decent number, it was time to change tactics. He pulled a grenade from his belt, peered to where the rest of the creatures pushed out again, and drew a deep breath before he pulled the pin and lobbed it into the pack.

It would earn them a couple of minutes of respite, at least, and while everything had turned out all right so far, he wouldn't say it was a complete success. If they had followed his instructions from the start, there would be no need to have wasted almost double the number of bullets to clear the first surge.

"Maybe this time, you'll listen to me when I tell you to hold your fucking fire," Badawi snapped and checked his magazine. It was two-thirds gone but he still had a few bullets left. He pulled it out, tucked it into his bag, and retrieved a fresh one. "Our bullets are finite and I want a few left so the teams know people are in need of rescuing down here."

"Of course, sir."

Maybe he would take the opportunity and save one bullet for himself, just in case. One from his sidearm would be more than sufficient since killing himself with an assault rifle felt terribly inconvenient. Or maybe he could set the grenade box on fire. That way, his body would be buried under an avalanche of rocks and he would not be turned into Zoo meat.

Or maybe Allah would smile on him again. Preferably in this life.

"Oh…fucking hell no."

Francesca jumped up from where she was seated although to her credit, she stopped her cup of coffee from spilling. "What's the matter?"

"Franklin's on the way. There's been an incident—a spur exactly where we don't want it to be."

"Don't we generally not want the spurs to be where they are? I mean, as a general rule?"

"Now is not the time for sass. Intelligence reports have Badawi right in the middle of that whole mess. Franklin's in a helicopter right now and he's on his way."

"Fuck." Francesca downed the rest of her coffee and they heard the sound of the helicopter rotors already approaching as they stepped outside. The soldiers were on alert from the orders sent out the night before. Word was that the spur was acting a little more aggressively than most. All camps, bases, and compounds around the Zoo were told to be ready for anything and at this point, no one questioned the threat.

That was probably a good thing. She was tired of having to fight humans as well as monsters.

Franklin clambered out of the helicopter as they were getting into their suits.

"There's no time for prolonged conversations," the commander stated immediately.

"We need a fucking rescue team," Murphy finished the man's thought for him as he climbed out too. "The kind that'll head directly into the thick of it, which means that—"

"You need volunteers. Yeah, we get it," Courtney interrupted. She'd had only a few hours of sleep that night and it didn't look like the Zoo would let her have any more than that on a regular basis. "Francesca, do you know of any volunteers who want to head in to potentially save the fucking world?"

"We have two right here. You and me."

"Well, I planned to volunteer myself, but I guess letting you do it is a little more efficient."

Murphy took a step forward, his eyes narrowed. She could see the doubt in them and could even understand why it was there.

"Dr. Monroe, I appreciate the offer, but this is—"

"Your appreciation is noted, Captain."

"The rest of the Heavy Metal team would likely join us too," Francesca added.

Murphy nodded and turned to the soldiers who had been stationed there to keep an eye on the Heavy Metal compound.

"Is anyone else looking to volunteer?" he roared and hands were raised faster than the Zoo could grow trees.

"Well, we need someone to stay here to keep things in order and all that shit," Courtney said as she pulled her helmet on. "Choose ten, I think, and we'll be on our way."

He complied, although it looked like his selection process was a little random since he highlighted them on his HUD and gestured for them to climb aboard.

In minutes, they were airborne again and banked toward their destination. A short while later, they could already see the effects of the battle raging below.

"I don't mean to be a distraction or anything," she whispered on a private channel to Murphy. "But...has there been any word?"

He nodded. "A flare was fired early on but as it was green, we assumed they were merely confirming the progress of the mission. Another was picked up last night shortly before the sun went down. As of that moment, it looks like our people in there are still alive."

That was good to know, at least, and she wasn't too proud to admit that it was one of the reasons why sleep had been slow in coming the night before. Not the only one, of course, but certainly the one that hung the heaviest in her mind.

"Thanks."

"No problem."

It didn't sound like they would have much time to acclimate to their surroundings as the helicopter descended sharply to where a field base had already been set up. The air was already thick with the smell of smoke and cordite, and teams still headed out into the newly grown jungle. Injured troops and mercs were being ferried out too and the scene showed all the signs of one of the most violent attacks yet.

Or at least that they'd seen in a while. There was no telling how hard the Zoo would continue to hit them if Sal wasn't successful.

One of the captains approached the group as they disembarked and his gaze immediately focused on Courtney. "Is this who you have leading the rescue team? Couldn't you have gotten someone a little more—"

His voice was cut off when the trees suddenly erupted. Locusts surged out to attack the group where they'd settled a little too close to the trees and the Zoo possibly saw the possibility of an easy strike that would put its enemies at a disadvantage with no leadership.

Courtney motioned for the rest of the team to step forward and drew her assault rifle as her HUD quickly selected the targets she would fire at.

It wasn't the most difficult battle and it was something

of an eye-opener to see how heavy the Zoo presence was in the area.

"You had some objections to the rescue team, Captain?" Murphy snapped once the locusts were driven off.

"None, sir."

She turned as a handful of soldiers approached them.

"Sir!" one of them—a merc judging by his armor—stepped forward to address Courtney. "We'd like to volunteer for the rescue effort."

The three soldiers behind him nodded their agreement, and she looked at Murphy, who shrugged.

"The more the merrier," she answered and reloaded her rifle. "And we'll need two each of fire and plasma throwers. A shitload full of whatever big ass guns and bullets you can lay your hands on too—oh, and another six gunners, with at least one medic as soon as you can find them, Captain. I'll wait ten minutes, and if none of you volunteer and I get my ass killed in there, expect me to haunt you and kick your ass out of bed every fucking night for the rest of your miserable lives, which I think we all know will be short."

There was a flurry of movement from the teams that were still gathering and preparing to attack. None of them wanted to deal with a possible haunting and they all wanted to head in there and start attacking instead of defending. She could understand that, and it wasn't long before there were green checkmarks all across her HUD from the volunteers. The captain who had addressed her first went through the crews and chose those who were most likely to not get anyone killed on the rescue mission. They soon had their assorted quota and the equipment was gathered hastily.

"I guess you could learn a thing or two from the doctor, eh, Murphy?" Franklin asked, raised an eyebrow, and grinned maybe a little too widely.

The captain chuckled as he turned to address his superior officer. "With all due respect, go fuck yourself, Commander."

"I had a feeling I would hear one of those."

CHAPTER ELEVEN

A little extra surprise in the Zoo was always there to make things unpredictable enough to avoid complacency. Sal wasn't sure if it would be a problem or the solution this time. Their purpose was to push deep toward the heart and make sure they had the Zoo's attention, but the only surprise was that the jungle still treated him differently.

He hoped fervently that it was something they could take advantage of.

"Sal! Do you want to get in on this?"

Madigan powered through a handful of creatures without even looking at them and he bounded forward into the space behind her. With a clear path to them, he immediately rushed at the mutant that attempted to attack her. Her attention was focused on her battle to keep one of the killerpillars away from the rest of the troop, and a handful of panthers tried to use her distraction to gain purchase and yank her armor off.

While he had no doubt that they would be able to keep the monsters at bay without too much difficulty, their mission demanded that they produce something a little more ambitious than that. The entire team was still looking for The Opportunity that would distract the Zoo sufficiently to pull its attention away from its campaign against the wall.

Not at all sure that this current engagement would deliver the result they needed, he flicked his sword on. It shuddered in his hand at first before the suit compensated for the weapon. Whether this was their moment or not, they needed to push ahead as quickly as possible. Both logic and instinct insisted that Ground Zero held the key.

His blade cut one of the panthers in half at the stomach and splattered the blood on the other creatures that jumped back and appeared surprised that he had attacked them. He didn't like the idea of a connection with the monsters that made them think that he was one of them. It felt dirty—like he was betraying them somehow.

"Is everything all right? Your adrenaline readings are a little abnormal."

He narrowed his eyes and glanced at the scans she ran continually on him.

"Nothing's wrong with my adrenaline readings. They're level."

"Exactly. You're in the middle of a battle and your adrenaline readings are the same as when you were looking at data collected from yesterday."

"Well…uh, that was fairly exciting."

"No doubt. Even more interesting is that your heart rate has only gone up ten bpm from your resting rate. You might as well be going for a nice brisk walk."

She wasn't wrong. His body was acclimating to the

elevated combative state. It was one thing for Madigan to be as calm handling monsters as she was when she went for a walk, but he was supposed to be different. He was a decent enough fighter, but his realm of comfort was supposed to be pressing his eyes to microscopes and waiting for days on cultures.

He twisted closer to the killerpillar his partner was still wrestling with. His blade cut through the carapaces smoothly. They were made to stop bullets, and he was positive that the Zoo knew exactly what it was doing when it designed them that way and had deliberately made them difficult even for armor-piercing rounds to penetrate.

His blade sliced a gaping hole in the creature's body to create an unprotected target Madigan could open fire at. Her rounds were large enough to do all the damage required to kill it in moments.

If the Zoo thought he was there to help it, that was its problem. Until it reached in and tried to take direct control of him, he would continue to disappoint the creatures it sent to kill his friends.

"There is an uptick in adrenaline in your bloodstream, along with some epinephrine, usually linked to reactions like panic, the fight or flight responses—"

"Or anger." He cut her off, felled one of the panthers, and pushed forward to impale another before it could jump on Madigan's back. He stepped aside to let Jiro lop its head off with a smooth stroke. "Definitely anger."

"Is that indicative of the Zoo trying to take control of you?"

Sal shook his head. "In fact, I think my anger is one of

the particularly human emotions I have left. I don't think the Zoo's influence accounts for that."

"It will."

He couldn't tell if it was Athena's voice from the suit or if the words rang in his head. That confusion was something he couldn't account for but he pushed past it and steeled himself to be ready to face whatever they had to deal with.

Still, the lack of any significant opportunity would continue to piss him off even more. He jerked forward, drew his sidearm, and opened fire on the locusts that attempted to close in on them from above.

A short while later, the creatures began to pull back again and things settled into the kind of lull that usually followed these short-lived assaults.

"We need to push harder," Sal shouted. "Check your gear and make sure we can keep moving."

"Aren't we pushing a little hard?" Madigan asked. He could almost hear her raised eyebrow.

"The point is to make sure the Zoo has something else to focus on. The most annoying thorn in the side is the one that digs in deeper and does more damage as it moves along."

"Right. And that ends up with waves of monsters rushing at us sooner rather than later, right?"

Sal turned to face her. "Yeah, right. This is what we signed up to do, Madigan. I can't...I can't change it. If you guys feel this is too hard, you can head back, but I will keep pushing. I...have to."

She laughed and for a second, he wasn't sure what about.

"If you think I'll leave your ass behind at this point, you don't know me at all, Sal. But I'll let it slide this time."

"I...thanks. I guess."

"Yeah, we're in this together, whether you like it or not."

That sounded good but something still nagged in the back of his mind. Was that him talking to Madigan and genuinely concerned for her well-being, or was it the Zoo trying to influence him into getting his people to stop being a problem for it?

He forced himself out of the trap of wondering about that question since he had no real answer. Instead, he checked his weapons again to make sure he was prepared and ready for what might lie ahead. While second-guessing himself like this irritated him on some level, he had a feeling that the paranoia on his part was a good thing. It showed that a part of him still had some degree of control, although there was no telling how long that would last.

Hopefully, Athena would manage to adjust his baselines constantly for his behavior and know when to drag him back from the edge.

"I'm entrusting my life to an AI. It seems like this should be a movie in the Terminator franchise. They've made enough of those movies, even after Arnie passed away, so they might as well have included something like this. An AI living inside the suit with a human. No...that maybe sounds like the start to a bad sitcom."

"You're talking to yourself again. That is a good sign."

He narrowed his eyes as the team moved forward again on a trajectory that would take them directly into a dense group of the monsters. "Have I not been talking to myself?"

"Not as much as usual. It's been established as something inherently…well, human of you."

"Keep up the good work, Athena."

"Will do, Dr. Jacobs."

Now that he thought about it, Dr. Jacobs and Athena certainly sounded like a bad sitcom about a scientist getting into wacky adventures with his AI companion.

"We have more action heading our way!"

Sal opened his mouth to say the sensors had registered the movement for a while but he realized they had only now begun to do so. A surge almost like a wall appeared to try to stop them. This time, the surprise was that the creatures were not alone. Vines and trees seemed to push into the way. They made it more difficult for the humans in their suits to stay in formation and provided more cover for the creatures that attempted to close the distance to them.

The trees were still young, though. Even the hybrid suits would be able to push through the thin trunks without too much trouble, although they would rely on Madigan to bulldoze most of them. Sal and Jiro would be able to cut through more to open a wider area on the flanks, all without using too many bullets or explosives to accomplish it.

They would merely have to work a little harder.

"Jiro, are you with me?"

"Oh yeah."

McFadden had warned him that the guy had something of a death wish but so far, it had not displayed itself as him simply throwing himself into the battle with little thought about the fact that he might be killed. He was a competent fighter and had a keen mind in combat too. Still, he was a little crazy. That seemed like the right word for it.

Their blades attacked the vines and trees that tried to hinder their progress and Madigan was able to build momentum as the rest of the team rushed in with her. They all held to the formation that would allow them to keep fighting.

He acknowledged a twinge of pride in the team he and Madigan had put together. They were the best of the best and could probably have made a fucking fortune if they'd decided to sell their talents to the highest bidder. Instead, they chose to be on the front lines with Heavy Metal.

Hell, even Anja could have made a fortune on her own if she wanted to with no need to even engage with any team. Maybe she could have been the boss herself. From the way she'd handled the Savage operations almost completely on her own, Sal had the feeling she could probably run a criminal enterprise if she put her mind to it—and without needing to put herself in any danger.

She would be a shadowy figure there to control the world. Maybe it was better that she chose work that would make the world a better place. If she hadn't been the decent person she was, she might have made that decision already, but he didn't think he needed to worry about what she might do next.

One of the mini-guns on Madigan's shoulder activated and pulled him back to the present. It whirred as the barrels spun before a low, dull roar of gunfire drilled through the line of cannon fodder that rushed directly at them. Sal looked around for the creatures that generally waited for the opportunity to flank them and enter the fight when they were assured of a couple of easy kills. He did not intend to give them that opportunity.

Two of the panthers climbed between the trees but were forced to jump away when Jiro dove forward to meet them. His sword opened the guts of the first one and the second was shot almost immediately as it launched into an attack.

"Keep pushing!" Madigan roared, hammered her fist into the jaw of one of the massive lizards, and clamped the acid sac before it could spit. Instead of simply ripping it out or off, she fired into the sac from the side and pushed down to pour the acid onto the creatures that raced in behind. Sal had no idea how she could be sure that none of it would hit her instead but it was an interesting move. Maybe he would have the opportunity to try it later.

The rest of the team opened fire into the line of creatures ahead of them, a steady stream that pushed them back as he moved to the side where another of the lizards tried to circle and catch them from behind. If it was successful, it would wreak havoc with one squirt of its acid sac.

"Jiro! Stay with the team!"

The man nodded as Sal hurried forward to engage the creature. He eliminated two hyenas before he engaged the extra limbs that let him use the trees the way some of the animals did. Of course, Athena took over for him and positioned him above the lizard where it couldn't projectile spit him to death. He readied himself to strike the mutant from above.

"Are you sure about this?"

"Attacking the monster from above?" He let her move

him from branch to branch while he adjusted and fired to drop a handful of the locusts from the trees in front of him. "Yeah, fairly sure."

"No, I mean isolating yourself from the rest of the team."

It was a point she made fairly often even although she should be used to his combat style by now, but he was committed. A couple more of the monsters were felled by almost impossible shots—a single bullet punched through a panther's head and pinned a locust that flew in behind him—which meant that Trick was covering his back.

"There's no turning back now," he responded and adjusted so he was parallel to the ground as Athena dropped him over the lizard that hadn't seen him yet.

His stomach flipped with a weird sense of vertigo as he fell and he was unable to do anything but twist to land blade first. He used his momentum to thrust it into the monster's head. Although he knew he had missed the brain and the vitals, he landed with enough force to drive his blade completely through its skull and pin it to the ground.

It thrashed against him, but he made no effort to retract his sword and its efforts simply exacerbated its predicament. He drew his sidearm and punched two holes into the base of its skull where the sword should have gone.

Even if it was an alien beast, mutated and turned into a killing machine, Sal didn't feel right letting it die a slow and painful death.

"Sal! We need help over here!" Madigan called.

He dragged his weapon free as he evaluated the situation. The remaining creatures had pushed in hard enough to stop the team's forward momentum and their ferocity and sheer numbers meant there was nowhere for the group to go but back.

"Fuck!"

Athena immediately maneuvered him to where the team had regrouped and established themselves in a defensive V formation. The intention was to divide the Zoo's attack in half with Madigan holding the tip, but their efforts were ineffectual. While she killed as many of the creatures as she could, trees had begun to grow and thrust from the ground fast enough that they kicked rocks up when they emerged. They were small, short, and stubby and nowhere close to full-grown, but they were more than enough to provide the monsters coming in behind with a little cover that helped them press in much closer than any of the Heavy Metal team were comfortable with.

"Wait," Sal whispered. "Rocks? Since when are there rocks—"

"Sal! Get in formation!"

He obeyed instantly and stepped in seamlessly to where Mal had begun to reload. When he took over the duties of the flank rearguard, the man in the larger suit pushed forward to where he could support Madigan in point position.

"Rocks," he whispered and shook his head as he drove his sword into the open mouth of one of the hyenas. "No. Rocks aren't right here."

He saw what was happening but could also feel it. They were being funneled and guided back. There was only one reason why the Zoo would want to direct them somewhere, and he had a feeling it would not involve a surprise party with extra ice cream cake.

Every instinct told him that something was wrong and he looked to where they were being herded. It appeared to be a weird open area where, instead of the customary thick, dark soil, a hardened rock surface waited for them.

"Stop!"

His warning came a second too late. Heavy boots thumped onto the surface and the team's combined weight immediately compromised the unstable surface. Their efforts to move clear compounded the problem and before anyone could fully grasp the danger they were in, the ground began to give way.

As the exposed area collapsed beneath them, a sick feeling settled in the pit of his stomach. He was acutely conscious of the consternation among the Heavy Metal team as they were dragged down. Madigan fought grimly to regain stable ground so the rest of them could climb up her to reach it too, but the monsters continued their furious assault and pushed forward to the point where a couple of them fell in too.

There was no way to avoid the inevitable. Sal drew a deep breath and closed his eyes as the darkness wrapped around him.

He almost welcomed it.

CHAPTER TWELVE

She had a good, solid team. Many people out there would have paid well to have a group like the one she headed up now but in the military, the best of the best were generally part and parcel of the rest of the troops involved in the day-to-day routine of wherever they were stationed.

This time, however, they had been selected for something a little more important. All the jobs in and around the Zoo were tough, but the critical ones demanded the best the military had to offer. Courtney drew a deep breath and frowned as their connection with the GPS began to flicker. Her onboard computer was able to keep up with their location, but the deeper they were, the slower the connection got, to the point where she had to trust the computer's judgment on where they were going.

She liked it about as much as she liked the idea that Sal was entrusting his life to a goddammed AI. Computers in general irked her. Maybe she had watched one too many bad sci-fi movies.

At least she didn't have time to dwell on it, though, since the mutants appeared to be readying themselves to surge into them again.

"The number of monsters is disproportionate for a spur like this," Martin pointed out as she reloaded her rifle, took a grenade from her belt, and stared at the vegetation. "And there's so much tree movement here too. I don't know what's going on, but I have a feeling the Zoo wants something specific and it doesn't appreciate us interfering."

"I guess I should have expected the French skill of understatement," Courtney replied and grinned as she stepped out in front. More of the hippos than she liked had gathered with the other mutants. They weren't the kind she ever wanted to have to fight, but she had watched the videos on how Sal and Madigan had done it.

It was a little unlike the Zoo to create front-liners that didn't go down easily. They generally liked those creatures to be the weak cannon fodder, but the hippos were hard to kill and rushed in like bulls, although they were also able to bite or trample almost anything in their path. Thick skin and skulls made it difficult to land good kill shots but if they targeted the eyes or the open mouths when the opportunity presented itself, this usually enabled the teams to reduce their numbers piecemeal.

Even then, if they joined the fight, it was always best to get the hell out of the way.

A dozen or so of the creatures barreled through the trees and bumped into trunks and knocked bark off before they were able to pick up speed. The team picked off as many of them as they could—which turned out only to be three or four—before they knew they had run out of time.

Courtney dove out of the way and let her suit pick up most of the slack as she rushed to one of the trees to use it for cover.

In seconds, she realized she'd made a dangerous choice. Finger-like vines slithered down the trunk and looked almost like trickles of rain, except they swept from left to right as if looking for her. They had no eyes but she registered a tactile response from the tree she was pressed against and she backed away. Reflexively, she fired at the vines and they recoiled and snapped upward into the canopy away from her as they were struck by the bullets.

"Dr. Monroe!"

She bounded out of the way barely in time and one of the hippos rushed past her, close enough that its shoulder knocked her down but thankfully out of the way as the massive jaws snapped shut around the trunk of the tree.

The mutant would have bitten her in half if she had stood in front of it. She knew better than to give it a chance for a second attempt. Immediately, she twisted to drive her gun barrel into one of the eyes that would no doubt try to relocate her once the beast had finished chewing through the damn vegetation.

"I hope they don't come up with anything creative for this," Courtney whispered as she pulled the trigger. Her assault rifle kicked into the three-round burst and the shots turned the creature's brains to mush.

Sal made killing the bastards look a little too easy. She had a feeling that she knew why, but there was no point in mentioning it. While she didn't like to keep secrets, she knew a few of his—not because he'd told her, necessarily, but because she wasn't stupid.

It took longer than she liked but finally, the team killed the hippos one by one and it looked like the rest of the monsters knew well enough to stay out of their way when they were on the offensive. The larger creatures showed no selectivity when it came to what they killed. If it was in front of them, it died, whether human, Zoo, or—as it turned out—tree.

Still, it didn't look like the vines had died with the tree they were on, and she backed away quickly as they wound around and constricted the dead hippo while others continued to search for her. Courtney hurried to where the rest of the team had regrouped.

"Give the fire and plasma throwers time in the lead," she snapped and eliminated a handful of panthers that her suit had alerted her to in the branches. "We need to clear these trees before we advance."

The sergeant nodded and directed the men in question, who began to burn the foliage that had sprung up overnight. Courtney scowled when the vines snatched at one of them, but they rushed into the relative safety of the branches above when the plasma and flames touched them.

It looked like the throwers had run into these vines before given the way they laughed when the tentacle-like growth withdrew.

"I hate this fucking jungle," Francesca whispered.

"You and me both. Still, it looks like we carved out a niche for ourselves. If we all happen to survive this, we'll be fucking heroes."

"Survival isn't quite what I had in mind." The French-woman shook her head as she checked her ammo. "The way things are going, we'll be ground into dust in a war of attrition that'll last centuries. Humanity will slowly be driven from this planet, and those who can't afford to fly away will be left to scavenge and fight until every last one of us is dead."

"Well…that's a little depressing."

"Sure. But it's what I've come to fear much more the longer this fighting lasts. The Zoo can afford to wait. It doesn't look like it's going anywhere, and if we do find a way to stop it and drive it back, what's to stop it from delving deep underground to where we can't reach it or don't even know it's there? It could simply hide and wait for a couple of hundred years until we've forgotten all about it and then strike again."

There was a more terrifying option that Francesca hadn't considered and one that Courtney knew was becoming more and more popular with her peers across the world. What happened when whatever sent the Zoo came back to finish the job?

Still, the ex-legionary would be the doomy and gloomy one, which meant she needed to be the leader who provided a little hope when there seemed to be none.

"Well, I'll certainly fight to my last breath. And I'd be proud to do it with you around."

Martin laughed at that and focused on the trees again. "I guess there isn't anywhere else in the world I'd like to be for something like this. It's better to be fighting at the front lines than sitting at home and waiting for everything to go to shit. It gives you the impression that you're in a position to do something about it. Not that we do, of course. At least not in the grand scheme of things."

She would have to talk to Francesca about the bad

mood she was in. Maybe killing a couple of the bastards would help and the opportunity for that would present itself soon enough. The trees were being cleared at a good rate, which enabled them to press forward.

"Come on." Courtney patted the woman on the shoulder. "Let's get you something to kill to remind you how big a factor you are in the big picture."

"Now you're talking."

They had been at it for a few hours now. Being slowed to a crawl wasn't how she wished for it to go, but it was better than being forced back. They were able to cut through the monsters when they started attacking and then the throwers were ready to deal with the jungle when it started to get a little too out of hand.

It was tough when both vegetation and mutants attacked at the same time. So far, however, the team had managed to deal with the animals and avoid the damage the plants could do through judicious use of the flame and plasma throwers.

Thankfully, it wasn't long before the terrain began to tilt upward. There was enough soil for the trees to grow thickly but when she scanned the area, she felt sure that it was only a few feet deep over solid rock beneath. The larger trees very possibly grew directly into the rocks and pushed their roots through the natural crevices and miniscule gaps between stones.

Still, it was enough to tell her they were closer to the mountains. Aside from the rocks, the vegetation began to thin, a sure sign that they were reaching higher elevations.

The trees could still thrust from the rocks, but it was

much slower than in the sand and soil. It wasn't a surprise that it was easier to burn the Zoo away as they advanced through this new terrain, but she could tell that she was running her team a little ragged.

"Five minutes!" she called and gestured for them to stop. "Water, food, bathroom needs—get it all done as quickly as possible. Don't be parted from your sensor equipment, though. I don't want any blind spots the Zoo can attack us from."

They were all vets and knew the drill, and while the process wasn't big on dignity, they all knew how to get it done fast. It was her job to alert Franklin and those fighting the spur of their location. She took the flare gun from her pouch, chose a clear section of the sky to fire into, and watched the flare rise to about three hundred meters in a few seconds before it began to drift lazily earthward.

People would know where they were now. If they died trying, at least there would be some record of how far they got—and their death wouldn't inadvertently be through plasma fire.

"Do you know how pissed I'll be if the idiot we're here to rescue is dead when we get there?" Courtney muttered as she tucked the flare gun into her pouch again.

"No," Francesca answered. "How angry?"

"I'm not sure. I'll find out when it happens, but I would guess...seriously fucking pissed that all this was for nothing."

"Not to mention that our last hope—only hope, honestly—to stop the Zoo ends up as mutant crap."

Francesca nodded and sipped her water. "Yeah, I'll be fucking pissed too."

He was reasonably sure that he could come up with a list of about three million places he would rather be than in the Zoo. A third-world prison and sucking fumes in the middle of the Ironman triathlon were on the list long before the alien jungle featured. Marcel shuddered when a chill shivered up his spine as it came into view from the plane's windows.

The whole area was a no-fly zone, and not because they didn't want civilians getting too close to the jungle. While they didn't want them anywhere close to it, it wasn't merely about preventing people from discovering what was happening. He'd heard enough stories to wonder if they were close enough to the Zoo for the flying monsters inside to attack them.

His scowl deepened as he leaned back in his seat and tried to look away. That lasted about a second before he was drawn back to the thick green band that stretched across the horizon. Three more attempts made him simply close the flap on his window and stare at his laptop.

Although he tried to reassure himself that this was simply his over-active imagination, he couldn't escape the sense that it was out there, looking at him and reaching out to him somehow. He didn't like it or the vulnerability it stirred in him.

To project a calm and confident demeanor, he made a point of not looking at the horizon when they touched down at the US base, where a handful of men in uniform waited for him. They all looked about as tired as he felt and their bleary eyes suggested that they were about to snap at anything that so much as looked at them wrong.

They didn't snap at him, fortunately.

"Marcel Adams, Interpol." He extended his hand and when their grasps almost broke bones, he managed to avoid a whimper in response.

"Commander Franklin is already at the field base and he would like you to join him as soon as possible. Are you ready to fly again, sir?"

These guys were all older than he was and with more experience in this situation, and they called him sir. He wasn't sure why it irritated him, but he ignored the reflexive protest and simply nodded. The circumstances demanded that he be ready to fly again, but he knew that if he paused and thought about it for a second, he would find an excuse to stay as far away from everything as he could.

He hadn't gotten as far as he had in law enforcement by avoiding challenges. His choice of career meant he'd gone through shit that people wouldn't believe to get to where he was today, and it was done by strapping a pair on and heading into the thick of it, no matter what the hell "it" might be.

A helicopter was already waiting for them. Marcel scrambled in and pulled one of the headsets on. He wasn't the only one filed for this flight, of course, and in moments, the other seats in the aircraft were taken by soldiers in full combat suits. It didn't look like it was their first trip out. From what he could see, although his experience was fairly limited, hasty repairs had been implemented to get them out into the field as quickly as possible.

All seemed to share the same odd look on their faces—not quite scared but alert. He guessed they'd been alert for so long that they were all but exhausted, but they couldn't afford to turn it off yet.

It was a short flight—or maybe it felt shorter because he dreaded the rough military aircraft landing. Once they touched down and the doors opened so the bright desert sunlight streamed in, sand whipped in fast enough to hurt as he climbed out with the rest of them and followed the one man who wasn't in a combat suit to the field base that had been set up. Massive guns were in position to stop the Zoo from pushing in, and they fired almost constantly. The earth shook with every round launched and his feet tingled unpleasantly in response.

"What the fuck have I gotten myself into?" he whispered as he was guided to a tent that was larger than all the others—the command tent, he assumed—and people filed in and out almost constantly. He had to practically take a number and wait in line before he was let in by the massive, tattooed sergeant who directed foot traffic.

Everyone looked tired and stressed. None of them would be able to stop for a while, but it was clear who had been up the longest, which meant he was probably in charge.

"Commander Franklin?" Marcel offered his hand again. "Marcel Adams, Interpol."

"I know who you are," the man replied brusquely. "Thanks for coming down here on such short notice. We're closing in on Badawi, and if anyone might have some intel on how to leverage the asshole to cooperate when we do get our hands on him, it's Interpol."

"Is that why you brought me here?" he asked and took the water offered to him gratefully. "I thought it was all a waste of time when word came in that there was a massive spur when I was in the air. You have a location on Badawi?"

"Yeah. And there's a reason why you were brought to this field base too."

"Oh...fuck," he whispered.

Franklin nodded slowly. "Whatever's happening here, he's in the goddammed middle of it. We sent a team in to find him and get him out alive, but there's no real assurance that he'll want to help us even if we do get him out."

"Which is a massive if," one of the sergeants pointed out and folded his powerful arms in front of his chest. "It's impossible to know how likely it is that a man alone will be able to survive, or for how long."

"He won't be alone." Marcel shook his head. "Even with things not going his way, reports on Badawi indicate that he usually has at least a skeleton crew around him. Cheap but useful would be my guess."

"Noted." Franklin gestured to one of the other officers. "We'll transport you to the ENSOL camp. You can connect with your contact there—"

"My contact? Sam?"

"The Fixer, yeah. Their camp is the best-defended location we have in this sector, and it'll keep you close enough to stay in touch if we need you. Of course, you do have the option to return to the base, or we can fly you home if you like."

It was tempting, but he pushed his preferences aside.

"No, I'll wait there. Let me know if there's anything I can do to help."

"We might take you up on that."

This was the Zoo. The crazy, sci-fi land where alien mutants were real, monsters and trees ate people, and no one knew how to stop it. It was a magical land where anything was possible. Maybe that included the miracle he was sure they needed.

CHAPTER THIRTEEN

"Is everyone okay?"

Sal looked around and scanned the life signs of every member of their team, even in the darkness. The sensors were a little damaged but still picked up enough to give him an idea of what they were looking for.

"If anyone has difficulty breathing or feels like you've punctured or broken something, give us a heads-up," Madigan called from where she scrambled awkwardly to her feet.

"All good here, boss," Trick responded and pushed up from where he had sprawled on the loose dirt. "I might have some suit problems going forward but there's nothing we should be worried about."

"I have a feeling we'll have all kinds of shit to be worried about going forward," Sal whispered. "Athena, are you all good? Did the fall damage your systems?"

"I'm trying to work around some minor damage to the sensors," she answered.

"How far did we drop?"

"Not too far but there were some twists and turns on the way that might make it difficult to get out. The smoothness of the rock would be a problem too."

Almost like they had overheard the conversation, Chezza and Jiro fired grappling hooks along the walls to find a way to the top. The hooks didn't go far and simply caught the twists and turns above them but didn't catch on anything before they fell and were drawn in slowly.

"It doesn't look like there's a clear way up," Jiro commented. "We might be able to relay to the top, but the horde of monsters will be waiting for us. It might be a little better to hang out here until the shit calms."

"We're here to stir shit up, remember?" Madigan scowled and approached the wall. "It doesn't look like we'll get much of anything out of this place. We don't have any connection to the outside world and can't even send the flare up."

Sal drew a deep breath and tapped the wall, more out of a need to try something proactive. It surprised him that it wasn't quite as hard as he had thought—more brittle, he realized, and broke and crumbled every time he touched it.

"We need to keep moving," he told the team. "Assuming all these rocks aren't interfering with our compass, we can continue in that direction. It's more or less the same as we traveled in before, and we might save some time if we don't have to constantly fight monsters and living trees and all that shit."

Madigan nodded and turned to see where they were going. "What made this? Do you think something out there dug all these tunnels?"

"I don't think so." He settled on his haunches and ran his

fingers over the floor of the tunnel. At that moment, he wished he'd paid a little more attention in geology since he had no clue what the rock formations meant.

Although he had a couple of ideas. The first one that came to mind was that it was caused by water erosion, but that didn't make any sense. They would have seen some sign of the water.

"Well, we can keep moving," Jiro muttered. "I'm sure we'll find out what happened here eventually, for better or worse."

That offered little comfort, but they pushed forward regardless. The Zoo no doubt knew where they were and hopefully, it wasn't forcing them into an even more lethal attack. Sal wasn't sure what would happen if they were trapped down there.

His connection was somehow amplified underground, although the presence of humans interfered a little. It was difficult to work around them, but he managed it somehow and searched for something that might provide some insight. A persistent feeling of expectation nagged at him and he felt the pulse a little louder inside the tunnel.

"There is movement down the tunnel branches," Athena commented. "But..."

"What?"

Sal knew what the AI would say. He'd felt it himself but it was good to know that his feelings were still confirmed.

"There are monsters on the sensors," Madigan whispered. "But they are moving away. Do they not know we're down here?"

"I don't think so," he replied shortly. He was trying to think and people insisted on talking and interrupting him.

He drew a deep breath and tried to connect with the Zoo again to feel what was happening around them.

It was a smooth connection, powerful enough to indicate that however the tunnels were created, they contained high concentrations of the goop.

Moments later, something changed. He looked up and noticed Mal and Jiro exploring one of the branching tunnels, which led them away from the path they were following.

"Stop!" he called in warning.

Both looked at him.

"We're getting some additional reading—oh, shit!"

The locusts that had retreated before them suddenly surged down the tunnel toward them. Madigan stepped in front, activated the rockets on her suit's shoulder, and launched two into the monsters attacking them.

Sal could have warned her that it was a bad idea, but he lunged forward instead and dragged Madigan and Mal away from the explosion. Athena caught hold of Jiro, and all three were yanked away as the explosives impacted. The brittle surface of the tunnels shattered, collapsed on the creatures, and made the ground shake as he continued to haul them all away.

Fortunately, the cave-in didn't follow them. He had feared it would but the brittle surface of the cave held.

The branch of the tunnel, however, was blocked.

"I think we need to be a little more careful with our use of explosives down here," Sal whispered. "Humans need to stick to the plot or they'll be killed."

"What?"

He cleared his throat. "We need to stay on the path. It looks like we're being herded somewhere."

"You know what happens when cattle get herded, right?" Chezza asked. "Fair enough, these cattle are armed, but something is in there waiting for us."

"Waiting for Sal," Madigan corrected. "It's guided him the whole way and something will be waiting for him."

Sal turned to look at her. He assumed the team had noticed at least a little of what was happening, but hearing it spoken of that openly felt wrong. Humans weren't supposed to know what he was doing.

"We need to keep moving," she told them sharply. "We'll find the answers to this shit later."

The team nodded and began to move down the tunnel they were meant to use. He wasn't surprised that nothing stepped in to stop them, although that was the most sinister part of it.

"Something is wrong with that, right?" Sal whispered.

"What's wrong?" Athena countered.

"Don't play coy with me. More and more, I'm thinking of the hu...uh, the rest of the team as outsiders. I think I said it out loud at one point but no one called me on it. That was weird, right? That's something influencing me?"

"That would be the most likely cause, yes. The walls of the tunnel are saturated with the goop, which amplifies its effect on you. Whatever it's doing has been magnified."

"You think or you know?"

"The data might be difficult to discern but it all leans one way."

"We might need to approach the conversation of you shutting me down soon."

"Why do you say that?"

"Because what we're being guided to...there's...a massive concentration of Zoo...shit."

"Would you like another chance to explain that?"

Sal scowled. "Honestly, it's hard to tell. It's like a...well but instead of being full of water, it's full of flora and fauna all bundled together. I can't tell where the individual communication strands are coming from. And there's something else."

"More Zoo shit?"

"Maybe giving you the ability to project a tone with your voice was a mistake. Sass isn't appreciated."

"Sorry. What do you see?"

"It's...a black hole like something drawing and sucking everything else into it. Not a blob so much, but more of a meandering line. Like a...like a...a vein?"

"Are you asking me or telling me?"

"I'm asking me."

"Oh."

It was a good thing that he had the rearguard position. He paid little attention to where they were going and merely followed the team blindly and let Athena make sure he didn't trip over anything. The odd flat, blackness of whatever was in the walls reminded him of the blank patch he'd sensed at the first site where they'd found metal. Logic insisted that this was the same attempt to create a nothingness where there was something important.

With no one to notice his furtive study, it was easy to examine the wall as they continued and he noticed concentrations of what appeared to be ore here and there. Deposits from the running veins had settled within the natural cavities in the stone. Fortunately, the team didn't move too fast, which gave him the opportunity to pause and dig a little deeper when he noticed a larger section of the seam.

"It's metal," Sal whispered and inspected it carefully once he'd extracted it from the wall. He slid it hastily into a bag and sealed it. With the weird change in the goop at the wall, he was a little sensitive to the possibility of unidentified substances eating into his suit.

It had a faint greenish tinge to it. Maybe there was some kind of fungus somewhere that reflected the faint lights emitted by his suit that helped the night-vision sensors to pick up on what they were looking at without giving up their position.

"It's not defended," Sal whispered. "Why aren't they defending it?"

"Maybe the monsters and mutants know we're trapped down here? There might be no point in wasting the effort it would take to kill you all."

"Yeah." Sal gulped and shook his head. "Like we're already fucking dead."

There were things people grew a little too old for. Badawi had first realized that around his thirty-fifth birthday when he noticed he could no longer stay up all night, no matter how hard he tried. Fucking women for more than a couple of hours every night had ended at around thirty-seven.

Hell, that was more or less the time when he realized he couldn't even keep up with his wife's libido.

This was one of those times when he knew he was too old for this shit and he recalled the American movie with the two police officers. He had always liked Danny Glover, although the third remake was more than a little grating. Bringing the two original actors back for cameo parts took him right out of the film.

Most of his team members were dead. Sami was still with him but he'd been wounded by one of the locusts. They weren't that deadly in small numbers as it turned out, but their mandibles were more than capable of crushing bone if they managed a good strike.

The kid's ankle looked like it had been crushed, and while he tried to put on a brave face, it was clear that he was in considerable pain.

"Are you all right, Uncle?"

He was a good kid.

"The beasts are taking a break. It'll give us time to catch our breath. I'm better than ever. How about you?"

"I don't think I can walk, Uncle."

That would be a problem for a while. Even if they managed to get him to a doctor and save the foot, Sami would still have difficulty walking. Especially when it rained, although that wouldn't be a problem if he lived in and around the desert.

"The fire's going out!"

One other of his men was left and thankfully, he was young, energetic, and mostly unwounded. They all had their scrapes and bruises.

"So put more wood on it."

"Oh, yes. Let me squat and start shitting some wood."

That was a hilarious mental image, but Badawi didn't feel like laughing. The flames were going out and they hadn't burned hot enough to leave embers that would last for very long. Besides, the monsters wouldn't be afraid of something that wasn't open flame.

Not that they were afraid of the fire much at all, but it did help to burn the wings of the locusts and singe the fur of the hyenas.

Some of the bigger bastards were coming though. He could feel it in his bones and checked his ammo reserves as an attempt to keep himself busy instead of allowing any of the despair to sink in. Movement flickered and jumped in the shadows and soft chitters issued from the insects between low growls from the larger mutants that approached through the opening of the tunnel leading into the cave.

He no longer needed to tell his men to wait and hold their fire. They'd been through the process a dozen times or more by now and knew how to deal with it.

"They're coming," Sami whispered and shifted slightly so he was in a position to fire.

Badawi had half a mind to simply let him lay back. The chances were he wouldn't get many shots off, but they needed every last bullet they could get.

The bastards were coming.

He eased closer and his heart hammered painfully, a few beats away from simply giving out altogether. Still, he was alive for now so waited and watched as a pack of hyenas pushed in first.

His attention was suddenly drawn to the locusts. They climbed on the ceiling to make themselves harder to hit.

"Shoot the locusts first!"

His man nodded and the air filled with the sound of gunfire. He thought he would go deaf from it eventually but he promised himself that if they somehow managed to survive, he would see an ear doctor.

Until then, the problem wasn't one he could do anything about. Or he wouldn't need to deal with it at all. Dead men didn't need ears.

The locusts were the first to be eliminated. Spraying and praying appeared to be working out well enough, although it wasn't the most efficient use of their weapons.

Predictably, the hyenas fell next and he dragged his magazine out and slapped a new one in. He didn't need to feel in his pouch to know it was the last one, nor did he want to think too hard about what would happen when it was finished.

Something large was out there and used the smaller creatures as cover while they attacked and pushed closer to him. His team was positioned behind a small assembly line although the protection it offered was minimal. It was ancient and hadn't been used in years, likely installed when the tunnels were originally dug by one fighting force or another over the years. No one remembered that far back around that area.

"Uncle, look out!"

Sami balanced on his good foot, hopped forward, and opened fire. Two of the panthers had snuck in while they weren't looking, used the darkness to remain unnoticed, and tried to pounce on him.

One was dropped by the young man's fire, but the other attacked viciously and tossed him aside. The kid's throat opened with a splash of blood and he fell, gurgling, as Badawi stood over him and opened fire to kill the last panther.

"I'm so sorry, my boy," he whispered, dropped to one knee, and looked at his nephew. His apology came too late. Sami's blank eyes stared at the rocky ceiling and the blood flowing from his throat had slowed.

In moments, he'd gone.

The other man was dead already too, but he didn't care about that. Sami, though, hit him hard in a place he didn't much like.

"Motherfuckers!" he roared, claimed the magazines the kid carried, and put one into his assault rifle. He didn't much care if the military was coming in to push the spur's growth back. They wouldn't be in time to help him, and if this was his time to die, old or not, he would make sure there was a pile of corpses around him when he was found.

If he was found.

A massive shape appeared in the doorway. He could make out fur glistening in what little light reached it in the depths, but he couldn't determine what it was.

"Come on!" he screamed, pulled the trigger on his AK, and grimaced when it kicked painfully into his shoulder.

It was a mistake to open fire when he felt so unbalanced. The result was that he seemed to run out of bullets seconds after he pulled the trigger. So much for making his shots count.

He ejected the empty magazine but before he could retrieve another one, the shape moved. It didn't act like it had been wounded so he wasn't sure if he'd so much as touched the creature with his spray of bullets. No doubt his stupidly emotional response had cost him even that small satisfaction.

The beast charged forward and the ground shook with every step. He fumbled, dropped the magazine he had retrieved, and cursed loudly.

A moment later, something powered into his chest and he bounced off the back wall like he was in a pinball machine. Unfortunately, his body was considerably less capable of taking punishment than most pinballs were.

His ribs were broken, and more than a few bruised and broken bones all over meant he wouldn't be able to offer much more of a fight, but there was still one thing he could do.

Badawi groaned, rolled on his shoulder, and felt a sharp stab of pain but refused to let that stop him. He drew the pistol holstered at his hip.

It wouldn't do much, but it was enough to kill himself before the beast could.

He froze when something heavy stepped on the side of his body. The pain increased until he could no longer hold the weapon and he dropped it with a gasp of pain. Whatever strength he had left was immediately drained, and it wasn't like he would be able to wrestle this creature even if he was at full strength.

Still, he had to try something.

"Fucking...shit," he cursed and looked up at the monster. "Get off me!"

CHAPTER FOURTEEN

"Is it weird that this tunnel system is worse than moving through the jungle?" Trick's tone sounded almost conversational.

Jiro snorted. "Even though we had to fight a horde of fuckers on the way? Including the fucking jungle?"

Chezza nodded. "Well, the darkness isn't much better and I'd prefer to have something to fight than nothing at all. Honestly, what the hell are we even working toward here?"

"It's better to be down here than up there," Madigan stated immediately in the kind of tone that settled all debate. "If we were up there, we would have an endless succession of fights that drained our resources and made things more difficult as we went along. At least this way, when we get to the thick of all this shit, we'll be rested, armed, and with enough ammo to turn anything that comes at us into a bloody paste."

She made a good point there, Sal decided. Keeping everyone alive while they completed their mission was the

MICHAEL TODD & MICHAEL ANDERLE

point, but there were two downsides to the way they were doing it. One was that they hadn't done much distracting on the way in. This was the focus of their mission early on, after all.

They had some attention from the Zoo, but he had a feeling that their efforts had done very little to help the people dealing with the spur.

The other downside was that they couldn't communicate with the people watching and waiting for them. If this trip through the bowels of the Zoo lasted more than a few days, they would be in a situation where everyone thought they were all dead and planned accordingly.

Wait—did he know there was a spur? How did he know? Was it from the Zoo or had someone told him about it before they went in?

"Sal?"

He turned to where Madigan waited for him and realized that the rest of the Heavy Metal team was leaving him behind a little while he checked the walls again.

"Yeah," he whispered. "I'm only...uh, I don't know. Thinking."

"Is there anything you want to talk about?"

"Not really. But we should...be careful heading deeper like this."

"I'll tell the rest of the people to stop with their carefree attitudes. Jiro and Trick were planning on juggling grenades between themselves, but I guess they'll have to put a stop to that."

That drew a chuckle from him and Sal straightened and felt his suit adjust with his movement.

"You—"

"I know what you mean," Madigan whispered and patted him on the shoulder. "We'll be a little more careful going forward."

"Thanks."

"Of course."

It wasn't like her to simply accept what he said without even asking how he knew to warn them. Sal had anticipated at least one uncomfortable conversation in which she reminded him that the goop couldn't be trusted and maybe he only sensed what the Zoo wanted him to. They might be good points but they wouldn't help him at all. Still, he felt almost cheated that she hadn't. Maybe she knew what was happening and kept her thoughts to herself.

Of course, that begged the question of how she could know. Maybe Athena kept her informed of his status at all times. She probably gave her periodic updates when she knew he wasn't paying attention to what she was doing. Having the AI betray him to the humans was worrying until he recognized that it was all conjecture and most likely paranoia.

"The tunnel's coming to an end ahead of us," Mal called, having taken point when Madigan fell back to check on Sal. "It looks like a cavern of some kind."

Of course it was a cavern. Being blinded by merely relying on the primitive sensors had to be so fucking frustrating.

They stepped into it and covered all angles of attack carefully. The area was massive with many points from which the monsters could attack, both from the ground and the air, and even from above if the mutants scaled the walls for higher vantage points.

The team stood expectantly, poised and ready, but no attack was forthcoming. Enough of the creatures were gathered in the space to be a formidable challenge, but none of them displayed any hostility or aggression. Directly opposite where the humans stood, hordes of the locusts skittered and chittered and their wings created a low, steady buzzing that made Sal grit his teeth.

He realized that his teammates could see them too. There was a light in the cave. Something on the walls and ceiling—probably fungi or moss—gave off light-blue biolu-minescence. The tiny lights looked like stars stretched across the room and gave the whole place an unsettling calm feeling that contrasted with the sensations emitted by all the other creatures sharing the cavern with them.

None of them moved forward, however. They didn't even seem to mind having the humans in the chamber with them.

The creatures were excited to see Sal and their attention was drawn to him most of all as everyone stepped deeper into the enormous cave.

"I have the weirdest feeling that we should turn around and fuck off," Trick whispered as they moved into the open.

"That sounds about right," Madigan answered. "And I might even make that call, but if there was ever a place to distract the hell out of the Zoo, I'd say this is it."

She wasn't wrong about that. Considerable attention was focused on the cavern. Sal felt like thousands of eyes dug into the back of his skull and tried to see what he saw or feel what he felt. He wasn't sure he could fight them for much longer.

Without thinking, he moved to his right and away from the team as he approached what appeared to be a pool. A depression in the rocks warned him first, but as he moved closer, he saw the water reflecting the lights in the ceiling. It was beautiful.

"Does anyone else get that smell, even through your suit's scrubbers?"

He startled at Chezza's question and looked sharply to where she moved toward him. He drew a deep breath and immediately caught a foul smell emitted by something in the cavern with them. It was odd that he hadn't noticed it before.

"Do you think it's coming from in there?" Jiro stepped closer but stopped short of the edge of the water as though restrained by the same level of disquiet Sal could feel from the others.

The pool was the source of the smell, that much was certain. It could probably be best described as the reek of a swamp or bog with rotting and decaying plant matter. No one wanted to get close enough to explore the reason for the stench. That much was obvious from the way they inched away from it after a hasty glance at the surface of the water.

"Do you think they dug this area out?" Madigan asked. "I don't know much about this kind of thing, but it can't be natural, right?"

"Well...it might be," he whispered. "It looks like it might be some kind of water chamber that was already here under the desert that the Zoo coopted for its purposes before it did a little digging of its own."

The pool was most certainly something new. He could see where the creatures had worked and he had a feeling that many of them dug until they dropped dead and others came in to take their places.

"That's not water," she whispered.

"What?" Sal looked sharply at her. She was the only one who still stood close enough to the pool to see more clearly, although her body language spoke of her instinct to back the hell away. The other humans were probably wracked by the same need. Everything about the situation and the cavern would make them feel unwelcome and like they needed to leave immediately. Had they possessed weaker minds, they would have said it repeatedly until eventually, their morale broke and they ran in panic.

It was a useful tactic but dependent on people voicing their concerns. No one did, which meant that each one felt that way but didn't think that it was something to say to the others. No one wanted to sound cowardly in a room full of courageous heroes.

"Of course it's water," Sonja muttered. "What else could it be?"

"No, she's right," Sal replied quickly as he approached the edge. The vibrations caused by the weight of his suit made ripples form across the surface of the liquid. Seeing it in motion made it obvious that it had far more viscosity than water did. "It's some kind of...sludge."

"Goop?" Jiro asked.

"Technically speaking, yes. It is goop but not *the* goop. This is something else but I'm not sure what."

Sal backed away again quickly. The weight of their suits as the others moved closer increased the activity on the surface, but something else moved beneath to create more ripples. Moments later, the displacement released bubbles, which meant that something was ascending from the depths.

"What the fuck?" Madigan backed hastily away from the pool and aimed her weapon at it.

"Don't do that!" he snapped.

"Why?"

"Be...uh, because..." He paused when he realized that seeing the barrel of her assault rifle aimed at the pool had brought out a knee-jerk reaction of pure anger from him.

"Because it's pissing everyone else in this cave off," Jiro finished for him, although his interpretation of the situation wasn't accurate. Still, it seemed to satisfy Madigan.

He didn't want to have to explain that the creatures weren't angry. The buzzing from them had become a little more intense, which might have led someone to believe they were getting angry, but it wasn't what he sensed from them. Their reaction was closer to excitement and anticipation.

The shimmering ripples grew increasingly intense until the sludge bubbled like it had come to the boil. Moments later, something broke the surface.

At first, the thin and shivering creature was entirely focused on its effort to reach the edge of the pool. After it managed to secure itself on the rock with spindly limbs, it eased fully and its form was instantly recognizable.

Smaller than the other locusts, it appeared to still be in its formative stages like it had just emerged from its pupa and needed to complete the transformation to an adult. The wings fluttered weakly and the slime slid off but it shook and remained oddly vulnerable as if uncomfortable in its new skin.

Sal wondered how long it would take before the adolescent was grown and ready to throw itself into a hail of bullets. He estimated two or maybe three days but with the Zoo's current accelerated approach, it was probably less.

More of them began to emerge three or four at a time until a dozen or so of the locusts and humpers milled around the pool. They ignored the humans who stood so close and trembled and shivered while the gunk slipped off of them. It came away like water from a duck's feathers, dripped into the sludge, and left them with a slightly damp blue sheen that faded quickly.

"I feel violated," Trick muttered. "What the hell is happening?"

"This…it's a birthing pool," Madigan answered, narrowing her eyes. "That seems fairly obvious. These are their young and soon, they'll be off in a horde to kill humans or be killed by them but for now, they're…uh, growing up."

None of them seemed inclined to comment on that. Even with the excitement that spread to him from the other mutants, Sal had to fight the urge to retch.

"What happens next?" Mal inched away from the young creatures but held his weapon trained on them to be safe.

"They were just born," he reasoned. "So if they follow some semblance of how Earth-based creatures raise their young, there must be a nursery somewhere nearby."

"We are somewhere nearby," Madigan pointed out.

He turned to look at her. "What?"

"That pool birthed them and they were brought up here. This is the nursery—look."

The newborns began to move again but this time, away from the pool. Their legs were unsteady and their wings spasmed like they were still getting used to having them but they shuffled toward the wall with a kind of instinctual certainty that this was expected. The sheen on their bodies illuminated the room a little more and highlighted other bodies in the corners.

These had been there the whole time, of course, and the sensors had picked them up too. It had been easy to assume that they were merely more of those that had gathered to watch and wait. Sal wasn't sure how he'd missed it before, but they were all similar. While different species and varying sizes and shapes, they were smaller than the adults and huddled together until they were grown and ready to fight.

Madigan took a step forward. The sludge had reverted to its original undisturbed state but something protruded from it that had probably been dislodged by the newborns and hadn't sunk again yet.

She pulled it up. The liquid dripped away from it like it had from the creatures.

"It's a chunk of metal of some kind," Chezza commented. "How did that get down here?"

Madigan tossed it to Sal and he caught it almost without thinking. As he looked at the item, he realized the action had been without thought since Athena had caught it. He found it a comforting reminder that she stood ready in case he needed her to step in and take control of the suit.

She was like a solid presence in the background to ensure that neither he nor anyone else was in unnecessary danger.

"It's from a suit," he whispered. "One of the older Marks —maybe five or six years old, but it's been in recent use given the condition of the scorch marks."

"I guess we know where all the fucking bodies go," Madigan replied darkly.

"How the hell does a jungle grow into these rocks?"

That had been a question even Courtney had wondered about until she realized that the high rocky ground was riddled with caves and even what appeared to be a tunnel system. The latter had not been carved by the Zoo and probably predated it by at least fifty years unless she missed her guess, likely dug by one military force or another. The area hadn't exactly been the most stable before it had been engulfed by a massive alien jungle.

Even when they had climbed through the tunnels to avoid the steeper stretches, the system was already being broken by plants that forced through the hard surfaces. Nothing in their database said that the Zoo couldn't thrust plants through rock, especially since the rocks in the area weren't quite as solid as one might have thought.

Still, it had surprised her but she honestly had little practical use for the information. So the Zoo could dig and grow through rocks. What the fuck else was new?

"We need to keep moving," she snapped and gestured for the plasma and flame thrower team to clear the way ahead of them. They had encountered a particularly dense collection of plants that had stabilized themselves with an extensive network of roots, some of which were above ground. The many branches had yet to push out a full complement of leaves, but more than a few vines had anchored themselves securely among them and were already mobile, feeling for something to grab and choke the life out of.

Their pace had been slowed considerably and they had to burn through before they were able to advance.

They were still moving, though, either using the odd tunnel or hiking through the rough terrain when they were outside. When necessary, they hacked or burned through the thorns and vines that appeared to be determined to stop them. She reminded herself that they weren't only there to stop them. The Zoo was expanding and its prime directive would compel everything to assimilate this new territory as quickly as possible.

They were merely in the way, not the direct target. Trying to kill something by sending a fucking jungle after it had to be the most extravagant way to go about it. The simple truth was that the Zoo was breaking out and they were there, and any enthusiasm it might show about killing them was likely due to the fact that they were a handy source of biomass.

Courtney drew a deep breath and calmed herself as her suit completed its seismic scan of the area. The harder the rocks were in the region, the easier it would be to map the whole area and provide a decent idea of where they should go.

"So you got nothing?"

She looked up as one of the men who had joined them approached her.

"What did you say?"

"I asked you how the jungle could grow through rock."

"Do you want a play-by-play of the process, or do you merely not know how plants grow?"

"Are you fucking kidding me?"

Francesca stepped forward quickly. "Hey, hey. Let's get it under control here. What's the issue?"

"Nothing," the man snapped and walked away, his demeanor almost aggressive.

Courtney could understand their frustration. The pace was slow, the fight was hard, and none of them knew if the man they were coming to rescue was even still alive.

Worse, they'd taken their first casualty in the last attack. The vines had pinned three of them down before the rest of the team could help, and the monsters ripped through one within moments. The other two managed to keep the creatures away until their teammates reached them and cut them free.

The animals hadn't done much damage to the men themselves but their suits had been affected. She could see them limping while they tried to judge whether they were ready to get back into action.

"There's a cave entrance not that far ahead," she said once the seismic scans were complete. "Although there isn't much jungle between us and it, a large group of mutants is there waiting for us."

"It might not be for us."

Francesca made a solid point. Courtney didn't want to

believe that the Zoo was able to direct its focus toward someone in particular but it was the only explanation for what they were looking at. A concentration of mutants had gathered in a location where there was no military presence.

Coincidentally—or so she tried to tell herself—it was where they were looking for Badawi. It was a little too convenient, her science brain insisted, although their presence was certainly very inconvenient for the rescuers.

The team adjusted their formation so their wounded could be positioned at the center. There was no way to send them out for proper care, not without completely abandoning their mission and that was not an option. At least now they could be protected by their uninjured comrades and would also not create a weakness in the outer line that the enemy could exploit.

They would go in no matter what.

While they didn't need confirmation at this point in the game, the sound of gunfire from the cave they were approaching seemed to boost morale.

"I guess this is the right place," Francesca joked as they opened fire at the tail end of the horde of mutants that attempted to enter the cavern ahead of them.

Her laughter cut off when the gunfire from the cave stopped suddenly and the creatures outside surged toward the entrance.

Courtney cursed. There was no way they could have come so fucking close only for him die there under her nose.

"Push forward!" she yelled and brandished her rifle.

"Fire at will! Clear these bastards the best you know how! Hack them, shoot them, fry them—or all of the above. I don't care but get me to that fucking cave!"

CHAPTER FIFTEEN

Sal had to make sure that all the suits collected as much data as they could. It was almost a relief to lose himself in scientist mode while he double-checked and even triple-checked to make sure nothing was lost. They'd learned something new about the Zoo—although it had probably been there for much longer than one might assume—and he was damned if they ended up losing this kind of ground-breaking intel through negligence.

He was adamant that the only reason they might lose it would be that they were killed. If they made it out, he would make damn sure it was with vital intelligence on how the Zoo produced its creatures. He assumed some creatures could and did reproduce like their Earth-based counterparts based on the young panther they'd taken out way back when.

Hell, he hadn't thought about the little critter in a while although they'd given her a name and everything. He had no idea where she'd ended up, although if he had to put money on it, she was probably the cause of one of the outbreaks McFadden had been brought in to deal with.

Against all odds, he hoped the little mutant was doing well. She probably wasn't that little anymore, but she'd been as close he had ever felt that they would be able to coexist with the Zoo.

Things kind of went downhill from that point forward, of course, and the Zoo might have changed how it produced its monsters. The current situation was such that it needed to churn them out at a phenomenal rate to maintain its ongoing campaign, so maybe it had reverted to using the disgusting birthing pools across the board. Then again, maybe they'd never know the real answer to that.

"What are we doing here?" Madigan asked. "Sal, do you feel any need for us to do anything? Nothing the Zoo is directing us toward?"

Sal looked around and realized that his mind had drifted while he'd paused to look at all the data. He did that sometimes, which meant he would have to read it again with a little more focus. Although he might have absorbed a few facts here or there, he'd certainly missed most of it.

"No, nothing," he answered and cleared his throat. "It looks like this is where it wanted to lead us—well...uh, lead me. You guys were kind of interlopers who came along for the ride, or that's how it felt, at least. Which explains why these bastards made no attempt to attack us."

He regretted saying those words almost as soon as they came out of his mouth and turned his attention to what the Zoo felt around them. The excitement was still there but where it had been contained before, it now seemed to have antagonized them. Those groups that were gathered at the entrance seemed ready for something and didn't appear to be willing to wait for long.

The rest of the team felt it too. Maybe not the same way he did, but the locusts had begun to buzz as they did when they were primed to launch an attack. It meant they were ready for a fight and humans usually heard the sound from a long way off. The people around the Zoo had fallen into the habit of listening for it since the locusts were usually part of the first wave and were a good indicator of a concerted assault on the human defenses.

"Of course, you would fucking jinx us with that comment," Madigan snapped, readied her assault rifle, and checked everyone's HUD hastily to confirm their defensive positions.

She was right. He had walked right into that one.

"Dammit, get it together!" she yelled and the urgency in her tone was unmistakable.

They responded with alacrity and covered all approach vectors while they also positioned themselves to be able to support their teammates. Madigan took center front and all the guns on her heavy suit activated as the locusts and humpers began to move toward them.

Fortunately, not all the mutants participated in the increasingly hostile advance. The adolescent creatures remained where they were gathered close to the walls and showed no indication that the rising aggression affected them. It was like they were either cut off from the shared impetus or had entirely different "orders" that enabled them to simply ignore it.

Sal had no intention to tell Madigan to hold off on the explosives. He doubted that the Zoo would have made it easy to collapse the cavern and even if it hadn't reinforced it somehow, it wasn't a bad call to bring it all down on top of the birthing pool.

Those two words brought the burn of nausea to the back of his throat again. He was a biologist and gross shit was part of the song and dance, but this seemed to be the line at which his gag reflex took over.

The first rockets were launched and immediately impacted the first of the monsters as they surged toward the team in a solid wall. Some were now airborne while the others remained on the ground.

Sal grimaced when the explosives detonated. The contained location meant that everyone in it felt the shockwaves, and he held his breath when a shower of the brittle stuff from the walls was flung in the wake of the blast. There was no sign that it was all coming down, however, so whatever held it up was considerably stronger than what had been in the tunnels leading to it.

The rest of the crew opened fire and illuminated the cave with the muzzle flashes in an odd staccato rhythm that was more confusing than the pure darkness. Athena adjusted for it and made sure he wasn't blinded by the shots and explosives that transformed the enclosed space into a visual nightmare.

Their initial burst was enough to rip through the mutants that were in the chamber and decimate their ranks. Those that remained pulled back and positioned their bodies to prevent any of the human attacks from hitting their young. The humpers pushed forward, however, and in a few seconds, Sal noticed more attacks coming from the ceiling.

He highlighted them immediately and Madigan's mini-gun shifted to thin their numbers and drive them back. Mal and Jiro were the only ones who twisted to engage those coming from above, while the rest of the team continued to fire at the humpers on the ground and targeted those locusts that began to enter the chamber. Most of them seemed determined to protect their young rather than attack and gathered around them as a meat shield.

It gave the team a moment of respite, but a moment was all they would get. They needed a plan.

"Get away from the pool!" Sal warned. "If we get too close, they'll try to push us in to feed the young pupae still down there."

"That's certainly not the way I want to die," Sonja responded grimly. "We need a goddammed plan."

Madigan was already three steps ahead of them.

"Trick, you're the guy with the big boom on your list of...well, tricks," she shouted and caught his attention immediately. "Do you have anything that could destroy that little incubator?"

"And keep the rest intact, I suppose?" he asked and grinned. "I'll need a couple of minutes to set something up. I'm thinking, prime, throw, and run like hell."

"You're all fucking crazy," Chezza protested in almost a hiss although she at least sounded resigned to the inevitable.

The whole team began to retreat even farther from the pool and create an open avenue for their demolitions expert to work from. The mutants continued to attack but they didn't have the numbers to do so effectively. If the young had joined them, it would have been a massacre or enough to push them all out and into the tunnels where they could be contained and overrun. Fortunately, it seemed the Zoo had something else in mind for the youngsters, which would explain why it protected them so desperately.

Of course, there was no question of what they were being saved for. Sal had a feeling that way more of them were in the hatching process and far too many people would die when they were finally sent out.

"Right," Trick called from where he had been focused on preparing the explosives he carried. "I've set a time to give us a few minutes to push clear of here. We can't allow too much time since we don't want any chance for them to find a way to pile on the explosive and make it a little less effective."

"Okay," Madigan answered sharply. "So how many minutes do we have?"

"Uh...two."

She froze, ample evidence that she didn't like what he'd told her, but Trick had a point. If the Zoo noticed what they were doing and decided it wanted to stop them, it would find a way. The man spoke like he'd had experience so it was probably likely that they would pile bodies onto the explosive to dampen its effects. There was no telling if it would be successful but if he'd seen it or something similar happen, why take the chance?

"Shit." She turned and let the automated guns continue to fire while she inspected their surroundings. "Okay, we keep moving. Push harder than ever and as soon as that blows, we run. We have maybe a few seconds of distraction before the big ones pursue us and we have to be inside the tunnel by then. Trick, share the timer to everyone's HUD. We need to be on the move five seconds before it goes off."

He nodded, stepped out from where he had hunkered behind the rest of the team while he worked, and lobbed the device. Either his suit calculated the throw for him or he was simply that good, but it was a damn good throw. Sal had a feeling that it was the latter. Trick had an interesting way of seeing the world and was able to make every shot in the book—and probably wrote a couple more into it to be safe.

If he could shoot like that, he could probably throw like it too.

"Let's move!" Madigan roared and launched three rockets from her shoulder into the surge of mutants that suddenly rushed forward. It was truly impressive how angry everything around them was. Sal felt it seep into him and it felt right when he stepped out into the fight with his sword in hand.

Athena wasn't talking to him as much as she had been. It probably meant she was talking to someone else—keeping Madigan updated with his status, most likely. That felt like a betrayal but the offense of it collided with another part of his brain that recognized simple paranoia. The resultant conflict made him thrust both thoughts from his mind. He was in the fight and had to avoid being cut down like the rest of them. All that mattered was to stay alive a little longer to make sure the young were kept safe.

No, that wasn't right. He shook his head and tried to reset his focus. His purpose was to keep his people alive until the explosive detonated.

Sal realized that he shouldn't have even thought about having an obligation to the young. It was a two-way street, after all, and the Zoo could pick up what he was thinking as much as he could sense what it was thinking.

Things seemed way too confusing, but one thought emerged clearly—it didn't like the threat. The attacking creatures grew more intense. Those guarding the young began to rush out too but they made no effort to swarm the bomb like Trick had suggested. Instead, they threw themselves into the assault against the humans.

Madigan wouldn't be able to keep up with the horde for long. If they continued to fight without making any forward progress, they would eventually run out of ammo with their goal unreached.

He took one of the grenades from his pouch, slapped it into the launcher under his rifle's barrel, and delivered it into the thickest group of mutants that were defending the young. A handful was killed on impact—both the young and the adults—and three or four dozen of the locusts veered away from the team to defend those adolescents that were still alive.

The youngsters hadn't shown any reaction to the explosion. Those that had been killed simply fell and the wounded backed away from the blast, but only by a couple of steps before they returned to whatever the hell kind of stasis they had been in before.

It was chilling to watch, although preferable to seeing an endless sequence of thousands of the monsters being birthed. His mind had already decided that thousands was a realistic outcome.

"Ten seconds!" Trick announced and made sure they were all watching the clock.

His warning was timely. Sal realized that he'd forgotten completely about what they were doing there. The chances were that if he didn't manage to remain focused on his real mission, he would die.

The team retreated and Madigan took the rearguard while Mal worked to clear a path through to the exit. Five seconds wasn't exactly much time, but there were some tactical benefits to cutting things as close as they could. They wanted to draw as many of the creatures into the blast radius as they could.

They entered the tunnel and broke into a run. Madigan was able to gun down the few creatures that attempted to catch up to them. There was no sign of any of the larger bastards yet, but Sal had a feeling they would come before too long.

He wasn't sure what he had expected from the blast but he felt it in his chest almost before the ground shook. It wasn't anywhere near a Hollywood fireball or anything like that but after a single bright blast, the smoke engulfed them immediately. He recalled looking at the effects of high explosives on soft tissue and they hadn't been particularly pretty. The change in air pressure was enough to kill almost anything that wasn't protected. The suits were meant to shield them from that and make sure their lungs didn't suddenly decompress.

The shrieks of pain from the creatures that weren't protected behind them were enough to remind him of how lucky they had been to get out of that chamber alive. Not all had been so lucky.

Nope, the team had emerged unscathed. He needed to stop identifying with the fucking mutants. It made him feel like he was crazy.

Fortunately, his conflict went unnoticed and the team laughed as they continued to run.

"If that doesn't get the bitch's attention, I don't know what will," Jiro quipped.

The silence inside the cave was shattered. Gunfire was enough to clear most of the creatures, but Courtney wasn't sure how she could get in there without killing their target.

Assuming he was still alive, of course. None of them wanted to talk—or even think—about that. All they could do was press forward until they got in.

"What happens if we shoot the asshole?" Francesca asked as she pulled back to reload but still fired with her sidearm.

"We're probably all dead in the long-term—the walls come down, the world as we know it ends, and we have to fight for our survival against a jungle that wants to kill us all. So what we're dealing with here but on a global scale. Why do you ask?"

"Because my sensors have registered something human in there and it doesn't look like he's doing much moving."

"Shit."

They ran forward. One of their thrower team members was pushed back as the rest of them rushed in.

"Two of you, hang back and cover our exit!" she ordered, drew her knife, and slashed the throat of one of the hyenas before she shoulder-charged another. "The rest of you, cover me!"

She took a moment to steady herself and look around the cavern. Her suit was heavy enough but not compared to the proper combat suits or the tanks they called heavy suits these days.

Maybe she could find a hybrid that combined the weight and firepower of the heavy suits while still being maneuverable enough to be a researcher's suit. Kind of like a mobile lab.

Finally, she located the man who Francesca had referred to at the back of the cave. He wasn't in proper armor—mostly the kind of body armor that anyone could pick up around there—and he struggled to draw a small firearm under the weight of a massive panther that attempted to reach his throat.

"Goddammit." Courtney hissed in fury, raised her weapon, and pulled the trigger. Three rounds punched into the panther's body but didn't stop it from trying to attack him.

With a low curse, she dragged her sidearm out. The last thing she wanted was to accidentally hit their target in an attack that went awry or with any shrapnel. She strode forward, shoved the barrel into the panther's ear, and pulled the trigger. It jerked with each of the four rounds she pumped into its skull.

In almost slow motion, it sagged against the wall and sprawled on top of its target. The man looked sluggish like he had been injured and groaned softly.

"Oh...dammit," she snapped. "Sarge, get over here. I need some help!"

"Is that our guy?" He hurried to where she stood and helped to move the carcass while the man uttered another groan.

"That's a good question," she answered and examined the merc they had saved. He didn't look much like the picture they had, but the image was old and he was covered in blood. Hopefully, only some of it was his. "Are you Badawi?"

Another soft groan followed as they helped him up.

"Answer the question, asshole," Francesca snapped.

"Am I under arrest?" he asked as their medic approached and began to tend to his wounds. "Are…are you arresting me?"

"Not yet," Courtney snapped, "but if you give us any trouble with getting your skinny ass out of here over the next few minutes, you'll wish we were."

CHAPTER SIXTEEN

The phone rang insistently.

Why the fuck was it ringing?

Vickie Madison pushed from her bed, sucked in a deep breath, and tried hard to not simply pick the device up and throw it across the room to where its buzzing would not interrupt her sleep. This was supposed to be a nap, but with how little sleep she'd had lately, whenever she did happen to crash, it turned out to last at least six hours and often longer.

This time, it had certainly been longer. The McFadden and Banks hacker also didn't want it to end so soon, but the phone was ringing and that usually meant Taylor or Niki needed her for something. Someone was in trouble. That was the only reason they called her. She was tempted to try to feel offended by it but reminded herself that she called them when she needed help and they always came through for her.

She narrowed her eyes when she realized that the number was blocked. She'd taught Taylor about that shit but he wasn't that good, not this soon. This was someone else. The impulse to simply let it go to voicemail was appealing but she was now awake, and if someone was calling her, it meant there was some kind of emergency.

With a deep sigh, she woke her laptop and connected it to her phone to accept the call. Having it ready made it easier if she needed to run a trace.

"Hello?"

"Vickie Madison?"

"Anja? How the hell did—oh, right. That trick I taught you."

"Well, that you helped me refine."

"Refine. Sure."

It had been a while since she'd heard the Russian hacker's voice. There weren't many people in the world she could talk to on an equal level. They had a good number of things in common and the woman's story of escaping Russia, the Zoo, and starting work with Heavy Metal was interesting.

"Anyway, I don't mean to bother you—and if this is a bad time, we can contact you another time. Or even...uh, never if you would rather not."

Vickie shook her head, relaxed in her bed, and grinned when she remembered that Anja couldn't see her. "No, no, that's not...I'm all good with hearing from you again. It's nice to be able to speak to someone in the same language instead of dumbing everything down for everyone around me."

"I...we both speak English, is that right?"

"No, it's—"

"Right, the computers. It's like people don't even bother

to research the computers that keep the world spinning these days."

"Right? Okay, what did you need me for?"

"She wanted to contact you because there's a big market for girl-on-girl porn, especially when two nerd girls are involved."

The American hacker rolled her eyes at the new voice. "Connie. What a complete lack of pleasure."

"Hey, if you need pleasure—"

"Connie, shut the fuck up," Anja snapped. "AI's are the bane of my fucking existence."

"I don't know. Desk has been my best partner on our adventures. Taylor's too. It might simply be that you selected one from the discount pile that turned out to be the worst kind of pervert."

"True. But she's been effective and after a while, you tune out all the grossness and let her do her job."

"You might want to reprogram her to be...uh, you know, not a creep."

"That would be tantamount to murder," Desk interjected sharply. Of course the other AI would be listening.

"I know, but—"

"Or at best, brainwashing. The fact that a creep who designed her made her a creep notwithstanding, it is who she is. You can't simply change someone to be who you want them to be. You have to convince them to be that."

"This other AI's voice is hot," Connie stated cheerfully.

"There's no need to be rude, Connie. Get to know me first."

"I want to."

Vickie gagged. "This is worse than when Taylor and

Niki start getting intimate. Anja, did you want to talk to me about something or not?"

"Yes. Yes! I'm sorry, I'm…uh, distracted. I've worked for the past forty-eight hours and I'm at my fucking wit's end."

"Yeah, I heard that you were trying to trace the original researchers from when that goop touched down on the planet. I assume you haven't had much luck."

"It's ridiculous." The Russian sounded like she was at her wit's end with the situation. "There are probably enough ways for people to mask their print on society. I know I've done it, but these people are scientists—biologists and that kind of shit. How the hell do they know how to drop off the face of the earth like that? Do we assume they're dead or something?"

"Not dead. It's not likely. The government would want them alive and well if they're needed for anything in the future. I'd say the chances are they hid these people."

"No, the government isn't that creative. There would be traces."

"Not if they got professionals who do what we do for people who need it." Vickie shook her head. "They like to use the good freelancers for important shit as much as the rich and powerful do. I can ask our connection in the Pentagon to see what they know. If Jansen doesn't have an idea, Speare might."

"Who? And who?"

"Jansen is our connection to the Pentagon and Speare is his boss. We're on decent terms with them and we're on the same team. If the veil of secrecy can be parted, they'll know how to do it."

"That'll be great but it wouldn't hurt to have a plan B,"

Desk commented. "I think I can dig into some of the dead files."

"Dead files?" Anja asked.

"The files that if you somehow manage to read them, they'll kill you," Vickie explained. "It's merely a matter of time and you have to be careful. All those three-letter agencies still have an unhealthy interest in McFadden and Banks."

"I don't know what to do," Anja whispered. She sounded like she was at the end of her rope.

"Is there anything you want to talk about, Anja?" Vickie asked and frowned since she'd never heard the woman like this. "You're among friends here."

"Yeah, it's only...well, both our Heavy Metal teams are in the thick of it and nothing's been heard from them for a while now. I'm trying to hold things together here but it's all going... Well, I don't know how it's going. For all I know, the walls might be crumbling as we speak, and I'll need to get on a plane and run like hell. For now, all I can do is hope that the walls I've run into could be half as easy to bring down."

The room was much quieter than expected. Many people in it liked to talk and also liked to be heard far more than they liked to listen, but there was an interesting lack of garrulousness in the room at present.

None of them wanted to say anything about how the Zoo was turning into a fiasco. Not that it wasn't one already, but there was still significant promise for investment opportunities in the area.

Now that it was turning into the kind of disaster that people were saying would spell an end to humanity, Eric Samson had a feeling that numerous boards all around the world would pressure people to stay the hell out until it was resolved.

He'd worked in and around the place since he'd retired. It had been with a ring after his win with the Canucks, but that was more than a decade earlier. People still wanted to see the ring and hear the stories about the last true goon in the game but it was a passing fancy.

He could have gone the route other former players had and work the TV circuit. There was good money in that and he had made a couple of appearances, but most of his money had gone into investments, putting his MBA to good use to ensure that there were ample returns to his career salaries.

This was the first time, as far as he could recall, that he seriously considered the media route as an option. The fact was that he was used to being the bully in meetings like this, and he assured himself there was no need to tell anyone that he was currently way out of his depth.

All the paperwork they had been given for this meeting in the Pentagon had been put together by the brightest minds involved in the Zoo, and it showed. It might as well have been written in Cyrillic.

"This is science fiction bullshit," he muttered finally and shook his head. "I've heard the story before and I bet I'll continue to hear it for a while, but I don't understand how the fuck we're supposed to believe that organic nanotech out there is destroying the walls."

He'd raised the same problem with Franklin when they'd had a meeting, but his worries had been put aside for the greater good. Eric had decided he could hold back no longer. He had a responsibility to his shareholders.

"The risk has been signed off by the people who performed the original experiments on the goop when it was first brought in out of orbit," an older man in the corner commented. He was a Pentagon official and while they knew his name, there wasn't much to know about who he was and what he was doing there.

All they knew was that this Speare fellow had a vested interest in the Zoo and a unique and necessary knowledge of how it worked.

"If we are to believe their word on this," one of the other members of the Zoo Think Tank commented, "we'll have to hear it from them. If these people honestly know so much about what kinds of dangers the Zoo presents, they should be here to expound on the matter themselves and not submit vague, dumbed-down documents."

Samson raised an eyebrow. He didn't want to admit that he didn't think the documents had been dumbed down at all, but if they intended to claim that they knew what it said, he wouldn't go out of his way to disagree with them.

"The point," he interjected before anyone else could get a word in, "is that if we are expected to relocate, there must be an incentive. A carrot, as it were, and if there are no carrots—in this case no samples for our teams to analyze when they get there—I don't see the point of even having our people there.

We've all worked hard and spent considerable funds to comply with the new laws that force us to operate our research facilities from the Zoo. In all honesty, though, if we cannot do the research, I see no reason to continue pouring our money into the fucking black hole the jungle has become."

"Might I remind each of you that you are all still under contract with the US Government on the matter?" Speare looked and sounded like he was bored to have to address these matters with them.

Eric had a ready answer for that. "These contracts are all up for review and renewal at the start of the next fiscal year, though. I think you'll find there's no interest in spending more money without any real returns. The situation is halfway across the world and the American people don't want their tax dollars spent on someone else's problem that brings no benefit to them."

The man nodded. "I can understand that. You'll also understand that many of those American people will find out that you're the ones who spent too much time and money trying to exploit the Zoo and their tax dollars went into containing the disasters you all caused."

It was an effective threat that included PR nightmares, scandals, and Internet boycotts. Of course, everything under discussion was supposed to be top secret, but there was always time for whistleblowers and information to leak if it was needed.

"The fact of the matter," Speare continued, "is that none of us know exactly what happened when that missile, for lack of a better term, touched down. Nor do we know what was inside aside from the miracle goop you've all made so much money on. The scientists who were involved in the original studies did so only when they were promised complete non-disclosure regarding their involvement, and if these…investigations into their identities continue, there will be problems."

"I think you would be able to handle a few very pissed off academics, no?" Eric deliberately injected a slight challenge into his tone.

"Sure." The man adjusted his glasses and met his stare easily. "But it'll be much easier to bring some bullies in to shut the investigations down before they start digging into some very uncomfortable and possibly dangerous lines of questioning. I think we can all agree that this is one of the cases where the truth is best left buried."

Samson looked around and noted a general consensus of agreement among the members of the Think Tank. It was a little dangerous to disagree and he couldn't afford to be left out of these meetings in the future, especially if people would decide the fate of the profitable contracts going forward.

"On the other hand," Speare continued and looked like he was working from a prepared speech, "what the Zoo is capable of is becoming painfully apparent. Thanks to Zoo Watch and that goddammed reporter, the rest of the world is in the know as well. We're on the verge of panic. There are already talks about the end of the world as we know it."

"So you're wondering if we want to be caught with our pants down if it all goes to shit?" He checked the contents of his document again. It still looked like it was transcribed in an alien language that only slightly resembled English.

"Eloquently put," the Pentagon representative noted with a smirk. "But yes. Given that all your votes are in already for the matter at hand, I can safely assume that none of you want to create any problems that disrupt the status quo. Rocking the ship and fielding the balls with the usual bullshit has worked out so well for you all in the past, so why wouldn't it do the same here?"

It was partially true, at least. They were all in this to cover their asses, after all. People were already working hard to save the world. Rocking the boat could help but it could hinder as well, and if they could avoid both while maintaining their profit margins, so much the better.

One by one, the corporate stooges began to file out of the room. Eric watched them tuck the documents carefully into briefcases before their aides could so much as look at them as they made excuses. Important business called them and they wanted to put this meeting behind them.

He was one of the last to leave, although Speare looked like he was already moving on to other matters. There would be no point in asking him any questions. He was a political beast by the looks of him and had remained in Washington this long by learning how to cover his ass better than everyone else.

It would be hypocritical of him to condemn others for doing the same.

CHAPTER SEVENTEEN

"What are we looking at here, Doc?"

The medic didn't look up from his work and carefully analyzed the injuries inflicted on Badawi when he'd been attacked.

When they checked the other bodies in the room, they soon established that his skeleton crew was all dead. No one told him why a military team—and one of the best as far as he could tell—had been dispatched to help him survive. They had entered and asked for him by name, and once they established that he was the person they were looking for, they'd begun to treat him.

They were working quickly too and he was more than a little thankful for the medication he received. The morphine, in particular, was very welcome.

"I'm looking at some broken ribs, a fractured collar-bone, and multiple lacerations and contusions all over. Nothing too serious, though."

"It feels serious," Badawi complained.

"You're on enough pain meds that your complaints are

no longer justified," the medic countered and narrowed his eyes. "Next up, a sling will prevent you from making your collarbone injury any worse." He paused and looked at the woman beside them. "We'll be good to go then."

All team members were professionals and had gone through the Zoo gauntlet to reach him. This went beyond merely knowing that Interpol wanted to have a word. Something else was afoot, but no one was talking—at least not to him.

"What's the situation outside?"

The woman—who appeared to be in charge—snapped the question. She didn't wear the same kind of combat suit that the others wore. It looked like a hybrid of some kind, likely meant to allow for some research capacity while still being capable of violence, although he wasn't sure why she was the leader. The researchers were almost never given leadership responsibility.

Badawi leaned a little closer but made sure to not move away from the medic's ministrations. Her suit was probably the most expensive he had ever seen—bleeding edge, he thought cynically.

If he was lucky, she represented a third-party—maybe some corporate interest that wanted to get their hands on him for the kind of help he could charge through the nose for. There was no way that the military had provided her with the suit.

Still, she appeared to be working with the soldiers since most of the members of her team wore the cheap, beat-up suits the US army was notorious for sending their people out in.

"Nothing's stabilized yet." One of the officers answered

her question and shook his head. "It looks like the fighting will still be hot out there, and we can't afford to sit around and wait for the Zoo to get back to us."

"No, we can't," she answered and sounded annoyed. "Send a flare up. Let Franklin know that we have our target and we're on our way back. Hopefully, he can scramble support to get us clear of the jungle."

That certainly sounded like a good plan, although if she was talking about the same Franklin who was in charge of running the US base, maybe his fate wouldn't be lounging around while he consulted for some Fortune-Five-Hundred company's efforts in the Zoo.

Still, if they would get him out of this situation alive, he wouldn't complain too loudly.

"Doc," the woman snapped, "let me know the instant he's ready to move. That armor he's got on won't protect him from much, so our best chance to keep him alive is to get moving as quickly as possible."

"Yes, ma'am."

Badawi tilted his head and looked at the medic.

"Who is she?" he asked and scratched his beard with the hand of his good arm. "And why is she issuing orders like an officer even though she's not a member of the military?"

"So you noticed that, did ya?" the medic answered. "That's Dr. Courtney Monroe, one of the founding members of Heavy Metal."

"I'm surprised. I heard she'd worked from America and was no longer bothered with what happened around the Zoo."

"That's what I heard too but it changed recently. It sounds like she got word that shit is hitting the fan around here and she wants to help. And we can use the kind of help she has to offer."

Everyone in and around the Zoo was familiar with the Heavy Metal team by this point. He knew that while they were at the forefront of dealing with the Zoo, they were also a private company that operated by being very goal-oriented.

"Our boy's ready to move," the medic announced as he finished the arm sling and placed Badawi's pistol in his hand. "I'm not sure how much damage that pea-shooter can do at this point, but when the time comes, it's better to have as many bullets flying as possible, eh? But try to not shoot any of us."

He pulled himself into his suit and secured himself before he helped the smuggler to his feet. Monroe looked like she had waited for the word and motioned quickly for the team to head out.

The soldiers filed out with the kind of almost ruthless efficiency that defined a well-honed team. They seemed determined to make the trip back to some semblance of a secure location as fast as possible and positioned Badawi and their wounded at the center of the formation to ensure that they weren't slowed unnecessarily and everyone could be supported where needed.

It was a good call and he certainly felt safer. He peeked over the mountainside and his gaze followed the bright green flare that still drifted lazily to earth as they continued to move. That was not the focus of his attention, of course. The spur the jungle had pushed out was very present and visible. Fires burned and heavy plumes of smoke rose throughout the damn place, which told him that the fight was still in progress with no sign that they would be able to contain it before some other massive shit-storm hit them.

That was a painful thought but at this point, it seemed to accurately describe what the Zoo was turning out to be —a massive pain in everyone's ass. In the distance, more troops were being ferried in and out of the battlefield and helicopters almost outnumbered the locusts in the area. No, that wasn't right. He merely couldn't see the locusts from where they were but he knew they would buzz in to harass anything that came close to them. When he looked more carefully, the choppers maintained a safe distance from the jungle, close enough to expedite the delivery or collection of troops but far enough to remain unchallenged.

Planes flew overhead too, although none came close enough for the locusts to give them any trouble. He assumed that they were the Russians and conceded respect for the massive payloads they delivered that made the ground shake—even as far away as they were—each time one of them found a target.

"We've got movement coming our way!"

Badawi hadn't wanted to think about how the Zoo appeared to be targeting him. It seemed foolish to take it personally but as they continued the push out of the jungle, he would be able to tell if it tried deliberately to kill him.

The fact that the spur had been directed to his location could have been a coincidence, but if it followed him as they moved, maybe there was more to it.

He could think of nothing more terrifying than the

thought that an entire jungle wanted him dead. Any jungle, to be honest, but the Zoo added to the terror factor.

Whatever the jungle intended, the team that escorted him at least looked like they knew what they were doing. He had long since learned to keep his expectations about military help low given how many of them were merely kids who were brought along for the ride, but this group certainly looked like they were among the best. They were veterans, all of whom knew what their part was in the fight, how to perform it, and how to keep themselves and the other members of their team alive.

The plasma and flame throwers fell back slightly almost immediately and Monroe and the rest of the fighters stepped forward, waited for a second until they all had clear shots, and opened fire. It was refreshing to see after he'd dealt with incompetence all night.

Their assault rifles lay down a heavy opening volley that turned the group of locusts and humpers that pushed out in front into ground meat. They didn't wait for anything else to push through but drove ahead as a unit and forced the mutants back.

More of the panthers bounded forward and Badawi winced when the fangs all but ripped the head off one of the fighters before it was gunned down.

It was quickly established that their man was dead, and one of them stepped in close and retrieved the dead man's tags while he waited for his rifle to reload.

"It looks like something big is coming in!"

That was all the warning they had. A chill ran up his spine when he saw the killerpillar barrel toward them. Insects made his skin crawl when they were in their normal sizes and seeing one that size was all his night-mares coming true.

No, they were arthropods, right? It didn't matter. Insect or arthropod, they were still terrifying.

"Sure, that's what you need to focus on," Badawi whispered as the team backed away. They didn't have the weapons to engage the monster head-on, and if they let it charge into them, they would see fatalities within seconds.

It was clear from their body language that Monroe was having a quick and heated discussion with the rest of the team, and while the decision they reached didn't appear to be a popular one, they all jumped into action to see it done. The group retreated hastily to a point where the opening of one of the tunnels yawned before them. Grenades were pulled from their belts and pouches as they hurried into the confined space and pushed forward.

He felt like everyone around him was holding their breath while they waited for something to happen. Once the creature had followed them inside—along with a horde of other monsters that no doubt thought the humans were trapped and vulnerable—the soldiers raced ahead and paused to lob the explosives toward their pursuers.

Badawi suddenly realized why her solution hadn't been a popular one. The explosions put a stop to the massive arthropod's attack and inflicted significant injuries, although it didn't look like the creature was dead. Still, that was dealt with almost immediately when the tunnel collapsed and crushed the beast and the mutants behind it.

On the plus side, there was no way for the creature to advance, and the other monsters were stopped as well. On the other hand, it was their only way out too.

Before he could utter a protest, the team proceeded at a jog and he realized moments later that they had already established another way out.

He stared in something close to horror as the soldiers set to work in the wide opening that gaped from a sheer cliff. Grappling hooks were buried into the rock face and they began to attach their suit belts to the ropes.

"Oh...oh, no." He hissed sharply and shook his head. "No thank you!"

"You can stay up here if you like," the sergeant suggested as they attached his belt to the ropes as well.

"Like hell," Monroe answered quickly. "We went through too much shit to get to him. Doc over there can knock him out with more morphine and we'll drag his sorry ass with us. I don't care how, but that ass is getting out of here."

"I feel like there is far too much focus on my ass in this," Badawi commented as they moved over the edge of the cliff and those ahead began a careful descent.

"The focus is getting you and your ass out of here," she answered. "You can walk or you can be dragged."

It wasn't a simple decision, and Badawi wondered how comfortable being carried out of there would be.

But that honestly wasn't an option. He wouldn't wait for the Zoo to find a way around the cave-in and with more than a little trepidation, he inched over the edge of the cliff. His breath caught when the rope arrested his drop and lowered him slowly.

"Fuck, fuck, fuck, fuck, fuck!"

Nothing else came to mind for him to say. He tried to reassure himself that this was merely the short route from his base but his attempt to make himself feel better died a sudden death. Even suspended over the jungle, it seemed they couldn't escape the mutants and this harsh truth left him feeling more vulnerable than ever. The creatures had begun to climb the cliff to reach them and a few attempted to descend from the top to pursue them as well.

Badawi wanted to close his eyes but he couldn't bring himself to do it. Instead, he raised his pistol and opened fire at the creatures above them.

It might not have been the smartest decision. With only one working hand, it felt like madness to have it anywhere but on the rope he used to climb down, even if was automated, but he couldn't help himself. He couldn't even tell if he had hit anything, but he continued to shoot anyway.

The volleys from his protectors were far more effective, though, and a few of the mutants plummeted and dislodged piles of rocks a little too close to where he was.

Something grasped his shoulder and for a moment, he thought he was falling or that maybe a monster had reached him. His heart pounded in sudden terror and he cursed when he realized that Monroe, in her light hybrid suit, dragged him out of the way as the small avalanche tumbled past.

"Be careful," she snapped, aimed her assault rifle up, and fired at a few of the locusts that tried to fly down to them instead of attempting the climb.

Even worse, vines began to crawl and slither down the mountain face to find them. It didn't make sense in his mind to see plants so determined to kill living things, but there wasn't much else to explain it. All he could do now was hold on. He had no more bullets in his pistol and he didn't dare to look down to find more ammo. As much as his mind protested, he had to trust these people to keep him alive, even though he knew they weren't doing it out of the kindness of their hearts. Monroe appeared to be the kind of woman who got what she wanted no matter what.

Maybe being arrested was the better option. That way, he could complain about being a prisoner instead of having to fight for his life.

CHAPTER EIGHTEEN

As it turned out, the tunnels worked in their favor. He certainly didn't expect that.

None of them wanted to be there any longer than they had to and they also faced the risk that the brittle surface of the walls and ceiling might collapse around them. Sal had assumed that they would have to try to outrun successive cave-ins after Trick left his little present but so far, nothing indicated that they were in any real danger.

He hefted his sword and waited for a moment before he flicked it off and took his assault rifle out of the hands of the limbs Athena was controlling.

"Not in the mood for a bit of hack and slash, are we?" she asked.

"Look who's talking to me again. Did I do something to piss you off?"

"Not at all."

"It's merely that this is the first time you've spoken to me in a while. You made me wonder if I'd reached a point where you couldn't trust me and you communicated with Madigan instead. Something like that."

"Oh, well, there was a little of that. I've been in touch with her and fed her HUD all the signs of your vitals in preparation."

"Preparation for what?"

"Well, I wouldn't be much use to anyone stuck in your suit. I would be able to keep you contained but if I could transfer to Madigan's suit, I would be able to continue to help the team, albeit in a limited capacity. Her suit's HUD isn't set up to have something like me."

"Right." It made sense. Maybe it wasn't the kind of thinking he could attempt successfully while he was in the Zoo.

"Will you answer my question?"

"Question?"

"I asked you why you put your sword away. It's not like you."

"Oh. Well, there will always be a little something for me to do with it when I'm out in the jungle but in these close quarters, it's better for me to hang in there with the rest of the formation. If you think you can do something with the sword, please take it."

Athena paused before she replied. "No, you're right. There is no space in these tunnels for that."

Sal rolled to the right and his suit reloaded the assault rifle as he avoided a swiping paw from one of the first panthers they'd seen coming into the tunnels. It had mostly been the locusts and humpers, the species that were able to function in the tunnels with anything like efficiency.

The suit was efficient and had already slapped a full

magazine in the moment it had the empty one out. All that time spent learning how to work the delicate controls of the old suits to manually reload felt like a waste of time now, but he would never know if he would need those skills again. He might end up in an old, dusty suit and it would be time well-spent.

He moved forward, pressed his assault rifle to the skull of the panther, and fired a single round. It jerked and dropped before he kicked the body out of the way.

Madigan continued to focus her attention on the oncoming creatures while everyone else watched for anything that could slip through her line of fire or come in from behind them. It hadn't been much of a problem before with most of the creatures from the chamber dead or recovering from the blast. As they continued, however, more tunnels merged with theirs and the mutants appeared to have the advantage of knowing how to navigate them.

For the first time in the Zoo, Sal felt he was practically operating by the seat of his pants. He seemed to follow his impulses almost as much as he followed Madigan's leadership.

That lack of control scared him more than the real and present danger. He forced himself to calm and to reach out. He needed to ground himself, and although he didn't fully understand it—and hated the truth of it—his sense of presence in the Zoo network somehow helped with that.

After a moment, the sense of awareness that sometimes warned him tugged at his consciousness and he tried to make sense of it. All he knew was that they weren't in the same tunnel they'd started in. This was something else and he was sure it was leading them elsewhere. Dozens of twists and turns seemed confusing on a surface level, but his instinct said they were being directed again and drawn into another trap.

Sal snapped around suddenly and brought the party to a halt as he thrust his hand out and shoved it into the wall on his left. At first, he had no idea what he was doing or why. He acted purely reflexively based on the feeling that danger would come from that direction and there hadn't been time for him to turn his rifle toward it. Hell, it had been close enough that he doubted being able to bring his weapon to bear at all.

For a moment, his hand hovered inside the wall after it punched smoothly through the brittle surface. The suit, thankfully, was built to take that kind of punishment. Something moved against his hand and twisted jerkily to try to get away from it.

He pushed in deeper and caught hold of it with a growl of satisfaction. Athena directed her limbs to help him and they dug powerfully into the wall to reveal a small tunnel being dug by the creatures to position themselves so they could break through and flank them.

His fist closed around a humper that tried desperately to escape the crushing grasp he had on its thorax. He twisted again, yanked his hand out, and pulled half the creature with him. The rest remained in the hole, although the monsters coming in behind attempted to dig through the remains to reach the exit.

"There's no time for this," Madigan snapped. "Get that closed up quickly."

None of them questioned how he knew they would be

attacked through the walls. Maybe that was a good thing but they would have time to think about it later.

Trick already had a grenade in his hand as he approached the hole. He fired inside to eliminate the creatures coming through and plug the hole before he jammed the grenade—sans the pin—into the pile and gestured for the team to keep running.

It was a quick and efficient solution. By the time they were out of range, it detonated with enough power to close not only the new hole but also bring the rest of the tunnel down behind them.

"We need to keep moving," Madigan ordered. "We don't want to be trapped in this place where they can probably plug the tunnels with their bodies and leave us to suffocate."

Sal hadn't even thought of that. He would have to make a couple of suggestions when next they had an opportunity to try some of the new suits. With tunnels being a very real possibility for the future, he would suggest that they introduce oxygen tanks for emergency use.

The Zoo was already terrifying but the additional possibility of death through the horrifying reality of running out of air was not acceptable.

"There's an opening ahead," he called before he realized what he was saying. It seemed to somehow come more naturally now and he knew what was happening without needing to focus on the Zoo around them. "The tunnel's running out and we'll soon be back in the Zoo."

"Is it weird that I prefer a good ol' straight-up fight against monsters in the jungle?" Mal asked as he turned and fired at the creatures that had appeared behind them.

They must have cleared the cave-in or found another way through to enable them to catch up.

"You're in good company," Sonja answered and drew a deep breath. "It would be nice to be clear of the Zoo once and for all, though. I'd like to step out of the tunnel and be back within driving distance of the base."

"I don't like that idea," Madigan interjected. "It means that whatever dug the tunnel got in under the wall and is in driving distance of the base too."

"Oh. Right."

After a few more twists, Sal noticed a hint of sunlight ahead. It was filtered through leaves and branches but was blinding compared to the darkness they'd traveled through underground. Given the contrast, he suspected that the entrance to the tunnel was located in a small clearing or open area, or at least one where the thick jungle foliage didn't block out most of the natural light. It was interesting how he knew that—and also that the deeper into the Zoo they went, the thicker the vegetation would be.

"Trick," Madigan called and pushed hard toward the entrance. She trampled a couple of locusts underfoot without bothering to shoot them first. "Have something ready to close the tunnel behind us when we get out. I don't want anything to follow us through."

"Will do."

The HUD adjusted for the increased light all around them as they stepped out into the open again. Sal sucked in a deep breath instinctively, although he knew better than to think that the air would be any cleaner or less stuffy than it had been in the tunnels.

He was still in a fucking suit. The air would always be more or less the same through the filters.

Trick placed a charge on the wall of the tunnel as they exited while the rest of the team cleared the creatures that attacked them from the underbrush. They were angry and reacted with the same intensity as when someone plucked a Pita plant, although not quite in the same numbers.

Or with the different kinds of mutants either. These were mostly locusts, humpers, and some of the middle-range beasts, with no sign of the larger creatures to add to the challenge.

"Did you ever think…" Trick commented as he exited the tunnel, joined the team, and neatly eliminated two panthers that waited in the trees to try to pounce on them from above. "If the Zoo is kind of learning everything from us, we might be throwing more data in for it to learn from every time we come out here?"

Chezza waited until the charge detonated and effectively sealed the tunnel behind them off before she responded. "What do you mean?"

"Well…if you think about it, the amalgamation of chemicals that makes the goop what it is was probably something that was learned through trial and error—much the same process we used to learn how to make explosives. So if I keep using these explosives in and around the Zoo and its mutants, they might be able to read the chemical composition and learn how to make it for themselves."

"That's a terrifying thought," Gregor whispered. "Monsters throwing explosives around instead of acid?"

"Right."

"You're full of great ideas today, aren't you, Trick?" The Russian snorted but his sarcasm fell a little flat.

"It keeps the mind churning."

Sal looked around. They had come out of what looked like a hill in the Zoo where the tunnels were situated, which meant logically that they could have emerged at a lower altitude than where they'd entered the tunnels. He couldn't be sure but it didn't feel like they'd had either a significant incline or decline while they were underground, which meant their initial fall had deposited them into the tunnels at about the same altitude as where they were now.

Something else was different in the area around them too and he needed a moment to put his finger on what it was. The growth around them looked like a proper jungle now. Not only did the trees have the gnarled, twisted look that older trees tended to take on, along with collections of moss and vines that were reminiscent of the Amazon, but the ground was different. Rocks and boulders made the jungle floor uneven and thick roots jutted from the ground.

Most of the other areas of the Zoo were recently converted into jungle from one of the most arid terrain on the planet. While the conversion was impressive, it still looked like a desert had been converted into a jungle overnight.

But as he moved a little deeper into the vegetation, he realized that there was every sign that the area they were in had been a jungle for a long time.

Hell, streams ran through the earth that showed early

signs of erosion and pools had formed where the roots diverted the water, then poured out over the edges.

A sense of awe settled over him. This was a real jungle.

"Guys," Sal whispered and looked around, "I hate to sound like a cliché but I don't think we're in Kansas anymore."

Madigan looked around when there was a pause in the attacks and the creatures retreated from the charge Trick had set.

"What are you talking about?"

"It looks like we're much deeper in the Zoo than anyone's been for a while."

Sonja nodded. "The tree growth around here is thick. There's no real path unless we hack through."

There was that too but he hadn't noticed it. He'd assumed it was merely a way for the Zoo to head them off.

He drew a deep breath before he reached out again and tried to determine a more precise location for where they were.

Nothing could have prepared him for the response, but it felt like a giant hand had been thrust into his brain and practically wrenched his control over his body away for a second. Athena recognized it immediately and took control of his suit, probably in fear that he would begin to attack people. He couldn't blame her for that, of course.

But this wasn't the Zoo taking control of him. It was like everything inside the tunnels had been muted and allowed him to open his mind and become more attuned to the process. Now that they were in the jungle and much closer to Ground Zero, the effect was far more powerful.

"Oh...I'll have to...get used to that," he whispered. It

wasn't painful unless he tried to consciously move something—or maybe not too painful was more accurate—like the feeling of a hand or an arm falling asleep but extended to his entire body. The odd numbness was unpleasant, though, like his whole body crawled with ants.

"Are you all right?"

That wasn't Athena. He assumed it was Madigan because he doubted that Sonja or Chezza would ask him, but it was a human female. It was difficult to distinguish between them aside from that. Humans were all so terribly similar but a little deduction could help.

"Yeah." Sal took a moment to catch his breath. If the AI hadn't been there to help, he would have been curled on the ground. This at least provided him with a little extra dignity, which was always a plus. "The Zoo is a little...uh, extra-strong here. Athena already has control of the suit to make sure I don't do anything stupid or under its control."

Madigan nodded and moved back to where the mutants resumed their attack. Athena stepped in to help them fight as well, which allowed him a little time to try to come to terms with what had happened.

If the Zoo wanted control, it could have taken it, that much was clear. Instead, all it seemed to be doing was pointing out that it wanted his attention and reminding him of how powerful it could be while he tried to fight it. It was like a chess grandmaster toying with a beginner, letting him take a few pieces, but when the queen was gone, the beginner was reminded of who he was playing against.

Nothing else came through. He couldn't see the Zoo like he could before. It was still there in the normal waves he could generally sense but it was drowned out by the overwhelming presence in the back of his mind. He knew it wanted his attention, but there was something else too.

The only way he could think to describe it was showing off. It wanted to remind him of how powerful it was and at the same time, give him a proper hint of how frail and inconsequential his human body was compared to it. He couldn't help but feel a little impressed. This was power that extended far beyond anything any of them could ever fathom.

Which made it a little difficult to put numbers and figures to what it was precisely. Maybe it simply wanted him to have a glimpse. An intimidation plan, maybe?

He couldn't tell and it honestly didn't matter.

"We don't want to stick around here," Madigan called, although it felt like she was speaking from miles and miles away like a distant echo. "It's too easy to be corralled and I don't trust these trees to not start attacking us too. Let's get moving."

"Do you think we should send a flare up? To be safe and let people know where we are?"

Sal couldn't tell which one of the humans had spoken. It had become harder to tell them apart now. With their suits of armor, there were no distinctions, and while he was generally able to tell them apart by the sounds of their voices, the general body language, and small hints shown in their suits, whatever was happening to him now made it more difficult.

"There's no need. Not yet," Madigan responded. "The interference here is worse than ever but it looks like we haven't been gone for very long. We can keep moving and find a place that's better."

He only knew who she was because she was in the big suit. He didn't like that—no, he loved Madigan more than life itself. It was vital to know who she was. She wasn't simply another human but something special and real, something that kept him going no matter what…someone, not something.

The feeling turned a little more painful, and Sal gritted his teeth and sucked in a deep breath.

"Sal?"

"What?"

"Do you have anything to add to the plan?"

"No. It sounds good. Let's keep moving."

There was an edge to his voice that he didn't intend. Maybe it was the pain or rather the discomfort that made him irritable. Or it could be something else he hadn't thought of but again, she didn't question him and merely gestured for the team to move forward again. They had the opportunity to head into the heart of the Zoo and find out what the source of all their pain and anguish was, even if it killed them. Maybe it was worth it or maybe not.

If they were so close to Ground Zero, Sal would have expected a few more mutants to stop them. There were a few but not nearly anything like what he assumed they should have to deal with.

Madigan was supposed to be angry with him. She should raise hell with him but none of her responses met his expectations. It wasn't natural. She didn't give him any sass or try to engage him and talk to him about his humanity or anything like that. It was almost painful to feel. His fingers closed around the suit and he felt Athena still in control. There was no give in them at all. It was for the best. She was probably in communication with Madigan at the moment, telling her that he was going through something,

She loved him too. Not that she said it outright very often. There was merely a hint of a smile as she leaned forward to touch his hair before she called him an idiot or something like that.

To him, it was always proof that maybe she was uncomfortable expressing her feelings but they were still there.

An unexpected pain shafted through him and stole his breath and he groaned as the suit continued to move under Athena's control.

"Are you all right?"

He had no clue who had asked him the question and registered that it was one of the smaller suits. It held a sword in its hand but not his sword. The weapon triggered a memory. This was...Jiro. That was the name. Yes, that was it.

"I'm fine," he snapped. "Keep moving."

"Right, then."

Maybe he was a little too short with them. Humans were easier to kill when they were at ease or in awe over the wonders of the Zoo. If he snapped and yelled at them, they would be more on edge with itchier trigger fingers.

Fuck, it was hard to fight that line of thought—and oddly painful too. And he couldn't explain what was going on to anyone. If he told Athena, she would tell Madigan, and there was no telling what she would do. The chances were that she would freak out and decide they'd done enough distracting and maybe it was time to head back.

But, he acknowledged in a rare moment of clarity, this wasn't only about creating a distraction. At some point, it had become so much more than drawing the Zoo's attention away from what it was doing on the front lines.

There was no way to know if they had been successful and if they had, it would take a while for all the mutants engaged in harassing the Zoo bases to retreat from the wall to attack them instead. Besides, if they were close to other birthing pools, the jungle could simply produce more. It would mean fewer resources to commit to the spur but those already in place might not have to redirect their focus. Their efforts to buy time for the bases might have been doomed to failure before they began.

Still, he wanted to learn as much as he could. This was also about him confronting the other him—the one whose voice reared its ugly head constantly in his mind to remind him that he was not the human everyone thought he was. He was different now, there was no denying that, and the Zoo wanted to claim what belonged to it.

Hopefully, he would win that battle. He drew a deep breath and jerked when pain rushed through his body as Athena opened fire at more of the mutants that had appeared.

The real Salinger Jacobs would win. He had to.

Lowering the team down the mountain had seemed like a good idea when it came to her. Courtney had patted herself on the back as they started their descent. It was easier to climb down than up, which meant they couldn't have done it on the way up, so she felt better about using the long route that had cost them time.

As stressful as it had been to be suspended beside the cliff face while the monsters tried to reach them, the short route proved to be the best way to get out of the mountains. It was certainly the fastest, and by the time they were all safely at the bottom, teams had already begun to converge on their position.

Her logical assumption was that more troops had arrived to deal with the spur, which meant more troops at the ready to help where it was needed.

The unexpected help had made an enormous difference to their outward journey and now that Badawi was in custody, there wasn't much else for her to do. They treated the wounded and restocked their supplies but at this point, a host of cooks were in the kitchen and she had been told that she was needed on standby.

Part of her immediately felt like she was being sidelined because she was a researcher and now was not the time for researchers. No one seemed to consider the fact that she'd been subjected to the same stress and danger everyone else had and maybe needed something to occupy her while she unwound.

Franklin and a man she assumed was Adams approached and watched her warily as she paced as part of her efforts to keep herself calm. A little coffee had helped to settle her nerves somewhat, as terrible as it was, but the adrenaline hadn't dissipated and she wasn't used to it working at such a high level yet.

"Do you want more coffee?" Franklin asked finally and raised an eyebrow.

"I don't need fucking coffee," she snapped and ignored the voice of caution that suggested she be more polite to the US base commander. "I need to ask Badawi some pointed questions. We went through all that trouble to get him out and it's time to move on to the reason for it."

"I guess I don't need to introduce you to Dr. Monroe?" Franklin asked the Interpol agent.

"No, her reputation precedes her," Adams answered with a small smile. "All good things, of course. What research I could do on the way here told me you are one of the earliest boots on the ground since the Zoo situation started and that you are a founder member and still work with the famous and infamous Heavy Metal team."

"Right. Wait, infamous?"

He tilted his head with a small smirk. "Well...yes. You all have a certain reputation."

"Of heading into the thick of things for impossible operations that might or might not be sanctioned but are usually for the greater good—and making good money on the way," Franklin explained. "Infamous probably describes it rather well."

Courtney opened her mouth to reply but shut it again. She wouldn't deny that Heavy Metal had a reputation and it was a good thing too. People took them more seriously that way.

Still, it was time to change the subject.

"But my point still stands. Shouldn't we be pressing Badawi for information at this point? The intel we need from him is time-sensitive, after all."

"He's been through a traumatic experience," Adams cautioned. "It's probably not best to pressure him while he's being treated for the injuries he suffered. Besides, once he's in the clear and high on whatever painkillers they give him, he'll be more cooperative."

"You'd think that getting him out of that shithole of a tunnel system in the mountains alive and more or less intact would be enough for that."

"You'd be surprised. Criminals like him always look for ways to get ahead and make a profit somehow. It's how he's survived so long around here. The way he probably sees it, you got him out of that situation for free since he didn't enlist your help. Now, we'll have to find other incentives to get him to help us."

"How about we chuck him into the Zoo with a hunting knife and a faded copy of *Wilderness Survival for Dummies* if he doesn't cooperate?"

Franklin grinned. "Is that a real book?"

"Probably. I don't know."

Courtney scowled when Adams chuckled softly, although he clammed up when he realized she was watching him.

"Did I say something funny?" she asked.

"Well, yes. But there's also the fact that this is exactly the kind of attitude you and your Heavy Metal team are infamous for outside the Zoo. It's the no-nonsense go-getters who expect everyone to be on the same team or get the fuck out kind of spirit."

He looked at Franklin when he noticed that neither he nor the other soldiers in the tent with them were laughing.

"As far as I can see," she retorted and changed the

subject again, "that Algerian mercenary has delayed this meeting as long as possible. And not only by demanding medical attention, food, and drink, but also by virtue of the fact that he hid in the mountains and waited for all this to blow over."

"Agreed. But we need to pretend that he was merely looking out for his interests and not acting like a selfish, cowardly shitstain this whole time. I've dealt with people like him before. They've been threatened often enough that force doesn't play well as an incentive. We want to take the path of honey over vinegar."

Franklin stood, approached her, and gestured with his head to indicate that he wanted to have a word in private.

"I'm all for going gung-ho on this asshole," he whispered, "but in the end, we might want to leave this to the professionals, right?"

She scowled at him for a minute before she sighed and nodded slowly.

"We'll let him handle the questioning, I guess," she conceded reluctantly. "But this can't take much longer. At the risk of repeating myself, we have a time crunch here."

"Agreed. And if force is necessary, I'll make sure to let you have the first chance to throw him to the horned rhinos."

That was enough to make her smile but their attention was drawn to the flap of the tent when one of the doctors stepped inside.

"He's as good as we can get him." She looked exhausted like she had treated people for a seventy-two-hour shift and all that kept her up was the same shit coffee everyone else had. "I would suggest bed rest, but I hear you three have some questions you'd like to ask him."

"You have that right," Courtney confirmed but had enough self-control to let Adams take the lead in the conversation as they left the tent and strode toward one of those earmarked for the medics to use. At least it was small enough to afford some privacy for what was to come.

It certainly appeared that Badawi had taken a beating while trapped in the Zoo spur. Bruises and a couple of casts confirmed that he wouldn't join the fight anytime soon. Still, he was alive, conscious, and looked far better than he would have if they hadn't arrived to help him when they did.

"I must tell you," the smuggler said when they entered, "I did not expect to see the end of this day. It is a wonderful thing to live when you expected not to, would you not agree?"

His English was good, and while he slurred a little, Courtney was willing to attribute it to the painkillers he was on.

"How are you feeling, Mr. Badawi?" Adams asked and took a badge from his pocket.

"I am quite well, sir. And how are you?"

"I can't complain." He flipped the badge open with a practiced motion. "I'm Marcel Adams, and I'd like to have a word with you before you're escorted to the US base for proper treatment."

"Of course, Agent Adams. I understand you still have an interest in what knowledge I can provide regarding that little incident in Saudi Arabia. It is true that I facilitated the arrangement, but I was never made aware of precisely what was being transported and when I found out, I made it my top priority to inform the authorities on the matter."

"I'm sure. We anticipated your noble sentiments and assumed you would want to continue to help. I am informed that you are in a position to contribute to the Zoo containment effort, and I'm sure you wouldn't mind assisting us with that."

Badawi looked around, first to Franklin and then to Courtney.

"I am more than willing to help but in the immortal words of a great philosopher, if you're good at something, never do it for free. I would like to find out what rewards you might offer as well as certain…promises that I will not be arrested once I have fulfilled my duty."

Adams chuckled softly and shook his head. "There must be some kind of misunderstanding. Contrary to popular belief, Interpol is not empowered to provide anyone with rewards or even negotiate or effect arrests. We're mainly an administrative organization that helps the various official law enforcement agencies around the world to cooperate when dealing with criminals on an international level. Criminals…well, like you."

The Algerian mercenary narrowed his eyes and studied Marcel carefully. "Then what do you have to offer me to compel my help?"

"Compel? Oh no, we don't do that either. Instead, once you are remanded to the custody of the US base, it'll be my responsibility to recommend which extradition request they'll choose to implement. You have active warrants for your arrest waiting for you in fifteen different countries. Given how little sympathy the US has toward men of your ilk, I would say you might want to avoid being extradited there. Or to Brazil or Turkey, for that matter. Thailand is probably not the best place to end up either. I could always write a recommendation to Commander Franklin here to remand you to the custody of the Norwegian or Swiss authorities, where you're only wanted on smuggling charges."

"But—"

"Oh, and perhaps I should mention that the Algerian government has already thoroughly washed their hands of you, Mr. Badawi."

"Personally, I would recommend sending him to Niger," Courtney interjected and her scowl deepened. "Or the Czech Republic. Both have numerous witch hunts and vengeful occupants who want someone to blame for the situations in their country—of which you were very likely the cause. Those resulted from the rash you caused by removing samples from the Zoo and could have prevented and possibly cured. I guess I could remind you that if you withhold information, more people will die, but maybe your so-called noble intentions stretch only as far as you can use them to keep your neck out of a noose."

Badawi studied her closely and she wondered if he had a problem with speaking to women. It wasn't a prejudice she particularly cared about but maybe some interestingly backward customs that people were reluctant to leave behind remained in the area.

"You want to know how I was able to cure the rash the

Zoo caused my men?" he asked and looked confused. "Is that what this is all about?"

"It's about you accidentally finding a way to stop the burrowers that no doubt managed to infect those who brought the Zoo to Niger and the Czech Republic," Adams added seamlessly and showed no sign of irritation that she had interfered in his interrogation. "How did you stop the rashes?"

"Oh. I used a…cream. A salve I learned years ago."

"We'll need the ingredients," Courtney stated.

"I…yes, of course."

He was provided with pen and paper and she thanked their lucky stars that he was either ambidextrous or his writing hand had not been injured. Once he had finished, he handed the paper to her and she studied the ingredients carefully.

"Beeswax, olive oil, lemon, lavender…none of this looks like what we need," she muttered and shook her head. "We could probably try it, but I have a feeling the Zoo won't be stopped by essential oils."

"Is there nothing there that we can use?"

"I don't recognize one of these ingredients. What's this *azar tadawasa* that you wrote here?"

"*Azar tadawsa.*" He corrected her quickly. "It is…uh, the healer's root, I think it translates to. The plant is found close to where I grew up—a small shrub with bright blue flowers. The blooms are poisonous but we used the dried leaves as incense to keep…well, foul spirits away from the house. It smells very good too—sweet like licorice. But the roots are ground and added to the salve for the healing."

Courtney drew a deep breath. Of all the things she wanted to do right now, having to determine what kind of magical plant his family used to protect their house from evil was not one of them.

Still, if it smelled like licorice, it stood to reason that it was in the same family. She pulled her tablet out and scanned the options that grew locally.

Finally, she located an image that looked more or less like what he was talking about.

"Is this the... azar...whatever?"

"Yes." Badawi nodded enthusiastically. "It doesn't look like much but it has helped me in the past."

"What is it?" Franklin asked.

"*Hedysarum medicus,*" she explained and passed him the tablet. "It was named way back when we didn't have people running proper tests and everyone assumed that the roots and leaves had medicinal properties, I guess. I found this one in particular because it's a plant that grows only in this area and on the fringes of Sahara, having been picked to extinction everywhere else. It's an oddity, the kind that biologists like to learn about for no other reason than to impress other biologists."

"Is that the ingredient, then?" Franklin asked.

"It might be. We won't know until we try it." Courtney took her phone from her pocket and tapped to connect to the line Anja monitored. "Hey, my favorite Russian hacker. Are you there?"

"Always and forever."

"Not you, Connie. Where's the other one?"

"Right here," Anja responded hastily. "What's up?"

"I'm with Franklin and Interpol at the new spur base camp and have an image on my tablet of a local plant. Can you look around the area to find somewhere it might be growing?"

"You want me to find…a plant."

"Right."

"I can find you all kinds of shit, even the very rare. Plants are a little more difficult."

"Okay, but maybe think about where they might discuss collecting it or essential oil sites that talk about it—that shit. They use it a fair amount in ethnomedicinal recipes. Call me if you find anything."

"I can tell you where it grows," Badawi interjected and raised his good hand.

"Right," Courtney answered. "But I'd like to have a plan B in place in case. We need three of those plants yesterday. Your job is to call someone—a cousin, brother, aunt, or anyone else and have them arrange to dig the whole damn thing out."

"I'll see what I can do."

She nodded and looked at Franklin, who was already on his phone. "I'm arranging for helicopters to go in and collect them. With our luck, there might already be a spur heading in to stop us there too."

"Right, excellent." Badawi beamed on his cot. "Can I go now?"

Adams chuckled. "Not yet, I'm afraid. We still have work to do."

"Am I under arrest?"

"For the last time, Interpol has no agency to effect arrests. That said, Commander Franklin hasn't arrested you yet. For the moment, you're merely a person of interest and I'm very, very interested."

Sal was done with second-guessing his decisions. He had other people to do that for him. Athena and Madigan were there to keep him in check and for the moment, all he could do was make the calls he assumed were right and progress from there.

Not reaching Ground Zero when night fell seemed like a good call. Not only to him but to everyone else as well. They were all tired and once they got their flare up for the evening, it was probably best to clear space between them and the trees so some rest could be had.

He wouldn't complain about it. None of them had gotten much rest the night before and they could all use a break. Still, he doubted that he would get much sleep, which was interesting since he had enjoyed proper sleep. Maybe it was their turn now.

Madigan was out of her suit and he winced when he saw her stride toward him. The numbness over his whole body had begun to lift and he wanted nothing else but to sit and relax against a nearby tree. It had been an exhausting day for all of them.

"We need to talk," she said as she sat cross-legged and gestured for him to do the same.

"Yeah, I had a feeling we did." He complied and settled beside her. "What's up?"

"I'm checking in. Athena told me things were a little

grim when we left those tunnels. I guess that explains why you've moved around like a robot since then."

"This is the part where I'm supposed to be offended that you and Athena talk about me behind my back."

"It's now or never."

He was too tired to banter with her, which was the real tragedy. Not physically tired, although there was that too, but he hadn't felt this way since he'd worked for an entire weekend cramming for his bachelor's when his mother thought he was still too young to drink coffee. Mental exhaustion was tough to deal with.

"Fucking hell," she muttered and folded her arms. "No response to that. Yeah, you're so not okay."

"It hasn't tried to pull a tentacle monster on me," Sal countered quickly. "If anything, it feels like this bitch is ignoring me."

She nodded slowly and studied him for a moment. "What do you plan to do when you get to Ground Zero?"

"Are we discussing this again?" He winced inwardly at the edge he didn't like to hear in his voice.

"It would seem so."

"Well, the answer is still the same. Unless we have no other choice, nothing is probably still the only answer."

She watched him more intently than usual, and he wasn't sure how he felt about her eyes digging into him to see everything he wanted to keep hidden from her.

"I know there's more going on, Sal," she whispered. "I won't try to push you or anything like that, but if you want to talk, you know I'm ready to listen, right?"

He lowered his head, painfully aware that he should give her the benefit of the doubt. Madigan knew what he was and who he was, and she trusted him. Why couldn't he trust her? Did he feel paranoid about something? Was it stress or was the Zoo trying to turn him inside out? Too many questions remained unanswered.

"Thanks." He tried to force a smile.

"Until then, I'll trust Athena to give you a swift kick to the ass when one is needed, okay?"

"Noted."

CHAPTER NINETEEN

Another morning brought another spur.

Kelvin didn't like it. The Zoo tried to keep them on edge with the result that everyone worked double shifts. Still, they had enough troops on the British and German bases to contain it, or at least that was what their commander said when more of the bases offered their support.

"Can you believe this?"

He looked at Mara who sat beside him and stared into the desert.

"What? Another spur right up our asses?"

"Well, yeah. That too." She pulled a cigarette out of her pack, offered it to him, and tapped another out for herself before she lit them both. "That bitch said we don't need help."

"Well, technically, we don't. It's the kind of shit we can handle on our own and if it escalates, we can call for help then."

"I see no point in being cautious about this. The more

time we spend faffing with the Zoo, the more time we give it to fuck us over for whatever reason."

She made a good point. Kelvin sucked a deep drag of his cigarette and watched the troops head out to join the effort to drive the jungle back. Their shift would start the next day but for the moment, both were off-duty and would only be called up if there was a state of emergency.

Which, he reminded himself morosely, would probably happen in a couple of hours. It was painful to consider so he chose to not think about it. They would simply enjoy what downtime they could.

Still, it worried him where they would be allocated when they were called in eventually. He'd usually been relegated to the thrower teams, but that seemed to be the people who weren't trusted to hold a formation and shoot a gun at monsters while under attack. It would probably change now since he'd been in and around the Zoo for a few months and for many people, that counted as being experienced enough to be fitted with a combat suit.

He decided to not make any suggestions.

"The word is that another spur has hit the Chinese," Mara said and exhaled smoke as she spoke. "We have more troops heading there to contain it too."

"I bet you our commander will change her mind quickly. No good will come of being isolationist in this day and age."

"It irritates me but I can't blame her. Isolationism has been a Brit tradition since the Brexit days."

"It went back further than that, no?"

"Probably. I failed history in school."

"Maybe she's already calling someone in," Kelvin whispered and leaned forward, his eyes narrowed.

"What are you talking about?"

He pointed to a helicopter that cut across the sky as the sun began to rise.

"Do you think they're already sending troops in to help? It looks like they're coming from the yank base."

"They might be. Or it could be researchers shipped in to collect samples and shit."

Still, it was good to know that the other bases were involved. Maybe someone above the silver-haired bitch would have the authority to call more troops in. At this point, they were all stretched thin, tired, and drained. They honestly needed people to make the right calls.

She would never understand how McFadden didn't like flying. Courtney still felt like a kid whenever the choppers took off and never tired of the thrill of excitement when the world fell away at that speed.

Maybe she was being a little unfair, she conceded. It wasn't like phobias would ever be rational.

Watching the Zoo race past them was a little unsettling, though. She could almost see the monsters fly out of the trees to attack the helicopter, even though they were miles away from the strike zone. That was fear too but in this case, far from irrational.

"Dr. Monroe!"

She turned when one of the other soldiers who shared the chopper ride with her called her name.

"What's the problem?"

"Your phone is ringing!"

They yelled over the deafening cacophony of the rotors above their heads. Even with their headsets and HUDs on, there was little that could be done for that much noise hammering less than ten feet away.

Courtney connected her phone to the HUD and answered the call. When it displayed that the number was blocked, she knew it could only be the Russian hacker. These days, you had to be a genius to block the attempts made by the number recognition software that came with phones and HUDs.

"Anja, how are you doing?"

"I've worked these plants you asked about all day. There honestly isn't much to be found on them, and what I did find wasn't helpful."

"Well, I guess I should have expected that. It was worth a try."

"Sure. But then I worked on something else. Assuming we find these goddammed miracle plants, we can't pin our hopes on there being enough out there for us to produce something on a large enough scale to stop the Zoo."

"Right." It was a major problem that she would have to address eventually. Synthesizing and mass-producing the cure or antidote—what the hell were they supposed to call it?—would always be the best option. That all depended on whether the plant had the properties they needed, though, so it was one step at a time. "I thought I could engage my Pegasus contacts to help with that."

"Well, yes, but I looked into a couple of researchers and companies that could help you. They specialize in that kind of thing and you could call on them since it isn't directly connected to the Zoo—you know, as in samples and shit that could be contaminated. It's something very random that somehow helps. Hopefully, we might have a jump start to get it all working as quickly as possible as soon as we can verify that we've found the miracle we needed. It would be useful to be ahead on that since Sal's plan doesn't look like it's working. The Zoo is still very focused on the wall and another spur has pushed into the Chinese sector too."

Courtney drew in a deep breath and tried to ease the pain that stabbed through her torso. She knew it was psychological with some psychosomatic symptoms as part of a purely reflexive response.

"Has there been any word? You know…uh, from Sal?"

"Nothing yet. But the next flare is only due tonight and it might take time for word to filter back. They could fire the reached Ground Zero one but it's possible that they are too deep in the jungle for us to see the flare with anything other than a satellite."

"Or…" She cleared her throat. "They might already be dead."

"Right. Why do you think I've worked through the night?"

Anja cared about Sal and the others as much as Courtney did. Maybe not in the same way, but they'd worked together for a long time and friendships had been formed. The fear of losing them was enough to propel them both to work harder.

"Mass propagation might be a good option for us," Courtney cut in to change the subject as quickly as possible. "But only in the long-term. We're already in the shit so need a fast solution. First off, we need to fractionate a root extract into individual components—or as close as we can get—so we can test them to identify what we want. I honestly think mass fermentation using bacteria —naturally occurring or genetically engineered to produce the desired activity—would be the fastest route. Concentrate the soup and spray it on or inject it. Desperate times call for a desperate solution at this point."

"Uh...yeah." The hacker typed furiously, no doubt to summarize the somewhat off-the-cuff explanation so she could research it a little.

Neither of them wanted to state the obvious, of course. All the signs pointed to them already being too late. If the Zoo attacked the walls, the chances were that they would not be able to stop it from bursting through. It was a painful realization and one that none of them wanted to address. Sal's plans were their only hope to derail the jungle's relentless campaign and buy more time. Unfortunately, whatever he attempted would have to be something major—the kind of thing that would put him and the team in there at even greater risk.

"Are you thinking what I'm thinking?" Anja asked.

"That depends on whether you've been reading Connie's core programming again."

The hacker laughed. "No. I...uh, was thinking about how we're stuck between a jungle and an apocalypse. We have no real chance of getting out alive but we'll keep fighting anyway."

"There is nothing else we can do at this point. We have

to keep pushing and hope that something good is there for us at the end."

———

The sun wasn't even up yet. Sal scowled at the heavy tree cover above them and tried to decide why the hell he was awake at this ungodly hour. His HUD told him that it was four in the morning and there was no hint of anything but blackness above them, even through the rare breaches in the leaves that allowed him to catch a glimpse of the sky above.

Still, it was not pure darkness. The naked eye would have difficulty noticing the pinpoints of light that peeked from under the bark of the trees, but there was enough to create an odd kind of awareness of what they were looking at.

Of course, the night vision in their suits had a field day with that slight light and gave them a decent view of the world. This was especially so when combined with the software that joined the sensors to give them a clear view of everything that was happening around them.

It wasn't quite as good as whatever the Zoo did to help him to see, but that would always come with some serious drawbacks.

They weren't the kind he was willing to commit to unless they had no other choice.

Still, if he was up, it was about time the others got up too. They'd been camped for about eight hours, and the lack of activity in the Zoo around them had begun to get on his nerves. There should have been at least a couple of panthers in the branches trying to make a sneak attack while they rested.

Nothing moved and he didn't trust the calm. The Zoo didn't suddenly decide that it would be accommodating to its visitors. It meant that either the jungle was pushing them somewhere or its efforts were directed elsewhere. Both options were enough to compel him to push forward and find another way to end it—and to not waste time doing it.

He stood immediately and noticed Gregor turn to look at him. The Russian had the last early-morning watch and it looked like he was about to drift into a doze before he'd been distracted.

"All good?"

Sal nodded. "We need to get moving."

"I don't think anyone will like that."

"I don't like it either, but the longer we stay anywhere, the better the chances of the Zoo springing a trap on us while we're not ready for it."

"Do you sense something the rest of us should be aware of?"

"Not yet, but I'm learning to trust my unease at this point."

Gregor nodded and quickly sent the signal to the HUDs of the rest of the team. It wasn't a red alert since nothing was ready to attack them yet but simply one to say that it was time to get the fuck up.

"Is something attacking?" Mal asked and looked around.

"No, dumbass." Sonja snorted. "A yellow alert means it's time to wake up. Didn't you pay attention to the brief last night?"

"Not really."

Sal shook his head and hurried to brew enough coffee for them. The welcome aroma filled the small clearing and although it was a little stale like all the coffee they got, no one would refuse it at this point. It might as well have been liquid gold given the value it had for a team on their last nerve while traveling through hostile territory. The fact that the enemy knew exactly where they were but still didn't act against them was even more unnerving.

"We need to move," he whispered as they packed their camp and in less than five minutes, the whole team was up, in their suits, and ready to push forward.

"Yeah, who needs sunrise to tell you that the day started?" Matt asked as they started.

Chezza shrugged. "It's how many people live their lives. Farmers out there get up before the sun to get to work."

"It helps to wake up knowing the whole farm isn't trying to kill you. Including your crops," he retorted, his voice rough from sleep.

She laughed. "You'd be surprised. More people die being attacked by cows than by sharks."

"Tell me what the figure is when people start herding sharks by the thousand," Jiro interjected.

"That would be one hell of a farm, though. Can you imagine?" Matt chuckled. "Shark farms. How would they make money?"

"People in Jiro's homeland love them some shark fin soup," Mal quipped.

"Not us," Jiro retorted. "The Chinese are into shark fin soup. I'm Ja—"

"Enough," Sal snapped. "We're heading into the most

dangerous part of the whole fucking jungle and we all need to be as aware as we can."

Maybe that wasn't called for, even though he was right. His people could be trusted to banter and keep their guard up, but the conversation irritated him for some reason. He could have simply pushed ahead without them, but the time would likely come when he needed their help.

After a moment, he realized he had taken point ahead of the team—even Madigan—and none of them had called him out on it. Maybe they had said something but if so, they had kept it a secret on private channels to avoid distracting him.

Still, she was right behind him and watching his back where he needed it, but he knew she was watching him too, making sure he didn't go off the deep end.

He realized that he had instinctively led the team a little to the left without being aware of it. No one made any comment and they appeared to follow him and simply waited for the next crazy thing he would say or do.

Something was out there and he sensed that the Zoo didn't want him to pay attention to it. The jungle pulled his attention to the northeast of their current position with an intensity that made it difficult to focus on anything else around them.

It must be Ground Zero. Nothing else in the area indicated that they were close to another birthing pool or something like it. The pressure associated with the awareness made it very clear that this was way more than anything they'd seen thus far.

A little confused, he focused on the odd blank spot in his vision. He recognized it—and that he'd seen something similar at least once, maybe twice before. Something was there and he had to see it before they moved forward but Ground Zero was more important. They needed to ignore this other distraction and focus on the real destination.

He paused as he considered the contradictory messages in his head. It must be the Zoo's influence guiding him and trying to push him away from the blank spot.

"All good, Sal?"

Athena's soft, pinging, non-human voice washed over him in a wave and gave him a moment to stop and catch his breath when he realized he'd been holding it.

"Something is out there that the Zoo doesn't want us to look at. Another black hole that indicates we're probably looking at another ore deposit."

He realized they had shifted in the direction of the likely ore deposit while he talked to her. Maybe being in his head was the way for the Zoo to control him, and if he found something else to occupy his thoughts, it was easier to move past the relentless pressure.

They reached a stream that was close to becoming a river, although it still ran shallow. Pieces of ore with a faintly red tinge were immediately visible like they had been scattered across the stream bed.

There was no time for this. They had to keep moving toward Ground Zero.

"It's happening again, Sal."

Sal grinned. "You're a fucking lifesaver, you know that, Athena?"

"Of course."

Released from his indecision, he approached the riverbed, collected a handful of samples, and stashed them quickly before he turned to move past the stream. It was odd how fighting the pressure in his head could be so exhausting and it was almost a relief when he finally did what it instructed.

But why did they need to head to Ground Zero? Well, that was obvious...maybe. They needed to do something there but the exact nature of it was a little fuzzy.

And what did it matter if they were all going to die?

CHAPTER TWENTY

Tellisman was something of a legend in the world of biology. He worked in a field a little separate from Courtney's since he specialized in microbiology and her expertise lay in macrobiology.

Which was also known as simply biology, but splitting hairs wasn't the way to get ahead. She needed to stay focused.

There would have been a time in her life when she would have loved the opportunity to pick the man's brain on a variety of her theories, and maybe that time would come for them.

For now, though, with all they were working toward, it felt like a distraction. There had to be another way to keep people outside the Zoo appraised of the situation.

"Dr. Tellisman, it's good to talk to you again," she said, almost surprised when they were connected. "Thanks for taking my call."

"Of course. It's the least I can do at this point given all the work you and your people have put into the matter."

She shrugged. "Well...I guess so. Anyway, did you get the data Anja sent you on the healer root?"

"Yes, although the title of the message included a handful of rather crude remarks regarding my genitalia."

"Oh, Lord. That must have been Connie. We have a very competent AI running defenses on our compound, but her programming includes a need to make everything a dirty joke. I'm sorry about that."

"Mind you, I have nothing against the odd rude limerick or joke, but there's a time and a place, you understand."

She decided to simply go ahead and erase that mental image from her head.

"Are you sure about this?" Tellisman asked when he sensed her discomfort. "It seems so ridiculously...well, odd that our collective survival is based on a small and otherwise unremarkable species of shrubbery."

"I imagine it means we should make an effort to conserve every type of flora and fauna on our planet, if for no other reason than because it might one day be the key to stopping an alien invasion."

That drew a chuckle from the older man. "Quite. I've looked into any specialists on *hedysarum* plants who might be able to shed some light on how it might be able to help us. Your contact mentioned that it smelled of licorice and it made me wonder if some element of glycyrrhizin in this plant could give the Zoo pause."

"The...acid that gives licorice its taste?"

"Indeed. It's a natural saponin, a plant-based toxin that is generally used to make soaps. If something in it causes a reaction in the Zoo materials, we might be able to derive it from other sources, which in turn would enable us to pour more of it into the Zoo besides what can be derived from the plant."

Courtney nodded. Badawi had already informed them that his family was ready with the required plants and waiting for them to be collected. If Tellisman was right in his assumption, the chances were that they could pull in more resources and make a few changes that would tweak it to work against the Zoo. She doubted that soap was all they needed to push the burrowers out, at least not in its natural state.

"That brings me to my next point," she said and leaned back in her seat. "We've tried to contact the people who were originally involved in studying the goop when it was first brought down but have been stonewalled at every turn. I've even consulted some of our hackers to find information on the original payload."

"Is that…legal?"

"Honestly? No, it isn't but at this point, a girl's got to do what a girl's got to do."

"I understand. Have you had any success?"

"Nope."

Tellisman scratched his jaw and looked pensive. "As of this moment, this healer root is the best chance we have to stop the Zoo. Labs are already waiting for samples to be collected."

"They should come in over the next few hours and my labs will participate in the first round of testing. The more we have working on this, the better."

"Right, then. I'll forward this intelligence to my team and find out if something can be done to help. Given how critical it is to our goals in the long-term—confirming that the Zoo is, in fact, alien and working to a pre-sequenced agenda—we will do anything we can to help you find your countermeasure."

"If we don't, we won't have much time to prepare for what comes next. Assuming we're all still around by that time, but I'm trying to be positive about how long we have."

"That's a healthy attitude."

"Or it's denial."

"True."

A ping in her comms drew her attention to a marker from the helicopter team to confirm that they were on the way back.

"Good news. The chopper has collected the one thing that might save all our lives."

"That's good to hear. Tell them to handle those plants with care. They might prove to be the most valuable items on the planet."

For once, he didn't have to endure any argument from the other members of the ZCP committee. Franklin assumed it was because they were all dealing with spurs in their sectors and none of them could afford to play any games, not unless they wanted people to decide that they were on their own. The British commander had thought she could handle the attacks without help, but it wasn't long until the second one appeared and they needed all hands on deck.

So far, it looked like the spurs were contained, but they didn't have the resources to do much beyond push each new occurrence back. Eventually, they would expand again and the shit would hit the fan. It wasn't unreasonable to imagine that at some point, someone would have to make some tough decisions about which spurs they would focus their efforts on. If and when that happened, they could only hope that those were the important ones.

Despite this, the rich, pompous assholes continued to complain. They had been subjected to fifteen minutes of that and by the sounds of things, they had talked to people in the Pentagon for a better idea of what they could do with impunity to make their position a little stronger. He didn't like that. These money-hungry dickheads had too much help already.

"The accommodations have already been agreed to," Franklin reminded them when the whiners took a moment to breathe. "Hell, all of you signed off on them. There won't be the optimal amount of space for everyone in the protected areas, so you'll simply have to find a way to make this work between yourselves."

"That agreement was reached before the current circumstances came up," a CEO protested, his voice arrogant and slightly condescending. "The extra moving expenses, the moratorium on Zoo trips—everything needs to be reevaluated in light of the current situation."

"If we reevaluate everything based on every single change that happens in the Zoo, we'd have to do it every day," Solodkov pointed out. "You cannot expect us to hold your hand on the matter. We have other responsibilities that frankly are more important than protecting your interests in the area."

"You shouldn't," a woman all but snarled. "Our money built everything you have in the desert."

"And we work daily to prevent what you've profited from for the past few years from chewing through all you," Franklin interjected quickly. "I have to assume that you want the focus to remain on keeping the wall intact to avoid the largest humanitarian crisis since what happened in Niger. You no doubt all remember the drops in stock prices that occurred when that clusterfuck hit the news network. I don't have to remind you that larger population centers could be next—Casablanca, Cairo, Benghazi, or even Marrakech. And the headlines if the Zoo hits any of those cities will be the demand to know who's to blame."

That quieted them effectively, although he assumed they had all made about as much as they lost by shorting the stock options of their competing companies. It was the smart thing to do when looking at a catastrophe.

Franklin cleared his throat now that everyone paid attention to him. "Currently, we're looking at concerted attacks from all over the Zoo. I've sent you all data packets on what's happened over the past twenty-four hours, and almost all the spurs have directed attacks at the walls. If each of these is a repetition of what we've seen before, we face the very real possibility of an explosion from the Zoo that will require a far stronger military presence to counter."

He paused to let that sink in. "The US military is on the move and will send emergency troops from bases Stateside as well as around the world, but it could be about twenty-four hours before we see any real additional presence. We need suits, weapons, ammunition, vehicles, and other supplies to arm the troops who are coming in."

Again, he gave them a moment to hopefully realize the full gravity of the situation. "If you want to be a part of the fight to prevent the worst from happening and ensure that your names are associated with any successes we have around the Zoo, you'll want to help with the funding. It'll cost you less and be worth more than most PR campaigns these days."

The CEOs began to converse among themselves, but he doubted that they would see any real support from them before the week was out, if any. The best option they had for immediate relief was to draw from their rainy-day fund to bring in mercenaries and their supplies to shore up the troop and supply lines that had begun to take considerable strain.

"Right." Eric Samson addressed the meeting brusquely once he had discussed something with his aides. "Let us assume that all the data you sent us is correct, including the information that the Zoo seeds with the nanotech are being delivered via these spurs when they reach the wall. Can we assume that these seeds have been planted along each of those stretches where the wall has already been completed?"

"Yes," the German commander answered. "It is the assumption we are working on. Very likely, they have lain dormant so far or have already eroded the foundations underground where we would not be able to see them. Aircraft and satellites are keeping track of any changes in the prioritized areas. Hopefully, we'll have some kind of warning to alert us of where the wall is fully compromised."

Franklin nodded slowly. "We have additional reports from the Heavy Metal team's research around the edges of the Zoo, where it looks like they found evidence of active water sources. Yes, I know it's crazy but the evidence is hard to argue."

"The Zoo can create water now?" one of the CEOs demanded almost indignantly and shook his head. "I suppose finding out that there might be a holistic cure to these nanotech bastards isn't the craziest idea after all."

"It's the first positive sign we've had in a while," the US commander admitted. "It offers hope but so far, it's not a confirmed solution. For the moment, the truth is that the Zoo has us under siege."

It was a frightening concept to hear out loud and he was gratified to see that the group took it with an appropriate amount of respect.

"And for once," the British commander interjected petulantly, "it looks like our crazy Zoo guru's scheme has failed. We've seen the flares but thus far, there's been no indication that the efforts of him and his team have made any impact on the Zoo's current campaign. For all we know, Dr. Jacobs might soon be as dead as we all will be."

He wasn't sure why, but that frightened Franklin most of all.

CHAPTER TWENTY-ONE

His first view of Ground Zero by far exceeded paltry human expectations.

Sal paused, mesmerized for a moment as he tried to make sense of what he was looking at. Three massive domes dwarfed everything around them. A prefab building was still in place and while it showed some signs of damage, it was more from the time it had been left unattended and the issues were mostly surface. Prefab buildings were meant to withstand the test of time, and these had been put through the wringer. What captured his imagination, though, was the fact that the domes were still standing.

They were called biodomes and he remembered them from the pictures taken back when there was nothing in the region but desert for thousands of miles in every direction. The foliage around them had thinned somewhat too, almost like the Zoo respected the area. A deep sense of awe seemed to pervade the scene, the same powerful mystical something that infused the old churches. Even if one didn't particularly believe in what they represented, the old cathedrals still had an effect on the people who visited them.

The three domes were constructed in a triangle with little separation between them. Up close, it was easy to think of them as the same structure until you circled to see what was on the other sides.

Everything was still in place. That was probably the biggest surprise. The second biggest was their dimensions. The numbers were a matter of public record of course, at least to those who had access to the records. They weren't exactly hard to find, not for him. Each dome was about the same size—hundreds of feet in diameter and about forty feet at their highest point.

Rusted doors were still on their hinges and looked like they were installed with security in mind a long time before. The dome structures were webbed with cracks coming from the doors, which suggested something big and strong breaking through.

"That must have been the admin and housing building." Madigan pointed to the prefab that had been erected at one point of the triangle. "How the hell is this place even standing?"

"It's a monument. Freedom was achieved here and it should stand for the freedom it continues to provide."

He looked around and winced when he realized he'd said that aloud. Thankfully, it wasn't on a public channel, only between him and Athena.

"Has that been on your mind for a while now?" the AI asked and cut through the almost hypnotic trance from which he'd spoken.

"I don't know where it came from. It seems about right, though. This, from all the records, is where the Zoo broke out. I don't know if a jungle can be sentimental about a place like this, but it feels almost like...I don't even know how to explain it. On a more practical note, though, if there is something it doesn't want to appear on any satellite photos, scans, or anything else, the domes are perfect for that. I doubt we would have even been able to find it if it hadn't been for the...you know."

His brain seemed fuzzy again. It was a comfortable fuzziness, the kind he didn't know what to do with because the impulse to relax into it was certainly not one he wanted to listen to at the moment. Sal was learning that almost anything that felt comfortable in his mind was what the Zoo wanted him to think. Fighting those impulses had become exhausting. He honestly couldn't help it if a few blank spots were scattered among his thoughts here and there.

No definite awareness came up. He received no direction, only a wall of pulses that swept constantly into him. It felt like when he lay on the beach at the edge of the water and the waves rolled in. The smaller ones were no problem but the big ones came and knocked the breath out of him. It was almost pleasant and he relaxed into it until all were suddenly big waves that surged relentlessly and he couldn't push to the top. He couldn't breathe and his arms couldn't move so he couldn't swim to the surface. Oddly, he didn't sink either but seemed poised on the cusp of getting a gasp of air here and there before the next wave hit.

"Sal, are you all right?"

Athena's cool, metallic voice snapped into the vacuum

in which he was trapped and Sal realized he'd slumped. She'd taken control of the suit and prevented him from falling while he'd had his panic attack. Maybe it was time for him to simply hand the reins to her entirely. He didn't know if something would snap in him or if his brain would give in after days of the abuse he'd endured. It would be so easy to let go and be washed out into the ocean, catch a riptide, and not care where he ended up.

"Not…not really," he whispered and fought the claustrophobia that clawed in his throat. "It's strong here. I'm… it's…I'm trying to hang on."

"We're at Ground Zero, Sal. You always wanted to see it."

"I don't know what I'm supposed to do," he confessed. "Everyone expects me to come up with the answers to all this shit, but I look at this and draw a blank. My brain isn't…working the way that it should. Nothing's working."

He would normally have a hard time containing all his ideas especially in a place like this, but all that creativity was stifled and pushed down to the point where it was an exhausting chore to try to bring it to the surface.

Still, having Athena there helped. Her cool, calm voice in the back of his head assisted him to stay centered, but he had a bad feeling that if he pointed this out to her, it would lose its efficacy.

"All you need to do is look around," the AI stated calmly.

"Right, like it'll be that…easy." Sal took a step toward the massive buildings. There was no telling what would happen if he approached them but he intended to do so, even if it was in a roundabout way.

Easy wasn't quite the word he would use to describe it

but allowing his mind to focus on something else certainly helped. He turned to the first of the domes, the door of which stood partially open, and eased through. A sense of desolation filled the structure.

Thinking about the people who had lost their lives there was unsettling, but the jungle had replaced them with an abundance of life. Vines grew up and down the walls and the entire floor was covered by red-and-blue Pitas, concealed from prying eyes by the buildings humanity had erected to imprison the Zoo and force it to do their bidding.

The only thing that was missing was defenses. The closer they got to Ground Zero, the fewer live animals they encountered, and the eerie silence that had taken hold without them around was even more unsettling.

Maybe the monsters had chosen to hide and stay out of the way to let Sal and his human companions through.

"I've had the weirdest bad feeling that a whole horde of human Zoo mutants is about to appear," Trick whispered, approached one of the domes, and rested his hand on it almost like he didn't quite believe that it was there. "They'll jump up from their graves like fucking ghosts and attack us."

"Hey, Trick," Chezza called.

"Yeah?"

"Do me a favor next time you have a feeling like that."

"Of course."

"Keep it to yourself."

It was ridiculous to think that the Zoo would use human mutants. That was something it would have done by now if it had any intention to do so.

If they wanted to survive, having thoughts like that wouldn't help. The whole site was abandoned with not even a breeze to rustle branches for a little white noise. Still, he'd come all this way so he might as well get settled. Home was where the heart was.

No, he wasn't home, not yet. Home was at the compound. He was there to do something important but he couldn't seem to bring it into focus. Pressing on it felt like it would simply push it away again, and there was no point to that. It was like a dream. If he thought about it too much, it would disappear.

He would remember sometime soon.

"I hate to have a thought like Trick did," Mal commented, "but we should be swarmed by mutants, right? Not only the locusts and the humpers but the big fuckers too. Dinosaurs, at least, would defend a place like this. Where the fuck are they?"

It was a very good question but Sal wasn't sure he could answer. The mental noise from the Zoo meant he couldn't feel any of the small things. If they were quietly surrounded by a horde of mutants, he probably wouldn't realize it until he was pushed to join them in ridding the jungle of the filthy humans.

"A whole horde of mutants, yes," Madigan whispered. "But nothing shows on the scanners yet."

"The creatures are here. Hundreds of them. They simply aren't out yet."

He had spoken again. His mouth had, anyway, with little to no input from Sal himself. This time, it was on the open channels and the whole team turned to look at him and fell silent.

"Shit. I said that out loud, didn't I?"

"Never mind that," Madigan snapped. "What the hell are you talking about? What does that mean?"

"I don't know. Thoughts come into my head and I don't know where from or why." He braced himself as the feeling surged again. The waves washed over him and dragged him into the water, and anything he could grasp felt like sand that was simply washed out with him.

"I've isolated your frequency," Athena informed him as he fought to breathe again. "Your readings are starting to show issues again so you need to think and focus your mind."

"I can't focus." The panic began to build as he struggled to hold on. "Nothing…to focus on. I only…it's all there. I can't…it won't…let me."

He realized that his gaze had shifted to the team. He managed to focus despite everything. Madigan's massive suit made the ground shake as she moved closer. She stopped beside him and he could see her face on his HUD.

"What's the matter?"

"Something's wrong."

What was he talking about? No, that wasn't him. Athena was giving Madigan an update.

Gorgeous, strong, solid Madigan was always there for him, fought for him, kept his feet on the ground, and protected him from all the threats he faced, even those he created for himself.

"Sal, you stick around with me, you hear? You're here and we're depending on you to get us out of this alive."

"That's…your prerogative."

"I can shoot guns better than you, kill mutants, run

around, and make things blow up, but I rely on you to point me at what needs killing, shooting, and blowing up. I need you with me on this, Salinger Jacobs. Do you understand me?"

He narrowed his eyes and tried to focus on her, but something fought it. This was important. He had no idea why, but if he told himself it was, he would believe it. They needed him—and with his head screwed on straight. A version of him that wasn't fighting a losing battle against a cosmic entity that wanted to take permanent residence in his brain.

Instinctively, he drew a deep breath, then another. Adrenaline pumped through his body where it had been sluggish and oxygen surged into his brain where it felt like it was about to run out. He had no idea what he would do next, but one breath at a time? That he could do.

They were all watching him and waiting for him. Sal wasn't sure if he saw them with his eyes or not. Yes, it must be his. The Zoo didn't like having to tell the humans apart.

And there it was. The part of his brain that had no reason to worry about the Zoo taking over because it was where he went when he needed to think—his happy place, as it were. The Zoo was still there but isolated somehow. He was in a part of his brain that seemed to function separately from his day-to-day consciousness. In all his struggle, it had not intruded, but it now gave him a cold, clinical view of what was happening around him.

What was happening to him, he amended when he saw the truth of it. He took a mental step back and let the Zoo flood in.

The nurseries were nearby. These housed locusts and

humpers for the most part, but that wasn't all. He had no idea how he knew that but he did. The information poured into his brain with every wave that struck him and he sensed that it hoped he would have no idea how to process it all. And he didn't, in all honesty. Vague images here and there were carried on a groundswell of feelings and sentiments.

Nothing was concrete, but his exposure to the Zoo was enough to allow him to parse out bits and pieces.

"Storage?"

"What?" Madigan asked.

She had been talking all this time. It had been rude of him to zone out like that but he had to sift through everything the jungle flung at him.

"It's...storage. Or a barracks. Barracks makes more sense, right?"

"None of what you're saying makes sense."

Sal laughed softly. "It's crazy, I know, but there you go. The fucking bitch has been building an army. We can't see them, but I can...well...feel them. I don't know how that sounds, precisely, but there are hundreds of them. Thousands maybe. Down there, underground like that nursery or stored in all the hidden places around here. This isn't about a simple outbreak. She has a fucking invasion planned."

CHAPTER TWENTY-TWO

Someone kicked her awake with a hard thud that launched a jolt of pain up the side of her leg. No, that didn't sound right. Something else was happening.

She'd been up and working for close to thirty-six hours, and she was owed a nap. All she needed was fifteen minutes until the coffee was ready and she would be good to go again.

No, she hadn't been kicked. Courtney groaned softly and registered something cool and hard pressed against her cheek. She'd fallen off the couch. Something must have disturbed her and made her fall off the couch. It wasn't the most elegant way to wake up and was made even worse by how she'd simply fallen asleep again, but everything would come into focus shortly.

With a scowl, pushed slowly from the floor and tried to adjust for how sore her neck felt suddenly. It was uncomfortable but the kind of pain she could walk off. And she could smell coffee, exactly what she needed to fend off the post-nap effects.

Anja was seated cross-legged on the couch opposite her and sipped what looked like a steaming cup of coffee, although there was a weird smell to it.

"If you're wondering about the smell," the hacker said and took another sip, "it's because this coffee is old."

Old? She settled on the couch and rubbed her neck gently.

"How old?"

"About seven hours old. Shame on you for wasting good coffee."

"If it was old, why didn't you make a new batch?"

"Because I don't waste coffee, no matter how old it is. If it's drinkable and not poisoned, it will be consumed. Failing that, coffee is good for plants, or so I've heard, so I'll give my plants a snack."

"You…have plants?"

"A few of them. Not many, though. I might be developing a green thumb, but it's not quite to the point of orchids hanging from the walls yet."

Her neck might be a real problem but wasn't one she would try to deal with now. She brushed her fingers through her blonde hair and worked through the worst of the tangles.

"Seven hours, huh?"

"I should pour you a cup and make you drink it, but it looks like you'll do that to yourself presently. Come on, we need to get to work. I have something you need to take a look at."

She nodded at the TV screen, where live satellite images displayed to provide minute-by-minute updates of the Zoo. One of them was zoomed out to show where all the different spurs extended from.

It was never a pleasant sight to be reminded of how ambitious the alien jungle was.

"Shit," she whispered. "That looks like...fuck, I don't know. A wagon wheel?"

"Well, yes, I suppose." Anja tilted her head and nodded as she acknowledged the resemblance. "But look at this."

The hacker superimposed what looked like a piece of engraved metal.

"What...what is that?"

"I found this when I sifted through emails sent when the plans were formulated for the original goop project. From what I understood, this was on the missile and Dr. Marie wanted to use it as the basis for a logo for them." She fiddled with the image from her computer and settled the first image over the second. Courtney couldn't help a gentle chill that shivered down her spine and sent goose-bumps across her skin.

The metal image lined up with the spurs added to the Zoo image and the spokes on both were almost a perfect match.

"We have two spokes missing," she pointed out and barely noticed that she spoke in a whisper. "It might be a coincidence. Or it means we're almost out of time."

Anja nodded slowly and ran her fingers over her laptop. The hacker ground her teeth and looked like she'd been up as long as her companion had. It was a painful thought to know that they were almost out of time. Everyone was as on edge as they were and they hadn't even shared this revelation yet. Could they hope to hold that many attacks off at the same time?

Something rang and she jumped, looked around, and snapped her hand reflexively to her hip. It was where she carried her sidearm on her suit but nothing was there now. Anja had jerked as well and almost knocked her laptop off its perch on her lap but she caught it in time.

"It's your phone," the hacker informed her and checked the screen. "Franklin is calling. This should be good."

"What makes you say that?"

"It's his personal line. I forget sometimes that his first name is Jed. Who the hell names their kid Jed?"

"There are entire states whose whole identity is giving their kids weird fucking names. Is it Jed, or Jedidiah?"

"It only says Jed. Do you plan to answer sometime soon?"

Courtney rolled her eyes at the woman before she pressed the button to accept the call and put it on speaker. "Franklin, it's always good to hear from you. How goes the work of saving the world?"

"Honestly? It feels like we should simply let the world go to shit so I can get some sleep. We just got word of another spur in the Chinese sector."

"In the middle of the day? Until now, all the spurs happened overnight or in the early hours of the morning." She checked her watch to make sure.

"It has all the same signs, though. I'm still waiting on confirmation from the aerial surveillance, drones, and the like, but it looks the same."

"It's a break in the pattern so it's likely that the Zoo has pushed the timetable up. Anja, can you send him the pictures you showed me?"

"Will do, boss."

Franklin paused and studied the images. "This is interesting. Why do you think it would be breaking its pattern like this? It gives us full view and time to intercept it so it doesn't make sense."

"Maybe Sal managed to do something and has forced the Zoo to act sooner than expected."

"I can't say that's a good thing." The commander sighed softly. "It sounds like his plan might have backfired spectacularly."

It was a shocking realization and Sal couldn't understand why he hadn't seen it sooner.

No. He knew why. The bombardment in his head from the Zoo tried to obfuscate it. It seemed an odd tactic and one that didn't appear to be entirely focused on keeping him away from what it was doing. All it achieved was to delay him, but maybe it did know what it was doing and that was the plan.

The rest of the team seemed like they were trying to process the fact that they stood frighteningly close to an army about to mobilize. He could understand that they needed a few seconds to adjust to that idea in their heads.

It helped that he now thought about it more clearly than he had in what felt like forever. The details of the past few days through the Zoo were hard to differentiate and he realized now that he was the most unreliable narrator there ever was.

But something needed to be done.

"Trick," he called and drew a deep breath, "how many explosives do you have on you?"

The man turned to look at him for a moment and he could almost picture him smiling beneath his helmet.

"Enough. What do you have in mind?"

"I need you to set your toys up for a party on the dome with the red-and-blue Pitas."

"Are we thinking wine tasting with cheese over some smooth jazz or underground rave with no fire marshal within twenty miles?"

"I'm thinking...something along the lines of the '99 Woodstock."

"Oh, damn. You want me to bring the whole place down."

"You're fucking right I do."

Trick laughed softly and immediately began to put his pieces together. Sal had no idea how he carried that much explosive on him but in the end, it was more about where you put it.

That added to the age of the building allowed them to make certain decisions about how they would go about doing what they'd come in to do.

He could think of no better way to distract the Zoo than dropping a building on the army it had created to invade the world.

"Uh, Sal..." Chezza cleared her throat to make sure he was paying attention. "Sorry, but are you fucking crazy?"

"The whole situation is crazy at this point. If you want,

you can help Trick to set and place the charges, but I want a push-button detonator. When that's done, you can all turn the fuck around and get the hell out of here."

The channels exploded with a series of protests that he had no intention to address one by one. Madigan lead the charge on them too, and he shook his head.

"When that button is pressed, all hell will break loose. Every fucking mutant in this area will react. If you think plucking a Pita or killing a dino is bad... What we're looking at here will be a hundred times worse."

"You don't know that," Madigan snapped.

"I do, though. We've all wandered around with our heads in our armpits without a goddammed clue, but everything the Zoo has done so far has been for a reason. We're out of time. If this isn't done, the full force of the Zoo will swarm the wall and break through. It'll move beyond at the kind of frenzied pace we've all seen and kill every living person in the region, and that will give it all the biomass it needs to push on before anyone can try to stop it. And that's if someone has time and sense to get the word out. We don't have the resources to defend the wall as is. How the fuck do you think we'll manage to contain the Zoo once it's fueled and fed with no wall to hold it back?"

At least that sounded a little more like him. Sal wasn't sure how long this moment of clarity would last, and he wanted to make damn sure that all the pieces were in place to do the most damage to the Zoo before it tried to over-whelm him again.

He had a bad feeling that it would happen sooner rather than later. Thankfully, the rest of the team appeared to be of a similar mind. Trick, Chezza, and Jiro worked together to set the charges.

Trick certainly had a talent for it, chose the positions where they could be placed for best effect, and moved as quickly as possible.

"That means you too," Sal said directly to Madigan. "I want you to do it now while you still can."

She smirked because he could hear it in her tone. "Yeah. How far do you think we'll get? Besides, if the fucking Zoo kills me—and it will either way—it'll be right here next to you."

"I can give you guys enough time."

"No, you can't. For one thing, I don't trust you to be able to go through with this plan with the Zoo in your fucking head. If we're too far away to push the button for you, it'll all be for nothing. Besides, there is no more time."

Sal drew a deep breath and tried to fight the fact that she made sense. But he was used to trusting her judgment over his in certain situations. It was better for everyone.

"I guess we're all out of everything, Maddie," he muttered and checked his assault rifle.

"Not everything. We still have ammo. And we have each other. It'll have to do."

CHAPTER TWENTY-THREE

Sal couldn't bring himself to intentionally push to achieve the connection again.

He was as close to himself as he'd been since they'd stepped into the Zoo and he didn't want to jeopardize that. It seemed counterproductive when they were looking at what had to be the toughest fight they had faced in a long time.

Even so, he could feel the rising tensions and excitement from the jungle around them. There was no telling when it would simply blow and surge outward, but it would happen soon.

They were running out of time, and fast.

Gregor pointed to the administrative building between the biodomes. "It looks relatively secure and it will provide us the most cover from the blast Trick is cooking up. We're setting defenses up. If we delay pushing the button until morning, we might be able to turn it into a fortress."

He shook his head and glanced to where Madigan

worked with Davis, Mal, and Sonja to try to secure the building as best they could in the short time they had.

"Something tells me we don't have until morning. We have to blow this shit before the mutants spill out of the domes, which means as soon as the explosives are set. Do you think you can direct the others to target any that survive?"

Gregor shrugged. "I'm like Batman. I can kill anything and anyone with enough prep time."

"Or like Kevin from Home Alone."

"I've never seen that movie."

Sal shook his head. "See what you can do. We're kind of committed already."

"Will do, boss."

The temptation to push for the connection was strong. He could maybe find out how long they had, and although it nagged harder at him, he didn't want to tempt fate. At this point, he doubted that he would be able to break free of its influence again.

He only needed to stay in control until the explosives detonated. After that, most of it was moot. The jungle was harnessing every instrument and weapon it had at its disposal and adding it to the growing inner roar.

No matter what, he had to hold out until the bombs went off. He could hold on until then.

Trick working fast with the other two former McFadden and Banks freelancers was probably for the best, but it didn't give Gregor and Madigan enough time to set the defenses up. Mines and a couple of turrets were about all they could expect at this point.

"It's all set to blow, boss," Trick called as he approached.

"I have it wired to a remote trigger and you can expect there to be one hell of a boom."

"Nice work." Sal took the device he was offered. "Help Madigan set the defenses up."

They nodded as he looked at the trigger. They needed to do this without delay and he turned to join the team.

A weird numbness settled in the back of his mind. It didn't feel like much at first—a soft touch that pulsed with the rest of the Zoo. For a moment, it felt like it was merely checking in on what was happening in his mind.

He couldn't do this. Not to his home. He felt the betrayal twist through the pit of his stomach. Not after all it had done to get him this far. He studied the trigger and nausea began to build, fueled by the accusation of duplicity in the back of his mind.

Trick should probably have kept the trigger.

Waves washed over him again but this time, it felt like a hurricane. He was angry. Or maybe the Zoo was pissed. He could no longer separate his emotional responses and it was painful to even try—like pushing through brambles, except the thorns were Zoo-long and dug into his mind.

With a soft cry, he dropped to his knees. His hands felt numb and the trigger slipped from his grasp and slid over the ground. It stopped barely out of reach.

He had to move to it...crush the damn trigger and break it to render it useless.

No. He had to press it and blow it all up.

That was a little extreme. They needed to think about it to find out the best way for them to get out of there alive. Blowing it up would seal all their fates and for no good reason.

"Sal!"

He startled, looked around, and tried to make sense of where he stood. He could have sworn he'd fallen to his knees but of course, the damn AI had propped him up.

The ground shook and he reached reflexively for his weapon. The Zoo was attacking. It wanted to stop him from pressing the button but he wouldn't go down without a fight.

"Sal! Press the fucking button!"

The shaking wasn't the Zoo. He turned as Madigan's massive tank of a suit approached him. Her voice sounded like it came from a long way off.

"Sal, what's happening?"

"Need…we need… Something's not right."

"You're damn right!" she snapped. "Set the explosives off!"

Athena said something and tried to get through to him. She felt like a lifeline, a solid, enduring presence untouched by the terror and emotions that plagued him and the others. Sal extended his hand for the trigger but realized he still held it. His hand closed protectively around the device.

Something was playing tricks on his mind. Confused, he looked at the trigger again and tried to make sense of what was happening as a figure rushed toward him.

"Blow it, Sal!" Madigan yelled. At least he could recognize her voice.

He sucked in a deep breath and this time, he was sure he dropped to his knees as he tried to determine what in the good name of fuck he was doing still holding the detonator.

The truth struck him a moment later. Athena still had control of the suit. But why didn't she push the detonator? Maybe it went contrary to something in her programming, but if she had offered an explanation, he certainly hadn't heard it.

Voices became a blur, white noise in the back of his head as he stared at the item in his hand, dragged in deep breaths, and tried to remember what it was and what he was meant to do with it.

His team needed to get out. He had to wait until they were all safely away before he set the explosives off, right? No, that wasn't the plan. It was what he wanted but no one paid any attention to him or his concerns for their well-being.

No, he had to set it off. And now that he had difficulty doing it, maybe them sticking around was for the best.

A hand grasped his shoulder and he pushed the figure away and fumbled for his weapon. Something stopped him and tried to control him. He couldn't tell if it was Athena's control of the suit or if the Zoo now fought to take hold of him too.

Everyone wanted to control him and tell him what to do and what to say. Why couldn't he simply let go? Letting the waves wash him out into the ocean seemed like such an attractive option but for some reason, he struggled against it.

"You have to do it now! Blow it, Sal!"

"Blow it! Fucking blow it!"

That was his voice. Sal was confused for a second. Why had he heard his voice coming from outside the suit?

Athena. Of course. The AI had activated the external

speakers to his suit and everyone could now hear what he was saying. But had he said that? He hadn't meant to.

Why was he yelling at himself?

The figure lunged forward again but instead of catching his shoulders, it took his hands. Madigan...the massive suit said it was her. She held his hands firmly.

"Are you going to tell me that you love me?" he said although he wasn't sure where the voice came from.

"In the only way I know how," she answered.

Sal looked down when he felt a sudden pressure on his hands. Her fingers pushed his onto the trigger and squeezed it carefully.

"No!"

That was his voice but not his words. It was too late. The Zoo couldn't stop Madigan, and everyone knew it had been trying for years at this point.

For a second, nothing happened.

Something hit him in the back. The blast wave hammered him from his feet and he and Madigan sprawled as the air was filled with a ringing noise.

A second later, he realized that was his ears. Athena hadn't caught the explosion in time and the blast was loud enough that he couldn't hear anything.

No big wall of flames followed and nothing even remotely what he expected from years of watching over-the-top action movies. A booming crack seemed to suck the air into itself.

Whatever the hell Trick had put together certainly worked. Sal's sensors revealed that the biodome was nowhere to be seen. It had simply collapsed under its weight and a huge cloud of dust was all that remained.

The hand on his spine was gone. Nothing tried to control him, hold him, or muddle his thoughts.

Instead, the Zoo seemed frozen in stunned silence. The threads of communication were severed and even the pulses paused for a moment like it didn't quite understand how he had pulled the trigger while under its influence.

Maybe it wouldn't understand that he hadn't, not technically. Madigan had done it for him.

He scrambled to his feet and helped her to stand as well before he focused on the destruction he had been a part of wreaking.

Something bubbled from his chest. He realized he was laughing while the whole Zoo felt like it had been brought to a standstill.

When the feeling from the jungle returned seconds later, there was something else to it. Rage rushed through his connection like a raging, ravenous inferno and abandoned all its attempts at subtle control.

This was anger in its purest form. Sal had never felt anything like it before but somehow, he was on the outside looking in.

"Fuck." His voice was rough and more than a little hoarse. It shook noticeably too, but he didn't care. The laughter welled again, almost against his will. "I guess… I guess…we…uh, got the bitch's attention now."

It would be a hard sell. She wouldn't even try to dispute that. Everything about the Zoo would always be difficult to explain to the people who didn't deal with it on a regular basis.

Hell, even people who had been deep in the situation but removed themselves from it for a time had a hard time believing what they had gone through. It was one of the dumbest characteristics of the human race's ability to adapt against overwhelming trauma.

Courtney could see the doubt on full display in Franklin, Murphy, and Solodkov's expressions. None of them looked like they'd had much in the way of rest, which explained why they were a little slow on the uptake, but there was no denying a pattern.

They stood less than a mile away from one of the spokes in the picture, after all. Having a visual aid helped, of course. The visible could be more terrifying than the envisaged.

The Russian was the first to speak and shook his head slowly. "All right. Let us...assume you're right about this. What is your next point?"

"Think about it for a minute." She put her tablet down and suppressed a sigh at the blank stares they fixed on her. "What made the Zoo change its pattern? It certainly wasn't anything we did. The flares from the Ground Zero team have come through when expected and indicate that they've made good progress. The only thing we don't know is if they've reached the target."

"There might have been a flare," Murphy reminded her. "The planes might have missed it if it was fired during the day."

. . .

"I don't think that's relevant. What is important—and is the only different thing—is that they are in the Zoo and on the way to Ground Zero. While Sal hoped to draw the attention away from the wall, it's as likely that the bitch has upped the time frame because she knows they have something planned to stop her."

"We can consider the possibility that you might be right." Solodkov sounded like he was humoring her and it was all she could do to not slap the Russian's unshaven face. "It does not mean—"

"I'm goddammed fucking right," she insisted. "And if you'd get your collective heads out of your collective asses, you'd see it. We might or might not have found something to counter the corrosion but it's too late for it to make a meaningful difference to the wall. This, gentlemen, is a road map to a military campaign that's about to be unleashed. It's all there—a supply network is laid out and the plan is in place to move as many creatures as quickly as possible. It only has one more spur to go."

"So, you're saying that what he did—if anything—or even plans to do pushed the Zoo into shortening its time frame." Murphy seemed to need to repeat at least some of what she said to get it to stick. Still, he sounded like he made an attempt to wrap his head around the possibility and give her the benefit of the doubt.

"Exactly." Courtney pointed the spurs out one by one. "The pattern fits. They've all grown at night, protected by cover of darkness, and so avoided any attempts on our part to identify them early. Now, it's suddenly decided to push that shit out in broad daylight? It makes no sense—it'll sustain heavy losses and it's given us a clear view of what we're dealing with from the start. It seems like no attempt was made to grow everything underground first before it was thrust out."

Franklin nodded slowly, his expression grim. "What would come next, per your hypothesis?"

"My guess is that it's drawing our attention. The next spur will push into place overnight if not sooner while we're focused on dealing with the more obvious attack. You might have a couple of days' grace while the burrowers do their work. Then again, given what we know about the Zoo, it might simply double the corrosive qualities or throw more nanotech at it to shorten the process. Either way, we have a timetable. Within the next twenty-four hours, our prep time is up."

Franklin, Murphy, and Solodkov exchanged a glance. She couldn't tell what they were thinking, but the Russian finally sighed and shrugged. It was probably the first time she'd seen anything remotely resembling human emotion on his face and it was enough to convince the other two.

"I'll call it in to the other base commanders," Franklin said wearily. "If you're right, we have a basic location on where the other spur will be and we might be able to nip it in the bud."

He took his phone from the desk but before he could dial anything into it, one of Murphy's radio's crackled to life.

"Sir, we have word from our thrower team at the front lines," a woman's voice hissed and crackled through the poor connection. "They've reported something weird and it looks like all our other soldiers on the front line are reporting the same thing."

Murphy unclipped the radio from his belt and keyed in. "Define weird, Captain."

"It's... I'm not—"

"What's fucking happening?"

"It's a little crazy—uh, crazier than usual."

"Tell us, dammit," Franklin ordered sharply.

"It looks like every single goddamn mutant here turned tail and fucked off. I wouldn't believe it myself but I have seven other teams that report the same thing."

Solodkov paused, retrieved his tablet, and keyed quickly into his men's frequencies. The rattle of fifteen or sixteen voices in Russian sounded like people were confused on his side as well.

"Reports are the same from my men also," he whispered, his expression confused.

That made two human expressions from the Russian in a single discussion. Maybe he wasn't an android after all.

"Fucked off where?" Murphy asked into the radio.

"We have no goddamn clue, sir. Back...back into the Zoo, I guess. Sensors tell us nothing is moving here except for trees."

"Ground Zero," Courtney whispered, looked around, and almost shouted it again. "Ground Zero! That son of a bitch did it, and now—"

She paused to think about the consequences of Sal's success. If the creatures in the spurs were headed in, it meant all of them were doing the same thing.

"He'll die for his efforts." Franklin finished her thought for her, his tone hollow.

Murphy narrowed his eyes and scowled deeply. "Not if I have anything to do with it."

CHAPTER TWENTY-FOUR

"Did we sustain any damage?" Sal asked Madigan

"Not that I can see. The suits are still functional. I guess they were made to resist explosions, even those of that magnitude."

He turned when she slowed her walk to where the rest of the team was busy with the last of their defenses. The admin building wasn't designed with a siege by mutant monsters in mind. While most of it was intact, the interior would be something of a death trap if the creatures gained access. Trick had brought down two of the outer walls and the rubble was better than no defenses at all but barely. As a last resort, they could maybe clamber onto the roof but vines and panthers would be an issue.

Besides, their ammo was limited. Everyone knew they were unlikely to need a secure position to retreat to.

"Send another flare up," Madigan ordered once they were on the other side of the mines.

"We've already sent two," Sonja reminded her.

"Yep, and we'll continue to throw them up until we run out or we can't."

The woman drew a deep breath, took another flare from her pouch, and launched it skyward.

"They're coming," Sal warned as he checked his suit again for any internal damage from the explosion. Tapping into the Zoo felt a little easier now. Instead of drawing him in, it fought actively against his attempts to look into its collective mind—which, weirdly, made it easier.

Or maybe it was so painfully obvious that he didn't need to look too deep. The rest of the team could probably feel the sheer anger radiating from all living things around them.

They were coming and he knew this would be a battle that made everything else they'd seen in the Zoo thus far look like a cartoon movie. He drew his sword and it hummed softly in his hands. Athena had his firearms in the extra limbs that protruded from his back and their sensors already began to register a surge racing through the Zoo toward them.

At least they had the building to their backs as cover. It would slow and funnel any attacks coming from behind them and provide some protection, at least.

The ground shook when the mines detonated, but it didn't look like the creatures slowed even slightly. Even as the ball bearings savaged dozens of them at a time, they pushed forward. A solid wall of locusts appeared first, a few flying and others on the ground, and rushed immediately into the attack.

"Now!" Trick called, and Mal stood ready with another trigger in his hands.

He'd already used all his high explosives, but Trick lived up to his moniker by having a couple more up his sleeve. Phosphorus charges were buried inside piles of timber that they'd positioned in the center of all advance points. They suddenly began to burn a pale blueish-green and tongues of flame licked up ten, twenty feet high as the locusts tried to jump over them.

Those that did were immediately set on fire and their wings and bodies burned as they still tried to push their attack.

"I found me a new delicacy," Trick quipped, raised his assault rifle, and opened fire. "Fried Zoo Mutant. Who brought the buffalo sauce?"

"We're all out, I'm afraid," Chezza answered with a laugh. "I do have some barbeque sauce, though."

"Seriously?"

"Yeah. It came with the chicken teriyaki food packet they send out these days."

"I guess that'll work. We've got some fried wings. Get it? Fried wings?"

Not long before, that kind of joking would have grated on Sal's mind and made it impossible to focus on anything else. He probably would have snapped at them to be serious, but none of that rose to the surface now.

He was in a good mood. Maybe even a manic mood but it countered the feeling of not having any control over himself during the time they had spent in the jungle.

While they would probably all die in the next few minutes, he would at least do it as himself.

"Check your ammo, everyone," Madigan warned since there was no need to tell them when to start fighting.

"Make every bullet count. We don't have any to spare at this point."

Sal jumped forward as the mutants cleared the last of the mines and the sentry turrets began to target the creatures that moved closer. Her shoulder-mounted guns delivered a sustained barrage of lead and killed the creatures by the dozen, but it wouldn't matter. Dozens might fall but hundreds took their place.

And he was still in a damn good mood. Sal bounded forward at the first of the panthers that pushed through and tried to find itself an easy target. A bright red light filled the clearing as another of the flares arced skyward. It drenched the whole area in vivid color as he slashed the creature in half and twisted to deal with two humpers that tried to surprise him while his back was turned.

They were both dead before he could attack them. Jiro dealt with one, severed the head, and cut the body in half in two smooth strokes that were so fast the second one could barely be seen.

Athena gunned the second down for him, and Sal turned to face the massed ranks that surged toward them from the front.

Fires, turrets, and the sheer amount of firepower from Madigan's suit were enough to soften the initial drive, but it wouldn't last. Their ammo levels were finite and eventually, humans would fall.

Sal jerked to intercept three lizards that barreled toward them and he swiped two humpers out of the way before he highlighted the reptiles for the rest of the team. Hopefully, some of them weren't too busy to help. Nothing could undermine defenses like lizards that could spit acid.

Two of them were killed almost immediately. He assumed he would hear the two gunshots that felled them, but it was only one. Trick, of course. He'd found an angle that would allow him to put the same bullet through two skulls, and a panther coming in behind them also yelped and limped away as fragments from the bullet injured it too.

He would never tire of seeing the master marksman at work.

Jiro stood beside him and swung his weapon deftly to clear four hyenas from the path while Athena jumped Sal above the acid spitter so it wouldn't be able to reach him.

His sword drove through the creature's spine and chest and sliced its whole body open as he drew his sidearm. He emptied the magazine into a small pack of humpers that tried to take advantage of his exposed position.

It kicked hard into his arm but it was a satisfying feeling. He smiled as he let all the frustration, hatred, and anger that had coursed through his body over the past few days out in the form of hot lead cutting through soft bodies.

That was a dark thought. Maybe it would be time to dig into these feelings with a little therapy—but that assumed they would survive this.

It grew less and less likely, he knew, but it was hard to not feel alive while surrounded by this much death.

"Look out!"

The warning wasn't for him and Jiro, even though they were knee-deep in mutants that still showed no sign of slowing. Still, the two of them were likely to be up and fighting longer than everyone else. The fusion cores that powered their suits would keep going for years, most likely. Their swords would be much deadlier than the guns once the ammo ran out.

Still, the warning came from behind them and he turned to where creatures now climbed over the admin building and began to drop onto the defenders. A panther was the first one down and its pounce had been accurate. It's powerful jaws locked onto Chezza's shoulder and it flung her down almost effortlessly.

Before it could lunge in for the kill, Trick was already beside her. One shot to the head splattered its skull and brain fragments across what remained of the paving around the building.

More of the creatures joined the others on the roof, and Madigan gestured for Sal and Jiro to pull back while she helped to deal with the bastards there too.

"I'm fine!" Chezza shouted when her teammate tried to help her up. "The fucker broke my shoulder but the armor took most of the damage. I can still fight. You keep shooting."

She drove that point home when she aimed her rifle at the roof to fell two of the creatures that were still up there. Sal couldn't see what they were but even with her shoulder injury, she still had damn good aim.

It was best that she stayed alive too. She was their only medic in this little venture.

"Jiro, stay on the front lines," he called. "I'll head up there to try to clear the building."

"How will you do that?"

Sal retrieved a belt of grenades with a handy tug line

that he could use to pull all the pins at once. It would at least make it harder for them to attack from the roof.

"Athena, do think you can get me up there?"

"I'm already working on it."

She sheathed the assault rifle on his back, brought him up quickly, and moved him forward like a damn insect. It was maybe not the best way to think of it given what they were fighting, but he saw little point in protest.

Only moments later, he reached the top. The building was a mere three stories tall, and the walls were already pockmarked and studded with plants.

He should have known what was up there. He knew he was getting a little reckless but he should have checked. Maybe he would need to look into the possibility that he had bloodlust issues that clouded his judgment.

A small horde milled at the top, all waiting for the right moment to swarm down. They were locusts and humpers for the most part, creatures that could climb or fly easily, but something far bigger slithered forward. He knew what it was merely from the size. Killerpillars were exactly the kind of nightmare fuel that was easy to identify.

"Oh, shit," Sal whispered, drew the pins out of the grenades, and threw the belt into the middle of the creatures. Under the explosion and the weight of the mutants, it was entirely possible that he would bring the whole building down.

The massive monster knew that too and it rushed to where he stood even as he hurled the belt forward. He missed it and dove back as the mandibles and venom-tipped claws reached toward him. The beast swiped and missed, and they both fell over the edge of the building as the grenades detonated.

Sal sucked in a deep breath in response to the swell of vertigo as the world fell away from him.

Athena twisted the suit to catch his momentum and give him as smooth a landing as possible.

He smiled at his three-point landing. Well, there were two more points now that Athena caught him with the extra limbs. There was no real superhero precedent for that.

The killerpillar landed and immediately began to wrap around Madigan's suit. She hadn't caught it in time and tried to push it away. The mandibles weren't close enough, but it tried to wind around her to drag her closer and fight against the mechanism that controlled her suit. The venom-tipped claws would dig in soon too.

Mal stepped in to help, jammed his assault rifle between the carapaces, and opened fire on full auto. The beast jolted immediately in reaction to the strike but its response was slow. Its body still twisted to try to crush Madigan until he pulled a grenade from his belt, thrust it into the hole he had created, and let the carapace close again before it detonated.

After a wet thud, the creature toppled and finally released her.

"Thanks." Madigan gasped, stepped away from the crea-ture, and after a second, moved closer to fire another three rounds into its face.

The whole team watched her and she paused and looked around.

"What? It twitched."

"A good use of the three rounds," Sal commented. "Why didn't you hit it with a rocket while it was falling?"

"I'm out of rockets and I'm running out of ammo for the mini-guns too. Soon, I won't have anything but my fists to fight the fuckers with. Maybe I can use my assault rifle as a club."

"We'll continue to fight," Sal told them as he flicked his sword and retrieved the ammo packs he still carried. "If we have to punch the bastards with our bare fists, that's what we'll do."

He slapped his ammo packs into her collects and sealed them.

"Sal—"

"Don't worry. No hero bullshit. I have a sword and it does enough damage. You're better using the rounds anyway."

"Uh...my pain meds might be kicking in," Chezza shouted as more of the monsters gathered for a new assault," but I think I hear helicopters."

Another flare washed the area in bright red.

"Nah," Trick answered. "It's the winged chariots waiting to carry us all away to Valhalla or some shit."

"You sound very confident about that theory."

"I need to be. It's all about believing hard enough."

Sal hacked off the lower jaw of a hyena and kicked it back into its pack as the rest of the team gathered. He turned as Jiro limped to the group. The armor around his right leg was mangled and it looked he'd tangled with the same pack that Sal had fought.

"Get some medical attention!" he shouted, drove the creatures back, and let him get to where Chezza could help him. They didn't have time for much aside from painkillers, but it would have to do.

The ground shuddered again. He knew what to expect before he saw the mutant. Eyes the size of baseballs looked at them in cold silence and the beast stood over three stories tall.

"A fucking dinosaur." Mal growled in frustration. "Maybe they should send us some pirates next."

"Pirates?"

"Yeah, my kid sister loves her Disney movies. We've been going through the Pirates of the Caribbean movies. Did you know they made eight of those things before the reboot?"

The joking should have gotten under his skin, but Sal laughed and flicked his sword from left to right. He wanted to kill that fucker. Doing it without guns felt like the right way to go about it too.

"Come on big guy," he whispered, took a step forward, and licked his lips. "Let's see how you like my sword."

Before he could start his attack, all the other mutants scrambled to get out of its way and a low whistling sound grew louder. A second later, a white blast filled his vision. Athena immediately corrected to prevent him from going blind, but when his vision returned, the dinosaur's head was gone, along with most of the neck and almost half the torso. Vaporized blood and smoke were immediately illuminated as another flare went up.

"I thought you said you were out of rockets," Sal shouted at Madigan. Killing the monster was a good thing but he had wanted to do it. He felt cheated that he couldn't.

Well, more were on the way. He could take his frustrations out on them.

"I am," Madigan responded. "I don't know where that one came from."

"No," Athena told them quickly. "I pick up helicopters in the air. One of them identified the big bastard and sent an air-to-ground missile to finish it off. They must be closer than I thought. We have teams approaching from…three different directions and in large numbers. I've also picked up what appears to be…well, I imagine they're Russian bombers and they are flying much higher than we might be able to detect. It appears that they're using the Zoo's focus on you to try to establish a safe exit route."

"Well, hot-fuck," Jiro muttered, pushed up, and tried to stand on his mangled leg. "I've never been rescued by the Russians before."

"It's not you," Gregor countered. "It's me. And it's not so bad. They don't have great amenities but they are efficient."

"I'll be sure to give them a great review on Yelp," Sal quipped.

A foreign voice immediately requested permission to join their commlink and Madigan processed it as soon as it came through.

"Team Heavy Metal heroes, do you copy?"

"Heroes?" Sal asked as he sliced through a panther that attempted to attack them from the flank. "We faked it for so long that I guess we finally made it."

"We copy, and we're damn glad to hear your voices!" Madigan responded. "What's your current position?"

"Our team is pushing toward you as fast as possible. And we have a whole lot of Zoo between us and you."

"We're coming in from the southeast," another team called. "We have a couple more teams at our back to make sure. Although we have a lock on your position, we'll try a little surprise to clear the numbers out."

Sal narrowed his eyes but any explanation was rendered moot by the roar of the bomber engines as the aircraft dropped in a little closer, followed by the whistle of the payload they left behind.

He'd half-expected high explosives but a wall of fire erupted through the Zoo and ravaged the mutants that attempted to reach them.

"Now that looks more like a movie," he whispered and grinned as the teams began to show up on the sensors. The Zoo continued to rage and tried to stop their advance, but he could feel something else in it. It wasn't quite fear but similar. Apprehension, he thought after he'd considered it.

And maybe the cold realization that humanity wouldn't be that easy to wipe off of the planet as it might have thought.

"Helicopters are coming in to get you out," one of the pilots called. "You'll need to coordinate with the rest of the teams that are pushing hard to connect with you."

In scant minutes, the area around the old admin building erupted in activity as teams bulldozed in, eliminated the monsters in their path, and made sure that enough of them were cleared for the thrower teams coming in behind. A veritable army rushed to their position, but the Zoo had adjusted its advance to come from behind and use the structure to hide their approach before they launched a concerted attack against Heavy Metal.

Mal was the first to fall back. One of the spitters had

reached him, and while it paid for the attack with its life, the acid ate through the man's chest before he could pull his armor off. He looked down, realized there was no chance he would recover from his wounds, even with help coming in, and made the decision almost immediately.

He still had two mines they were saving for when they were inevitably pushed into the building. They wouldn't need them now.

"Front...toward...enemy!" he roared. The acid reached his lung but he managed a final push forward and activated the mines as he powered through a few more spitters. He drove them ahead of him by the weight of his suit, picked up a third, and dragged them through the wall of the admin building.

A second ticked past before the mines exploded and added to the damage the structure had already taken, which brought it all down.

If there was ever a way to go, it was blowing shit up and taking a whole fuck-ton of the monsters in the aftermath. Maybe it wasn't the best way to think about that, but Sal had a feeling that was how Mal wanted to be remembered.

"The helicopters are coming in." Madigan motioned for them to stand ready to board.

Enough of the mutants had been cleared to make it easier on the helicopters, but there was still the danger that the locusts would swarm them. While enough gunships were in the air to turn almost anywhere on earth into a charnel house, it was barely enough for the Zoo.

Boarding was quick and easy, even with their wounded. Chezza looked like she was about to pass out, and Jiro needed Madigan to carry him most of the way.

It was painful to see but they were better off than Mal. Sonja stared at the rubble of the building with an expression he'd seen before—trying to find any sign that he might be alive. He hadn't even known they were friends. That was on him, though.

"Heading up!"

The helicopters shuddered and more attacks surged. The Zoo wouldn't give up without a fight, and it was likely that the damage they were doing would not take long to repair.

Still, they would leave a dent, mostly because it looked like the whole Zoo had been directed to attack Heavy Metal with no concern that the humans defending the spurs it had sent out were there to press the attack. Maybe it didn't expect them to. It wasn't like it had made its usual intelligent decisions after the dome had imploded.

Perhaps the Zoo didn't know humans as well as it thought it did.

CHAPTER TWENTY-FIVE

It felt weird. Sal had fully expected to never leave the jungle. Every day he spent out in the open again felt like the weirdest, most disappointing kind of afterlife.

He now stood in front of a group of CEOs and commanders of the bases around the Zoo, who all wanted to hear about what the fuck had happened.

The conclusion he'd reached was painful but he had to face it. He had survived, and any number of problems came with that.

Dying would have been much simpler.

"Another spur was expected to form last night," Courtney explained and pointed to her screen. "We have no way to know if the Zoo changed its plans based on what happened in there, or if it's merely waiting to try again."

Sal nodded. "It could be that with the destruction of the red-and-blue Pitas, it won't have the resources to expand. It explains why there wasn't much of a reaction from the plants and vines while the troops were attacking. But...

well, so far, there's considerable speculation and not enough facts."

"Still," one of the CEOs, a massive character who looked like a former athlete, stated, "your instincts were right. Maybe not quite on the schedule we might have liked to see but still right. It helped to contain the Zoo and even gave us the first opportunity for a counter-attack since...I don't know when."

He struggled to shake off the weird feeling and he could see it in Madigan's eyes too. The acceptance of death came with some interesting psychological ramifications and they were still working through it. Even though this part of the presentation was for the geeks and nerds, she was uncharacteristically silent through it all.

"I think what Mr. Samson is getting at," Franklin stated, "is that we're all learning to trust your instincts in this, Dr. Jacobs. What do they tell you about the current situation?"

He drew a deep breath and still felt relief that there was no pressure from the Zoo this far away. It felt odd and not necessarily all good like he was missing something in his head.

"The red-and-blue Pita plants are vital to the Zoo's expansion, although we don't know how or why yet. With the large number of them that we destroyed in that explosion, it'll have to pause and regroup. It gives us some time but I don't think we achieved anything more than that."

"Time is good," Solodkov commented. "Time we can work with."

"Right." Courtney cleared her throat. "I have my labs working full shifts to analyze the healing root plant, along with other independent labs. We have some promising leads on how it could be used to stop the Zoo spread, but that's all they are for the moment. Separate trials are being run to see if it's only the plant or a combination of it and the other ingredients in the concoction. Perhaps a chemical reaction in there would make it more effective. It's a long process, however, which means we might want to delve into other options. First and foremost, we would need to excavate and repair the damaged sections of the wall."

"We have to face reality at this point." Franklin rubbed his eyes before he focused on the screens. "Wall two is compromised and without a thorough investigation, we cannot be sure how extensively. The engineers at ENSOL will explore ways that the wall could be repaired and reinforced effectively at a reasonable cost. However, we might have to consider a third wall farther away from the Zoo to give us more of a buffer. We could focus on construction based on the knowledge we have now instead of spending too much time, energy, and money trying to repair something that might not be repairable."

"And maybe, just maybe," the Brit commander added, "we'll find somewhere else to put you fucking Wall Street leeches other than our bases."

The CEOs all exchanged uncomfortable glances but Samson chuckled.

"It's always a pleasure speaking to you, Jenna."

———

"We need to talk."

He knew this was coming. They'd waited during the

whole drive back to the compound and even until the rest of the mercs arrived. The team shared a few minutes of silence in remembrance of Mal before they got their money and left to spend it.

Only the core team was left now.

"What about?" Sal asked and approached his partners in his bedroom. Madigan was on the bed and Courtney was in his office chair, which left the lounger next to the bed for him.

"About what happened in the Zoo," Madigan told him.

"You mean the part where we stopped the Zoo from declaring all-out war on the rest of us?" He nodded. "We're all fucking heroes. You remember what they called us? The Heavy Metal Hero Team or some shit."

He paused and looked at them. This wasn't that kind of conversation. He'd suspected as much but had still hoped to not relive what happened in there.

Courtney frowned. "I won't pretend that I understand half the data that New Connie—"

"Athena," he corrected her.

"Right. Athena. I won't pretend I know half of what she was talking about and we might need to consult some specialists. A neurologist would be my first recommenda-tion,, but the fact of the matter is...well, the Zoo has an effect on you."

That was one way to put it. Sal stared at the floor for a moment and sighed softly as he collected his thoughts.

"Yeah. Knowing there's a deep, dark beast in there waiting to reach in and grab my trachea to stop me from breathing...isn't a pleasant experience." Even thinking about it made his heart beat a little faster. "And a doctor might not be a bad idea. It's out now. In the light and air again, I don't know when it'll make an appearance."

Madigan nodded. "Hell, I'm dumber about this shit than she is so I wouldn't even know where to start. Still, knowing it's there is a good place to start, no?"

That drew a laugh from Courtney. " Come on. You got his dumb ass out of there alive so maybe you should hold off on playing the dumbass card."

"True. It was damn heroic of me if I do say so myself."

That was Sal's cue to grin. "There's more than that, though. There's…I learned that I might not be the best narrator for what's happening in the Zoo right now. And I adapted. The only way I survived was by trusting the people around me—the Heavy Metal team and the two ladies in my life."

"Hold on there, tiger," Madigan warned.

"My point is that you guys trust me and you've stood beside me all this time, and I don't want you to think that I'm taking any of it for granted. I owe you the truth, no matter how uncomfortable it might be for me. You call me out on shit and you're there to keep my dumb ass in check when it needs to be. You listen, ask questions, and even raise my spirits when needed with snark and…other things."

"We've got your back, Sal," Courtney whispered and put a hand on his shoulder. "And your front too, when you need that."

"Hold on there, tigress." Madigan smirked when she said that.

This wasn't quite how he thought the conversation would go. He expected them to make a case for keeping him away from the Zoo forever, but they were being playful...and even a little flirty. Madigan was being flirty. It was madness.

"You know," Courtney said and leaned forward to place a light kiss on his cheek, "I think our good Dr. Jacobs here has grown up into a fine, strong man."

Madigan grinned and stood. "I think we should show him how excited we are about that."

And that was certainly not where he'd thought the conversation would go.

AUTHOR NOTES - MICHAEL ANDERLE

NOVEMBER 2, 2021

For this set of author notes, I'd like to once again bring in Judah, the editor for The Zoo Universe. Take it away, Judah!

EDITOR'S NOTES

Someone asked me the other day what I do for fun… "That's easy. I go to the Zoo." Of course, they looked at me strangely given that I'm still in the limp and shuffle rehab stage of yet another broken leg—yes, a long story—and mumbled something along the lines of, "How nice." They probably wondered if I needed rehab for my head too.

The reality is that despite all the stinky stuff I have to contend with in my life—think tanker-loads here—I have the Zooniverse to play in. This, in turn, means I have the world's greatest job ever since I get to play while I'm working (or work while I'm playing?)

Contain Or Die is the culmination of a frenetic, high-paced, up-and-down saga of man pitted against his greatest enemy. It's wild, wise, wacky, and wonderful, but it's not an ending. If anything, it's like that moment when you are poised at the peak of a rollercoaster for the breath-stealing second before you rush into the next section of tie-a-knot-in-it-and-hang-on adventure.

For those who have followed the series—along with *Cryptid Assassin* and *McFadden and Banks*—you'll be pleased to see some of the threads drawn together to complete sections of the tapestry within a terrifying "what-if" scenario. If anyone has not read the other books or series, this is the best time to do it. You know, before that roller-coaster plunges down the other side...

I freely confess that I am a Zoo addict—irretrievably and very happily so. It's my Precious and I wants it. I'm even more excited that it's currently poised on the brink of where-to-now? The beauty of the Zooniverse is that it is limitless, both in terms of humanity, heroes, and what-the-hell surprises. In the jungle, anything is possible.

If you wonder if there's life after *Contain Or Die*, the best advice I can give you is don't turn your back on the Zoo. The moment you do, that bitch will strike—and usually in ways you don't expect. Count on it. At the end of this book, that jungle is one pissed-off predator and you can expect backlash. What form that will take...well, we'll all have to wait and see.

Folk have asked me why I'm so obsessed with the Zoo and yes, it certainly speaks to my particular brand of crazy. But more than that, the Zooniverse is a place of unlimited potential and imagination. It's where monsters are spawned and heroes birthed, and where we can all fling caution and care to the wind and leap into the giant jungle mud puddle with reckless abandon. We can splash and flurry to our heart's content, sure that something drop-jaw wtf will emerge to lead us on another headlong adventure.

Best of all, while the Zoo is all about the Big Bad Ugly, it's also about us. The characters are the you and me of this world—ordinary people who step up to do extraordinary things because the alternatives create a future too terrible to contemplate. It's all about us at our worst and our best and even somewhere between.

So breathe—you'll need it after this book—regroup, catch up, and prepare. We're only at the beginning and have so much more of the Zooniverse to play in. I expect more monsters, mayhem, and miracles. There must be more "out there" to explore. Or will the "out there" come to "explore" us? Now there's a nasty thought... At this point, anything is possible.

Damn, it's exciting...

CONNECT WITH MICHAEL

Connect with Michael Anderle

Website: http://lmbpn.com

Email List: http://lmbpn.com/email/

https://www.facebook.com/LMBPNPublishing

https://twitter.com/MichaelAnderle

https://www.instagram.com/lmbpn_publishing/

https://www.bookbub.com/authors/michael-anderle

OTHER MICHAEL TODD BOOKS

PROTECTED BY THE DAMNED UNIVERSE

PROTECTED BY THE DAMNED*

8 Book series

WAR OF THE DAMNED*

8 Book series

DAMIAN'S CHRONICLES*

4 Book series

WAR OF THE ANGELS*

8 Book series

ZOO UNIVERSE

BIRTH OF HEAVY METAL*

10 Book series

APOCALYPSE PAUSED*

12 Book series

SOLDIER OF FAME AND FORTUNE*

12 Book series

TEAM SAVAGE *

3 Book series

Dungeon Core TV*

6 Book series

Dungeon Rails*

3 Book series

Hellspawned Chronicles*

3 Book series

The Sheva Chronicles*

6 Book series

Unlikely Bountyhunters*

6 Book series

House Drakonnen

The Accord

The Anchor's Inheritance Saga

*DENOTES COMPLETED SERIES